THE B...L

Also by Sarah Naughton

The Hanged Man Rises
(Shortlisted for the Costa Book Award)

THE BLOOD LIST

Sarah Naughton

SIMON AND SCHUSTER

First published in Great Britain in 2014 by Simon and Schuster UK Ltd
A CBS COMPANY

Copyright © 2014 Sarah Naughton

1 3 5 7 9 10 8 6 4 2

Simon & Schuster UK Ltd
1st Floor
222 Gray's Inn Road
London WC1X 8HB

Simon & Schuster Australia, Sydney
Simon & Schuster India, New Delhi

A CIP catalogue record for this book
is available from the British Library.

PB ISBN: 978-0-85707-866-7
EBook ISBN: 978-0-85707-867-4

Printed and bound by CPI Group (UK) Ltd, Croydon, CR0 4YY

For Bert.
Paddington Hospital's 'Most Beautiful Baby' 2006.

'Most of the witches that have ever beene
discovered have beene so by malice.'

Archdeacon of Colchester, 1644

September 1630

She awoke to the sound of birdsong. The room smelled strongly of rosemary and rolling onto her side she saw that someone had tied fat bunches of the herb to the bars of the cradle. Gingerly she pushed herself up, using the headboard for support, but the pain was not as bad as she'd expected. Though she was only sixteen her hips and pelvis were large and the baby had been small. A tiny purple thing with a slick of black hair that had sent a wave of disappointment through her for the briefest sliver of time. Then he screwed up his face and cried and she took him in her arms, all naked and wrinkled and slimy. For that moment, as he nuzzled his damp little head into her neck and his tiny hands batted her mouth, she thought she could never ever let him go.

But they made her.

They took him and cleaned him and bound him in swaddling cloths and put him to the breast of the fat wet nurse who had fed a hundred babies before him and loved him no more than a frog loves the eggs it squirts onto a lily pad.

A girl of your birth does not suckle a child, her mother told her; *it is beneath you.*

Frances swung her legs over the edge of the bed and cautiously stood up. This time pain clutched at her belly and she bit her lip to stop herself crying out. She didn't want them up here, not yet. She could not bear to watch Henry lean over the cot and pronounce her child an ugly wizened thing with a nose like its mother. She could not stand to see him poke his finger into that tissue-thin scalp and ask where it got such ill-favoured colouring.

His colouring was her own. Her hair was coarse and frizzy, the dull brown of leaf mould without the slightest glimmer of chestnut or gold. Even butter would not make it shine. The baby had the same fuzz of dark hair down the length of his spine that had so shamed her on their wedding night that she would not turn her back on Henry. But he had seen her embarrassment and kissed her back and called her his little woodland creature. He could be kind sometimes. And he was handsome. Too handsome. The glare of his beauty blinded people to his character, or perhaps made his faults lovable. And she had loved him so much. A crippling, dumbing love that had made her uglier and clumsier than she already was. It had stripped her of all wit and intelligence and made her mumble in monosyllables and trip over her feet.

Frances shuffled over to the cot, trying not to move her legs too much and risk disturbing the catgut stitches the midwife had sewn. She didn't recognise her body any more. She had always been plump but before her pregnancy it had been the puppy fat of a girl, and now it felt like the heavy deposits of middle age. Her belly was still so big she couldn't see the floor and stumbled, knocking a candlestick off the table. It landed with a loud thud and she peeped into the cot to check that the noise hadn't woken the baby. He was awake already, but had not turned towards the sound. He was gazing out of the window towards the edge of the forest where the treetops danced in the wind. Only as her shadow fell across him did he move his little dark head. His brown eyes lit up when he saw her and he made a gurgling noise in his throat.

'Hello, little one,' she murmured. 'Hello, Barnaby.'

He was to be named after her father: a brief gesture of humility on Henry's part, or perhaps a gesture of gratitude. Her father would, after all, bestow his entire fortune on his only daughter and, even ill-favoured as she was, Frances could have made a better match. At the beginning Henry had enjoyed teasing her, saying the opposite was true: that he could have had any girl he wished and she was lucky he had chosen her. But on the first night of their marriage, when he was too nervous to consummate it, he had told her that he loved her for herself, not just her wealth and status, and she believed him. He found his stride soon enough and within a month she was pregnant. From then on anticipation of the arrival of his 'heir' occupied all Henry's attention. He prodded her to make sure she was fattening up enough to nourish his 'son' and listened to her belly as if the child might actually reply to his inane prattlings. His father, John, was a shrewd businessman but Frances started to fear she had married a handsome fool.

It was too late now: she had chosen Henry and now she

must put up with her choice. Perhaps as the first mad surge of love for her child passed she would find some room in her heart for Henry again.

She could hear him laughing downstairs. He did that a lot. Laugh. Henry had a beautiful smile but an ugly laugh, like the yap of a dog. He had been laughing earlier as he told his friend Buck that he wouldn't have believed the baby was his, except that his wife was so ugly no-one else would bed her. Buck had laughed too, another ugly laugh. His own betrothed was pretty as a kitten and poor as a cellar rat.

Frances reached in to pick up her son but the door opened and she snatched her arms back guiltily.

It was Agnes: Henry's nursemaid when he was a boy, and now Barnaby's.

She was grey and brittle as a dead twig, with probing fingers that had no softness to them. Somehow she always made Frances feel like a naughty child. When Frances had suggested they had no need of Agnes, and that she could look after the child herself, Henry had snapped, 'And how would a great lummox of sixteen years know how to care for my son?'

She had cried then and he had apologised, but Agnes stayed.

The woman walked swiftly to the bed and looked inside.

'Where's the knife?' she said.

'I took it out,' Frances said. 'I was worried he might hurt himself.'

'Foolish girl,' Agnes snapped. 'Babies cannot even turn over until they're four months old, he'll hardly be able to stab himself. Where is it?'

Frances shuffled to the wardrobe and brought out the knife. A nasty, blunt thing, flaking particles of rust.

'When did you remove it?' Agnes said, grasping it and tucking it under Barnaby so that the sharp flakes scratched his face. Immediately he began to cry.

'Last night.'

'*Last night?*'

Frances nodded.

'So the child lay all night unprotected?'

'The iron nails are still there, see?' Frances pointed to the line of studs at the end of the cot. 'The Bible is beneath the mattress . . . and I used Henry's shirt to swaddle him.'

Agnes stared at her coldly then picked up the child as if he were a hunk of brisket. She narrowed her eyes and made an unpleasant chirruping sound with her tongue.

Barnaby turned his head in the opposite direction: he was looking for his mother. Frances stepped forwards to take him but Agnes hissed at her. She made the noise again, louder this time. Barnaby squirmed and cried harder.

Steeling herself against the pain in her groin and her fear of Agnes, Frances went over and plucked her baby out of the old woman's arms. At once he stopped crying and nuzzled into her neck, coiling his fingers into her hair and pulling until it hurt, which made her laugh. The laugh died when she saw Agnes's expression.

'What?' Frances said, lifting her chin defiantly. Barnaby was hers after all.

'When was the child baptised?'

'Three days ago.'

'Four days after its birth?'

5

'Yes.'

'You waited too long.' Agnes turned and walked back to the door.

'Where are you going?' Frances said.

'I must speak to Henry,' she replied and left the room.

Frances walked over to the window and gazed out at the forest. The sky was now overcast and the trees were black; they shivered in the wind and whispered to one another. She crossed herself and closed the casement. Perhaps Agnes was right. They were so close to the forest here. It was only sensible to take precautions. Tonight she would replace the knife. And the iron tongs. And she would sprinkle holy water on the window and doorframes.

She took the baby over to the bed and lay down beside him. As he gazed into her eyes she could see her face reflected in his dark, dark irises.

'The north wind doth blow,' she sang softly, *'and we shall have snow, and what will poor robin do then, poor thing?'*

Barnaby batted his hand at her face and she caught it and pressed it to her lips.

'He'll sit in a barn, and keep his head warm, and hide his head under his wing, poor thing.'

Barnaby's eyelashes were sinking and he made little snuffling sighs. His hand slipped out of hers to rest palm-up on the sheet, a perfect pink clam-shell. Frances watched him until she was sure he was asleep then, so as not to crush him with the weight of her arm, she slipped her hand under his, dipped her head until her coarse curls brushed his soft feathers of hair, and fell asleep to the sound of his breathing.

*

When she awoke it was dark. The fire had been allowed to die and the room was cold.

The cradle was a dark silhouette against the night sky. There was total silence. Fear jumped into Frances's mouth like a toad. She slid out of bed, not daring to breathe, and tiptoed over to the cot, her mind whirring as it struck up deals with Providence: if I don't creak a floorboard he will still be alive, if I get there in less than five steps he will still be alive; if the moon doesn't go behind a cloud he will still be alive.

She reached the edge of the cot.

It was empty.

Her breaths came all at once and she panted like a sick dog. Where was he? The wet nurse always fed him up here by the fire. Had they taken him away in a hurry? Was he sick?

The trees at the edge of the forest whispered and sniggered. Then the moon went behind a cloud and the room was plunged into darkness.

A chill gripped her like a dead hand.

Had Agnes's warning come true?

Had they come for Barnaby?

Then someone spoke downstairs; a raised voice.

Frances flew out of the room and down the stairs. Rounding the newel post at the bottom she burst into the hall and her insides turned to water.

There he was, tipped over the wet nurse's shoulder, as she patted his back to wind him.

She flew over and scooped him up in her arms, squeezing him so hard he burped at once.

Then for the first time she noticed the other occupants of the room.

Henry was there, and Agnes; but for some reason Henry's father John was also present with his wife.

They seemed not to have registered her arrival at all – all their attention was fixed on Agnes, who was speaking in hushed tones, as if a corpse had been freshly laid out in the room.

'I knew from the first time I laid eyes upon it that there was something amiss. You should have summoned me when the first pains came; I would have made sure everything was in place.'

Henry rubbed a hand across his face and said nothing. He was very pale. His mother was crying.

'As it is the girl tells me the child has been sleeping without the knife.'

All eyes flicked to Frances, then back to Agnes.

'It's plain to see the child is over-admired by its mother – this only draws their attention. Why in God's name did you not baptise it straight away?'

'We were waiting to see if it lived,' Henry said. 'It was such a scrawny thing after all.'

'And still is!' Agnes said. 'Despite its appetite. Martha tells me it is never satisfied and seeks to suckle all day long.'

All eyes turned to the wet nurse who immediately turned her attention to a milk stain on her dress and wouldn't catch Frances's eye.

'This is just one sign. There are plenty more. You have seen yourself how its attention is elsewhere when you try to engage it: it is fixed on the world we cannot see.'

Barnaby clearly had more wind because he started to squirm and whimper on her shoulder. She jiggled him but her movements were jerky with stress and it only made him worse. Agnes came over, her watery eyes glittering with malice.

'See how ill-tempered it is?'

'No he isn't,' Frances cried. 'All babies cry!'

'Ill-tempered,' Agnes repeated, as if she had not spoken. 'Its skin is yellow and covered in hair.' With a look of distaste she tugged the loose swaddling away from Barnaby's face. 'And look at its sly, black eyes. Those are not the eyes of a week-old child.'

'They are my eyes!' Frances cried. 'Dark brown, like mine!'

'That is the gaze of one of the immortals.'

Frances stared at her. The baby was dark and hairy like her, it cried like all babies, and surely constant hunger was the sign of a hale and hearty infant.

Agnes stood in front of the fire, casting a long shadow over the room.

'No luck will come to a family with a changeling child. It will drain away all your happiness, your good fortune and your wealth.'

Henry grew paler than ever. 'What can be done?' he said.

'There are some tried and trusted methods,' Agnes said. 'The fairies will not stand to see one of their own hurt, so if the changeling child is threatened they will at once rescue it, returning the original human baby that was stolen.'

'Go on,' John said.

'The first method is to hold the baby over a fire.'

'No!' Frances shrieked but Henry's mother shushed her angrily.

9

'Heat and fire are anathema to the changeling and it will fly away. The second is to force foxglove tea down its throat. In a human child this would burn out its throat: the fairy will simply—'

Frances didn't hear the final part of the sentence.

'Henry!' she shrieked. 'What madness is this? Get her out of my house!'

'*Your* house?' snuffled Henry's mother. 'You are wed now, girl, the house is Henry's.'

'Hush, Mother,' Henry said, then for the first time he looked at his wife and his face crumpled. 'You must have noticed something wasn't right, Fan? He won't look at me. He shows no interest in his surroundings. He looks so . . . so strange.'

'If you heat a shovel until it is red-hot,' Agnes went on, 'then shovel the creature up in it, it will at once leap off and run away. I know a woman who saw such a thing happen with her own eyes.'

'Get out of my house!' Frances shrieked. 'Or I will take that poker and spear your black heart.'

The room fell silent but for the crackle of the flames in the grate.

Agnes regarded her steadily.

'Sometimes,' she said quietly, 'a witch begets such a child by copulating with the devil.'

Frances shifted Barnaby onto her other hip, drew back her right arm and struck the old woman in the face. Agnes flew backwards onto the soft cushion of Martha's lap.

Frances was hyperventilating now, gasping such huge gulps of breath that she could not say more: though she wanted to.

10

'Get her upstairs, Henry,' John snapped.

She turned to see John and his wife fixing her with matching expressions of disgust. How things had changed now that they were married and Henry owned everything. Beside her the two women were struggling to their feet, spluttering their outrage. To add to it all the baby was crying.

'I will *not* go upstairs,' Frances cried over the cacophony. She turned on Henry, who now had vivid spots of scarlet on his cheeks as he stared over her head at his father.

'I am your wife, Henry, and I demand she leaves this house. And that fat milk cow along with her. I will feed my own s—'

Henry lunged forwards, grabbing her so violently that she bit her tongue and the midwife's stitches tore.

'Yes, you are my wife and you will do AS I SAY,' he bellowed, 'AND I SAY GO UPSTAIRS!'

She stared at him, the bitter taste of her own blood filling her mouth. Apart from Barnaby's cries the rest of the room was silent. Henry's parents were staring at them and she could feel the eyes of the other women on her back.

Henry swallowed then muttered, 'Do as I say, Frances, please.'

His blue eyes stared and sweat had plastered his blond curls to his temples.

'Do not let their words poison your heart,' she whispered. 'Please, Henry. *Please.*' Tears spilled over her cheeks and the room swam into a blur of shadow and firelight. She batted blindly at the pale figure of her handsome husband but he did not take her hand.

11

'I won't, Fan,' he said, moving aside to let her pass. 'I promise.'

She managed to get up the last few steps up to their room before a crushing exhaustion fell on her like an anvil. Pressing Barnaby to her chest she crawled to the bed, but she did not have the strength to climb up onto it. The floorboards were refreshingly cold after the heat of the room downstairs. She was sweating heavily and the cut between her legs seethed like a lime burn.

Manoeuvring herself awkwardly onto her back she sank down, tucking Barnaby into her nightdress to prevent him tumbling onto the hard floor. He was still crying, but without conviction now that he was nestled in her familiar warmth. She patted his back a few times and sighed words of comfort, but then her arm slipped off and her eyelids began to sink. She let her head fall to the side. The shadow of the cradle fell across the floor, crisp in the moonlight. Around it glimmered sticky patches where the urine had been splashed by Agnes, who had informed Frances confidently that this was extremely offensive to fairies and would repel their attacks.

Stupid Agnes.

Stupid Henry for believing her nonsense.

And stupid her for marrying him.

Frances's eyelids grew heavier but she forced them open.

The window that looked out on the forest began to rattle softly and as she watched, wisps of light crept in around the edges of the frame. They drifted towards the cot and gathered above it until the whole room was illuminated with ghostly light. A whispering began: the same sound the trees made in the dead of night when the wind was high. It pulsed to the rhythm of the light. She knew she was dreaming but forced her lips to move and the breath to rise up from her lungs: '*Our Father,*' she began, '*Which art in Heaven, Hallowed be Thy name. Thy kingdom come . . .*'

But before she could finish she was asleep.

Fairies plagued her dreams. Sometimes they would be no more substantial than dandelion seeds floating around the empty cot: sometimes they would gather round her bed, child-sized but wizened and sharp-toothed, stretching their claws towards Barnaby. She would hiss and spit at them and then sometimes they would grow and become Henry and his parents, or Father Nicholas, or her own mother, though she knew they were not real and would crook her fingers at them to make the sign that wards off the evil eye. Sometimes Barnaby would wake and look up at her and smile and say, 'Don't be afraid, Mama, you and I will never be parted,' and his voice was velvet, like the wing of a moth.

'I'm not afraid,' she would try and say but her mouth was filled with hard lumps, knobbled and papery like ancient fingers. She imagined they were Agnes's fingers, probing her gums, trying to pull out her teeth, and she bit down hard. They released a pungent juice that burned her tongue. Ginger.

She was sick, then.

She opened her eyes and squinted at the brightness of the room. A blur of colour to her left resolved itself into a vase of flowers. Henry had not given her flowers since they were courting. There was also a glass of water and a plate of dried fruit and sweetmeats.

Her heart leaped. Agnes would not tend her so well: she must have been sent away.

Candles were lit in the sconces beside the bed and the fire burned in the grate: with logs of applewood judging by the fragrance. Its leaping flames made the shadow of the cradle move as if it were rocking. But the cradle was still. And the sweet soft weight of her son was gone.

Her chest had deflated and no longer ached. There was no tenderness between her legs and swinging her legs over the bed did not produce a crackle of dried blood or a tug from the stitches.

How long had she been sick?

She padded across the floor and opened the door. As she passed the window she saw that the sky above the forest was lightening. It was dawn: surely too early even for the servants to be up, and yet their truckles were empty.

She peered into the hallway. All was quiet.

'Henry?' she called, suddenly afraid.

There was a rustle and a creak.

'I'm here, my love,' he called softly from downstairs.

'Where are the servants?' she said, stepping onto the first stair.

'I sent them away for a while.'

'And Agnes?'

'She's gone.'

As she descended the room opened up before her. Henry was sitting by the fire. She covered her mouth to muffle a gasp. His face was grey, his hair dishevelled, his clothes awry.

14

Her knees buckled and she collapsed onto the stair.

'Where's Barnaby?' she croaked.

Henry lowered his hand over the arm of the chair and swung it around, presumably in search of the bottle of wine that stood there. He knocked it over and it glugged a crimson pool onto the floorboards.

'Where is he?' she said again. 'Did you let Agnes take him?'

'I took him myself,' he said.

Pulling herself up on the banister she climbed down the last stairs.

'Where?'

He leaned forwards and pressed his head into his hands.

'It was agreed by the aldermen,' he said. 'Once Father Nicholas had got involved there was nothing I could do to stop it.'

She walked across the cold flagstones and stood in front of him, her breath coming in snatches.

'What have you done with my child?' she said.

He raised his head and looked at her. All his beauty had drained away and weakness and folly were written into every line of his drawn face.

'I did not let them hurt him,' he said. 'They wanted to use fire but I said no. It was Father Nicholas that suggested the midden heap, not me.'

He started to cry. Mucus drooled from his nose and he wiped it away with a grubby sleeve.

'The midden heap?' she said. 'In the forest?'

'That's what you have to do with changelings,' he said. 'You leave them on the midden heap overnight and the fairies take them back and leave your own child in their place.'

She stared at him.

'You left my baby on a pile of shit and bones in the middle of winter?'

Henry nodded. Now he was crying properly, ugly bestial sobs that shook his whole body.

'I . . . I didn't put him there.'

'Who did?' she said.

'One of the other men, I c . . . can't remember . . .'

'There were others there?'

He nodded: 'The whole village.'

'The whole village?' Her voice rose in pitch. 'And no-one tried to stop it?

'Only the furrier and his wife. She tried to pull the . . . to pull him off but we . . . they stopped her.'

Frances dropped to her knees in the ashes of the fire. Her son was dead.

She did not know how long she sat like that listening to Henry's grunting sobs. Eventually the fire died, its warm light replaced by the cold glare of dawn. Outside the birds chattered and laughed. She raised her head.

'Is he buried yet,' she said, 'or can I see him?'

Henry had fallen asleep. Black dribble seeped from the corner of his mouth to stain the seat cover. It would never come out. It would always be there, like a bloodstain, to remind her what he had done.

She knelt up and slapped his face. His skin was clammy and reptilian.

Henry awoke with a cry and blinked his crusty eyes.

'Is he buried yet or can I see his body?' she said again.

16

'No ... no,' he mumbled. 'He is not buried.'

'Where is he? I want to go now.'

He stared at her stupidly. Now she could hear voices outside. Many voices. They were approaching the front door.

'We only left him last night,' Henry said.

Father Nicholas led the procession. It would not be far. Only the hunters went deep into the forest, laying their offerings to the fairy folk, to whom the place belonged, as they went.

Henry and Frances went behind him. Their parents next. Her mother and father were pale but they stood tall and unashamed. Even they had not stopped this. As she walked out of the front door, with as much dignity as her anguish allowed, her mother had whispered: 'We all knew there was something wrong with him, darling, in time you will see this was the right thing ...'

The smell of the midden heap began to reach them. It was the stench of human and animal excrement, rotting bones and oyster shells, vegetable peelings, the stinking waste from the furrier and the tanner and the dyer. And laid on top of it all, like an offering to the god of foulness and disease: her darling child.

Though there was silence at the head of the group, those villagers bringing up the rear whispered to one another and occasionally there was a stifled laugh.

Father Nicholas began to chant.

'Yea though I walk through the valley of the shadow of death, yet will I fear no ill. For Thou art with me. Thy rod and Thy staff comfort me ...'

17

The trees murmured and bent their heads to another as they passed.

A knot of starlings burst, jeering, from a nearby tree.

The priest raised his voice:

'Thou preparest a table before me in the presence of mine enemies . . .'

A squirrel ran onto the path, rose up onto its hind legs and regarded them with sparkling eyes, before darting away.

'Thou anointest my head with oil. My cup runneth—'

And then something flew into his mouth. He stopped abruptly and began coughing and spitting onto the path.

There were concerned pats on the back from those up front and titters from the back. But Frances stood apart from them all, listening.

The breeze died a moment and even the birds grew hushed.

There.

The priest still hacked away behind her but in the pauses between his coughs she heard it.

She walked forwards then stopped. If she was wrong; if it had been the chirrup of a bird or the cry of a fawn, her heart would not stand it.

It came again. Strong. Lusty.

Now they all heard it and a hush descended on the entire party. The forest fell still as every creature from the tiniest wood grub to the noblest stag listened.

With a strangled cry she ran forwards, crashing through the trees, the branches tearing out clumps of her hair and sharp twigs cutting her face.

It was the healthiest, strongest, most furious cry she had

ever heard. She tore leaves and branches aside, stumbling and sliding on wet leaves. Now she could see the midden heap: a black mound in the trees ahead.

The cries grew louder, as if the child knew salvation was at hand.

How had he survived the night? Had it been especially mild? Had the stink of dung masked his own scent while predators prowled around the foothills of the pile? Had the fairies protected him?

Bursting through the final line of trees she began scrambling up the heap, her arms sinking into ordure, shards of pottery and jagged bones tearing at her clothes.

'Barnaby!' she shrieked.

She climbed higher and a fat arm came into view, the angry fingers clutching at air.

'I am here!'

Now she could hear the rest of them behind her crying out in wonder, *God be praised! It's a miracle!* And her husband calling her name, half laughing, half crying.

Now she could see the perfect hemisphere of his round belly above a tangle of blue cloth – naked: they had not even swaddled him properly – now his fat legs kicking. Fatter legs than she remembered. Now the top of his head.

She stopped.

She stared at him.

Her limbs turned to ice.

The morning sun broke through the canopy above and shone a single beam of sunlight onto his body, making his hair flash. Like a halo.

Henry scrambled past her, stopped and gave a hoarse cry.

The child stopped crying.

Very slowly, like a fox approaching a hen house, Henry crawled to the top of the midden. Then he stopped and his beautiful lips parted. The child reached out its fat arms to him. Henry threw back his head.

'God be praised!' he bellowed and the trees shook with his cry. 'My son! My own true son is returned to me!'

He scooped the child up in his arms and held it aloft. Below her Frances heard gasps and cries of shock as the villagers of Beltane Ridge took in the sight: of the handsome young merchant with the rich wife holding up, like an offering to God, his fine, bonny, pink-skinned, blond-haired son.

Frances felt herself falling backwards. The sky wheeled over her head and the trees lunged at her, and the last thing she saw was the bright yellow head of the boy that was not her son, glinting like a brass nail in the sunlight.

1
The Black Dog

The coney was plump and beautiful, with a peppery coat that glistened in the sunlight and eyes like pools of tar. Barnaby watched it from behind the trunk of the plane tree, waiting for the right moment.

At present the animal was too near a tangle of brambles and would bolt to safety if it caught the movement of the bow. He needed it to come further out into the open, but so far it had ignored the trail of grain he had left.

He was pleased with the bow. Since his and Abel's tutor had been dismissed the previous year he'd had far more time to concentrate on the things he actually enjoyed. He'd chosen yew because that was the wood Cromwell's army used for their longbows. It was incredibly strong and even when the string was fully extended retained its perfect arc. Too good for coneys. He would get his father to ask the baron's steward if he could hunt hares in the forest.

The coney made a single, slow hop away from the brambles. Then another. Towards the grain trail.

He slid an arrow from the quiver on his back and the barely audible rasp was enough to make the creature's ears prick. At this point, if Griff were here, the coney would be off; spooked by Barnaby's friend's noisy breaths and inability to keep his clumsy limbs still. Hunting alone had its advantages, although mostly it was deathly boring. He'd have to get used to it, however, because come harvest season all his friends would be busy on their parents' farms.

Slipping the fletch beneath the string he slowly drew the arrow back. The shaft didn't even tremble. He'd paid good money for these arrows and was glad he had done so. If he managed to make a clean hole through the back of the animal's neck he could make the fur into a hood for their housemaid Juliet. Thanks to his hunting skill Juliet was easily the best-dressed maid in Beltane Ridge. Although now that the furrier was dead he'd have to cure the pelt himself, which wasn't much fun.

The coney had found the grain trail, and now moved with the heedless abandon of greed, pale paws kicking up, pale tail flashing an invitation to any passing hawk.

Barnaby was about to release the arrow when a flash of white to his left caught his attention.

The other end of the trail he'd laid had been discovered too, but this animal was unlike any coney he'd seen before: it was pure white, with scarlet eyes and ears of the softest pink. The sun shone through them, making them glow. It must be young because it was still plump, its coat flawless and glossy. Invisible whiskers twitched as it nibbled the grain.

22

Very slowly he revolved on his heels until the arrow was trained on the back of the creature's plump neck.

Now this *would* be a gift for Juliet. Everyone would think it was ermine. He would have to keep the feet as proof she was not breaking the sumptuary laws: he was pretty sure servants were only allowed to wear rabbit fur.

The white coney dipped its head for another helping of grain and he waited for it to raise it again.

The black shape came out of nowhere, startling him so much that he dropped the bow. The white coney's shrill scream, like a child's, was drowned out by guttural snarling, then finally cut off altogether. Blood arced up into the blue sky and spattered down on the grass beneath the tree he was standing under.

Barnaby almost pissed his breeches. It was an alaunt. Most likely from the baron's own dog pack. Only last year one of these vicious hunting dogs had got loose and torn apart a shepherd as he tried to protect his flock. The man's family had received generous compensation but the baron refused to have the dog destroyed, despite the fact that it now had a taste for human flesh.

As the dog snorted and grunted its way through the coney's innards Barnaby did not dare move a muscle. In the height of summer his hair merged with the golden corn, but it was late spring and the corn was still green. Any movement would make him stand out against it as clearly as the rabbit. The dog threw its head back to swallow a chunk of meat and then, to Barnaby's shrinking horror, its black eyes fell upon him.

For what must only have been a few seconds they stared at one other, then Barnaby risked moving his eyes

23

to see if the tree was climbable. The first decent branch was over six feet up. The beast would be on him before he could even hook a leg over. He wouldn't even have the chance to pick up the bow. He flicked his eyes back to the dog.

It was still looking at him.

A breeze stirred the leaves above him and whispered in the leaves of corn. It was an eerie sound and the dog's ears twitched nervously. The seed balls of the plane tree danced in Barnaby's line of vision. If he snatched one down and threw it the dog might take fright; only for a second, but perhaps long enough for him to snatch up the bow. Slowly he reached up and plucked one of them. But it was too ripe. It crumbled in his hand, the seeds drifting off on their parachutes of fluff. One sailed gently towards the alaunt, and to Barnaby's surprise the dog skittered back.

The wind blew stronger, and the seed pods danced more frantically.

He plucked another and crumbled it in his hand, then let the wind take it. This time the wisps of fluff flew quickly, forming themselves into a single waving line, like a trail of smoke or a marching army.

The dog lowered itself onto its front legs and barked.

He picked another seed head and crumbled it. But he needn't have bothered. As soon as the first seed struck the dog's head, it let out a sharp whine, turned, and bolted. A moment later it was just a dark speck racing through the pastureland in the direction of the manor house.

Barnaby exhaled in a sob. His tunic was wet with sweat and his legs were too wobbly to support him. He slid down the tree trunk and sank his head between his knees.

Eventually, after a drink from his waterskin and the hunk of pie Juliet had packed for him, his strength returned. He went over to the trail of grain, but all that was left of the coney were a few scraps of bloody fur and the stink of fresh meat.

He stank too and the sun was giving him a headache.

In the distance the silver disc of the lake was too bright to look at. But however scorching the day its waters were always deliciously cool. He set off towards it.

The fields of rye and buckwheat he passed through would soon be ready for harvesting. His heart sank. Harvest time was always the most tedious part of the year.

The sun was low in the sky and he squinted into its red glare. Darting lights appeared at the edge of his field of vision and he paused to try and focus on them. As a child, before he realised it was just light distortion, he'd imagined these were his fairy guardians. Very occasionally he dreamed he was being watched over by other presences and, despite what he had been told about the spiteful and covetous nature of fairies, those in his dreams were warm and comforting.

In reality they could not have been, of course, because according to his father he had been so traumatised by his time in Fairyland that he was inconsolable for months afterwards. Those difficult first few days of his life were rarely spoken of, and though he suspected his father was secretly proud to have outwitted the Little People, his mother would not have it mentioned in the house. To

Barnaby it was all simply an embarrassment: if anyone new came to the village he would be pointed out to them and the story whispered breathlessly in their ear.

He came to the tree where they had hanged the witch and its branch creaked as he passed: it always did, even on a windless day.

Eventually the fields were replaced by bulrushes. Mating dragonflies weaved around their drooping heads. Bees and butterflies bobbed in the wild flowers. The scent of them was heady in the warm air, but as he picked his way to the lake edge the air cooled. The pounding in his temples diminished. Finding a firm section of bank he began undressing.

The insects soon left the yellow petals of the kingcups to creep amongst the gold hairs of his legs. He brushed them off and walked to the edge.

The lake was as clear as ice. Even further out, where it got much deeper, he could still make out the pale clay of the bed, flickering as brown trout or shadow-fish flashed by.

He bent his knees and dived gracefully into the water.

The first few seconds while his body adjusted to the sudden plummet in temperature were agony, but he forced himself to stay under until he was used to it.

Finally he broke the surface and set off at a brisk crawl to warm up. Soon he was enjoying the feel of the water rippling along his flanks. It was deliciously refreshing, and the meaty taste of the pie was replaced by the clean, green taste of the lake.

As he swam the rushes and wild flowers thinned out and a moment later the Waters' farm came into view.

Farmer Waters' fuzzy-headed daughter was sitting on the grass weaving a rush basket while her brother played nearby.

The little boy said something and held up a fat pink worm that writhed to escape his grip. His sister laughed then called across to him, 'Put it down now, and cover it or the birds'll get it.'

'Good for the birds!' the boy called back.

'But not for the potatoes, they need the soil to be worked.'

Barnaby snorted. She had spoiled her brother's fun for the sake of a potato. But his snort alerted her to his presence and she looked up, pushing her hair out of her eyes to see better. Underneath that mass of dark curls she was actually quite pretty.

When he was satisfied he had her attention Barnaby struck out to the centre of the lake, kicking hard and keeping himself high in the water to ensure she had a good view of his muscular shoulders. He made a few circles in the centre of the lake, then rolled onto his back and let himself float. Peering out from beneath his eyelashes he saw that the boy was now standing on the shingle beach watching him, the worm forgotten, but his sister had returned to her basketwork.

Barnaby waited.

She didn't look up.

'Coming in, little man?' he called across to the boy. The boy shook his head. 'Naomi says there's a pike in there the size of a ram.'

Barnaby's bladder contracted sharply. He scanned the clear water. Nothing but shrimp and minnows.

'Nonsense!' he cried, to draw her into the debate. She murmured something to her brother then got up and went into the house.

The boy lost interest and wandered back to the mud. The door of the cottage remained steadfastly closed and no face appeared at the window. The sun had dipped down behind the forest now and Barnaby was starting to get cold.

Were pike night feeders?

He swore and began swimming back to where he had left his clothes. He was about five yards from shore when his right leg spasmed.

He knew at once what had happened. He'd eaten that slice of pie too soon before going swimming and now he had cramp. Badly. His right thigh muscle was contracting in agonising waves and it was all he could do to keep the other limbs working to stay on the surface.

But they were not strong enough: the weight of the dead leg pulled him under.

The green of the sky merged with the green water and he completely lost his bearings. He kicked out to try and reach the surface but instead careened head first into a rock on the lake bed.

He gasped, inhaling water. He tried to cough but more water poured down his throat. Darkness seeped into the corners of his vision. Points of light spun and danced just out of reach. He watched his own hand move forward to touch them but it was too clumsy and slow. The lights seemed to whisper to him, and their voices were the music of the flint and mica rolling along the lake bed. He wanted to speak to them, but they vanished, leaving only the shadows and the cold.

A bubble escaped his nostril and he watched it lazily as it spiralled up towards the light.

But now a shadow blocked the light. An ugly, thrashing shadow that tore through the drowsiness that was drifting over him.

The pike.

He was so tired, but he had to fight.

It clamped its mouth around his wrist and he twisted free. A moment later it had him around the throat. Its jaws were powerful but strangely toothless. It wrenched him upwards and the pressure in his lungs became unbearable. He fought wildly as the drowsiness was replaced by pain. Still the colossal fish jerked him up towards the light.

His clawing hands found a soft part and the pike recoiled, with a yelp, but the grip around his throat didn't loosen.

The light became more and more glaring. The pain in his chest was unbearable. He could feel the fibres of his lungs ripping and hot blood filled his mouth.

His head broke the surface of the water.

The pike made a sound – or was it him? – a monstrous, heaving gasp followed by retching. Still he fought until eventually the pike, its nut-brown face haloed in wet curls, punched him square on the jaw.

The girl pulled him to the shore and dragged him up the shingle before collapsing on her back beside him.

By the time his own wrenching gasps had subsided and he was able to sit up, she was on her hands and knees coughing up clear mucus, like a cat bringing up a hairball. Ribbons of emerald-green weed were wound into her curls.

She must have felt his gaze on her because she turned her head and their eyes met. Her emerald irises were ringed by burst blood vessels.

'Thanks,' he said hoarsely.

As she spat onto the gravel he saw that his fingernails had raked three scarlet lines down her left cheek.

'Next time,' she wheezed, 'I'll let you drown.'

2
The Path

Barnaby limped home, bedraggled and bruised. The Waters girl hadn't even invited him into the cottage for a warming broth or a stiff drink. Neither had she sent her damned brother to get his clothes: his feet were sore and scratched from the thistles and coarse grass he had to pick through to fetch them.

At least he would get concern from his father and Juliet, though the best he could expect from his mother would be a *how silly of you, Barnaby.* As he got nearer home he began to cough, only half for effect: he was still feeling awful, as if someone had kicked him in the chest.

But no-one seemed to hear him. Certainly no-one came to the door.

He pushed it open and hobbled in. The parlour was empty. Surely they had not dined without him. He threw himself against the dresser to make it bang against the wall, then he leaned on it, wheezing, waiting to be discovered.

But it wasn't his father who came out of the kitchen. Nor even Juliet.

It was Abel.

There was an air of sly triumph in the tilt of his brother's chin that immediately made Barnaby uneasy. Was he in trouble for something?

'Father's been looking for you,' Abel said.

'Why?' Barnaby said, straightening up. All pretence of suffering vanished at once: they knew each other too well to deceive one another.

'The witch is dying,' Abel smirked.

'What?'

'Your precious Agnes.'

Barnaby blinked at him. His mouth opened but no words came.

Abel turned to go up the stairs. *'Woe to the women that sew pillows to all armholes and make magic bands upon the head of every stature to hunt souls.'*

'What's that supposed to mean?' Barnaby snapped.

Abel smiled. 'Agnes rejected the Lord God and put her faith in the potions and charms sent from the devil. God has punished her.'

Barnaby sprang forward, grabbing his brother by the scruff of the neck and spinning him round.

'Shut your mouth,' he snarled, 'or I'll snap your stringy neck.'

Abel's Adam's apple bounced up and down against Barnaby's knuckles but in his face there was no fear, only hatred and sly triumph. Barnaby hurled him aside in disgust and flew out of the door.

Agnes lived at the other end of the village in a tiny, neat

cottage that was always plentifully stocked with firewood and flour and fresh eggs from all the grateful families whose babies she had safely delivered. She was over sixty now and on recent occasions she'd winced at his embraces. He'd been steeling himself for the inevitable but all his preparations were as nothing as he blundered through the streets with tears streaming down his face.

Her little window was aglow with welcoming firelight and he couldn't repress the little skip of happiness his heart gave every time he arrived at her door. But then he realised: in May only the dying feel the cold.

He never usually knocked but now he hesitated, his palm flat against the warm wood. Was this the last time he would ever push open her door?

He could hear his father murmuring inside. If Henry could be brave, then he must be too.

The door swung silently open and he was struck by a wall of hot, foetid air.

He stepped in and closed the door quietly behind him. Agnes's bed had been drawn up to the fire and was surrounded by figures silhouetted against the flames. Two of the men were speaking quietly.

'She dies very hard,' one of them said. 'Are ye sure the cause is not game feathers in the pillow?'

'It has been checked several times,' the other murmured, 'and 'tis only duck and goose. Perhaps the evil eye has been put upon her.'

The other grumbled unhappily and moved away.

Now Barnaby could see the bed with his father kneeling beside it. Barnaby caught a glimpse of his old nurse's face and stifled a gasp.

The last time he visited she was as spry and sharp-tongued as ever, if a little yellow around the temples. Now she looked like a week-old corpse. The flesh had shrunk from her bones and the skin was waxen. He could clearly make out both bones of her forearm as it rested in his father's lap.

Had it been so long since he'd visited?

Then she saw him: her face lit up, and suddenly she became Agnes again. Her lips moved but he couldn't hear what she said. He stepped closer and the stench of death grew stronger.

He moved behind his father, laying his hands on Henry's shoulders while, just for a moment, he got used to her appearance.

'Now, what's all this fuss,' he said quietly. 'You're not just trying to get out of your chores, are you?'

Agnes gave a papery laugh – it was a phrase she had used to him on countless occasions.

'Yes,' she croaked, 'I am.'

She raised her arm from his father's lap and stretched her fingers towards him. It was all right now. He was ready. He walked around his father and knelt down on the floor beside her, then he took her hand in his own.

It was shockingly cold, and light as the shed husk of a spider.

'*Bye baby bunting*,' she sang, her voice reed thin and almost lost in the hiss of the flames, '*Daddy's gone a hunting . . .*'

But she subsided into coughing and couldn't continue.

'*He's gone to fetch a rabbit skin*,' Barnaby murmured, '*to wrap the baby bunting in.*'

34

The eyes that finally turned on him again were misted with death.

'You know . . .' he began haltingly, 'that I love you as a mother.'

He leaned forwards and kissed her hollow cheek and his tears dropped into her white wisps of hair.

'There, there, my love,' she murmured. 'It will be all right.'

'No,' he said. 'Without you I would have been motherless.'

'Do not judge her so harshly,' Agnes whispered. 'She couldn't accept the truth. She believed the changeling child to be her own and loved it as her own.' Her bird chest rose in a sigh. 'My one regret is that I could not save your brother.'

Barnaby wiped away his tears away and smiled. 'Oh, Aggie,' he said, 'Abel is no changeling. He's the spit of my mother's kin.'

She pulled him close and glanced furtively around. The other visitors, including Henry, were now speaking in low tones to one another. Seemingly satisfied they wouldn't be overheard Agnes breathed, 'He is the image of the other child: the one the fairies took when they returned you. Besides,' she lowered her voice until it was barely audible, 'only a changeling could be so odious.'

Barnaby gave a snuffling laugh. Conversations broke off and all eyes turned on him reproachfully.

'Watch him,' Agnes continued quietly when the low chatter had resumed. 'Bitterness and envy have blackened his heart.'

'And what could such a puling weakling do to me?'

35

Barnaby smiled, adding, 'besides hit me over the head with a Bible?'

When Agnes smiled her eyes twinkled as brightly as they always had. As a child he had been afraid of her sharpness but soon enough he had learned how to soften her edges.

'Now,' she said, 'be off with you.'

He would not have abandoned her but now that she had given him leave he could not wait to escape the thick air of the room. She held him a moment, her fingers gripping his wrist. He held her gaze until the blood rushed in his head, then finally she closed her eyes and her hand slipped from his.

He was pushed back as more people crowded in to say their farewells. He hovered for a few moments until the death rattle began. It sounded oddly comical. The sort of grunting snore his father gave after he'd eaten and drunk too much and fallen asleep in a chair. But then Father Nicholas shuffled out of the shadows and spread his black wings over Agnes's frail body like a crow over carrion, and Barnaby fled.

The funeral feast was to be held in her nephew's barn. His mother and Abel did not wish to attend; which was fine with Barnaby. Though Agnes had defended Frances, Barnaby knew full well there had never been any love lost between the two women. As far back as he could remember the atmosphere in the house had turned to ice every time Agnes arrived, with her characteristic five sharp raps on the door, which made Barnaby's heart swell with happiness, and sent Abel into a wild tantrum of howling and kicking. Once he had blackened their mother's eye as she tried to restrain him and for that he had received a beating from Henry, despite the fact that he had only been four at the time. Even as a five-year-old Barnaby had considered this harsh. But that was when he had loved his brother and still enjoyed trying to teach him to catch a ball and say *Please* and *Thank you* and *Juliet smells*. At the time Juliet's mother was their maid and Juliet and Barnaby, being almost the same age, would play in the meadows at the back of the house while her mother worked. On the few occasions Frances allowed it they would bring Abel along with them, and Barnaby vividly remembered the moment he came to dislike his brother. Frances had given Juliet a shawl of fine silk, brought back from Arabia by one of Henry's business associates, and she had let Abel play with it, tossing it up into the air and letting it fall on his face so that the sunlight was diffused through its rich colours. For a moment the two older children became distracted, trying to see who could make the most alarming screech by blowing along a stem of grass threaded through their forefingers and thumbs. When they looked up Abel was gone. Too small to see above the tall grass they ran blindly, crying out his name but with no response. Eventually they were forced to stop catch their breaths. By now Juliet was crying. But beneath her cries, and his own panting, Barnaby could hear a rustling sound. He hushed her and listened. It sounded like laboured breathing, close by. Was it Abel, too injured to speak? They set off again and a moment later burst out of the long grass, right next to the stream. Juliet wailed and Barnaby stared down at the rushing waters in consternation. Had Abel fallen in?

But there was that wheezing sound again, and now Barnaby recognised it: it was laughter.

A moment later he spotted his brother, crouched beneath a gorse bush at the water's edge, chuckling. His glittering black eyes swivelled up to something above his head. Barnaby followed his gaze. Pushed deep into the interior of the bush and torn to shreds by the thorns was the Arabian shawl. Juliet claimed afterwards that it had been an accident, that Abel had thrown it carelessly, but Barnaby knew the truth, and not just by the smirk that never left Abel's face all the way home. Abel had scratches all over his arms.

That night Frances and Henry had gone to one of the baron's dinners at the castle and Agnes was to babysit them. When she heard what had happened she sent Abel to bed with no supper and no candle. As the night darkened and Abel's whimpers of fear turned to sobs of terror she simply sat in the rocking chair by the fire, knitting quietly. Barnaby sat at her feet eating the marchpane animals she had made for him, torn between satisfaction at seeing Abel punished properly for once, and a sick relief that it wasn't him up there alone in the dark. From then on Abel would have to be taken out of the room when Agnes called, and his mother blamed the old woman for the fact that Abel started wetting the bed again and didn't stop until his twelfth birthday.

No, Agnes would not be sorry not to have his mother and Abel at her wake. In fact she might very well spin in her freshly dug grave if they did turn up.

The hour of the feast arrived. As soon he and his father stepped out of the door Henry rubbed his hands: 'We're off the leash for the night, Barney, my lad, and I for one feel like drinking a skinful and dancing a jig or two, how about you?'

Barnaby attempted a smile. His father had recovered from Agnes's death quickly, saying that the loss of an old person was a natural thing and not to be grieved, but Barnaby still felt as if he might burst into tears at any moment. The worst thing was that all his friends would be at the feast, including Griff's mouthy cousin, Richard, who always seemed to feel the need to outdo Barnaby when they were in the same company. If Barnaby drank a yard of ale, Richard would drink two, if Barnaby juggled three apples to impress the girls, Richard would juggle four.

The sound of fiddle music drifted through the evening air, accompanied now and again by the tinkle of bells. They quickened their pace, Henry keeping to the sides of the street to protect his tan suede boots from the dust churned up by carts. Barnaby regarded the boots enviously. He didn't see the point of wasting such finery on a man his father's age. Still, a bit of wheedling over some mugs of beer and Henry was sure to hand them over.

The fiddle music grew louder and a buttery glow lit the other end of the street.

Barnaby paused to adjust his clothes, delving into his boots and smoothing out his stockings – silk this evening, so wrinklier than usual – tucking his shirt into his breeches, then pulling the sleeves down so that they puffed out of his jacket cuffs. It amused him to see his father attempting similar manoeuvres, to very poor effect: his jacket wouldn't do up past the third button, his breeches strained at the backside and his fussy collar only accentuated his double chins. Still, he was better looking than most men his age and there were enough women who still flirted with him.

They strode up to the barn and passed through the wide-open doors.

Inside was ablaze with candlelight to prevent any spirits of the dead entering. A fiddler stood on a hay cart at the back, accompanied by an old shepherd with a pipe. A few children danced beneath them, one an infant barely walking who kept falling on its well-padded backside and having to be lifted and comforted. Barnaby's spirits rose when he spotted Griff, wedged into a corner with some other boys, a large pewter mug in one hand and a slab of cheese in the other. When Griff spotted him he grinned and waved the cheese. With a farewell pat on his father's back, Barnaby went over to his friends.

He drank quickly and by the time the red sky had mellowed to the blue of night he was drunk. A gaggle of girls on the other side of the barn kept glancing over, giggling and whispering into their hands. Among them was Flora Slabber, the butcher's pretty daughter. Barnaby had always admired her golden hair and cherry red lips and he had just persuaded Griff to go over with him when Richard appeared: stone-cold sober and with eyes that glittered with mockery at the shambling state of the other boys. Griff snatched his chance to get out of meeting the girls and went off with Richard to get some food. Barnaby took the opportunity of escaping through a loose panel in the back wall and stood in the darkness, gulping down the cool night air to try and sober up. He must keep his wits about him for Richard would certainly try and make a fool of him.

On this side of the barn there was nothing but farmland: lakes of silver in the moonlight, and beyond, the dark mass of the forest. He swayed gently as he stared into the blackness, trying as he often did, to make out any movement between the trees.

Just to the left of the trees a shadow detached itself from the greater mass.

Two figures were coming across the field towards him. A disc of light surrounded the head of the taller one, like a halo. As they came closer he saw that it was hair. It was the Waters girl and her brother. The moon had tipped each of her dark curls with silver.

So as not to look foolish he stepped forward at their approach and greeted them at once.

'Miss Waters, I must thank you again for saving my life. My parents are very grateful. Although,' he added with a grin, 'my brother is furious.'

She came closer before replying, climbing the slope up to the barn.

'The lake has strong currents,' she said. 'It's dangerous for weak swimmers.'

'I'm not a weak swimmer!' he spluttered. 'Last summer I swam a mile upstream to Braidwater.'

But she wasn't listening. She had bent to adjust her brother's collar and now straightened up and led him around the side of the barn to the main doors. He grimaced at her back. She might be pretty but what a sour stick she was.

Then the loose panel flipped up and his heart sank as Richard crawled out.

'Poor lamb!' Richard cooed when he saw Barnaby. 'Was it too hot for you, precious? Are you feeling faint?'

'Oh, shut up,' Barnaby sighed.

Richard smirked then took a step forwards and bowed low. 'My apologies, Prince of Fairyland, please don't turn me into a frog.'

Now Griff emerged from the panel. 'You're already slimy and warty, Rich, he wouldn't have to do much.'

Barnaby shot him a grateful glance.

'What you doing out here anyway?' Griff said, coming over and handing Barnaby a cup of mead. Now that he'd sobered up a little the sickly honey smell made him gag.

'Just getting some fresh air.'

'Can you see anything, Griff?' – this was Caleb, the blacksmith's son, as he too came crawling through the panel. 'Any lights or flames?'

'Nah,' Griff called back to him, 'Looks pretty dark to me.'

'What's going on?' Barnaby said.

'Caleb's brother got talking to a poacher in the Boar last week,' Griff said 'Reckoned he was out hunting in the forest and saw a coven of witches dancing with the devil.'

Caleb came beside them. One of his eyes was dragged down at the corner where a piece of hot metal had struck him and almost blinded him. It remained half closed while the other widened. 'It's true,' he said. 'The poacher notices this light and thinks it might be the baron's men so he creeps up and sees a ring of fire around the midden heap. All these figures are dancing around it and at the very top of the heap, spinning and whirling like a wildcat, is the

42

devil himself. The poacher hides behind a tree to watch them.'

'Did he recognise any of the figures?' Richard said, coming to join them.

'Only the Widow Moone,' Caleb said.. 'The rest were cloaked and hooded.'

'How convenient,' Barnaby said: he was used to Caleb's tall stories.

'Tell him what happened next,' Griff said.

Caleb glanced around him then leaned into Barnaby. His breath smelled of mead and onions. 'One of the women takes something from under her cloak. At first the poacher thinks it's a white cat, but then it starts to cry.'

'It was a baby,' Griff whispered.

'You don't say,' Barnaby said.

'The witch throws the baby up to the devil on the midden heap and the devil catches it and holds it above his head, chanting in this awful, hollow voice, and then suddenly these *creatures* fly down from the trees. But they weren't birds.'

'Or bats,' Griff whispered.

Barnaby rolled his eyes.

'Demons,' Caleb whispered dramatically. 'They fly down and land on the devil's shoulders and start tearing at the baby, like hawks tearing a rabbit. A moment later the crying stops.'

He paused and glanced around at his rapt audience.

'Then ...' he went on, his good eye even wider, 'the devil gets out this pen made of a raven feather, and stabs it into the baby. He brings it out all dripping with blood then he gets out a parchment and calls out in this hollow voice, "Which of you offers up your soul to the Son of the Morning?" And one of the women calls out "I" and she gives him her name and he writes it on the parchment. Then the next woman gives him her name and so on until all the witches' names are on the parchment. Then he says, "These names will be inscribed upon the very stones of hell where you will be enthroned as queens for the rest of eternity!" But suddenly the poacher feels something brush against him and he's so scared it's one of the demons he cries out. All at once the fires go out and there's total silence.'

The silence was mirrored by the group of boys gathered around Caleb, their round faces pale in the moonlight, their breath misting the cool air.

'Well, the poacher starts running and doesn't stop until he's out of the trees and when he gets out of the forest he finds that the whole of the night has passed and it's already morning.'

There was a collective exhalation and the boys straightened up.

Griff nudged Barnaby in the ribs. 'What do you think of that, eh?'

Barnaby gazed out towards the forest. It was just possible to make out a mist of bats swirling above the treetops, tiny as gnats from this distance. The story was probably no more than the drunken ramblings of a lowlife criminal but it had still brought goosebumps up on his arms.

'What happened to the parchment?' he said. 'That list written in blood.'

'What?' Caleb said.

'If they all vanished when the fire went out maybe the

devil dropped it,' he said, a grin spreading across his face. 'We should go and look for it tomorrow.'

'Yeah,' Griff said uncertainly.

'Come on,' Barnaby said, slapping his cowardly friend's shoulder. 'Let's go and get more beer.'

But as they walked back towards the barn Richard stepped into his path.

'Why not go now?' he said.

'What?'

'Into the forest to look for the list. There's nothing for you to be scared of, surely: not with your fairy friends to protect you.'

Barnaby sighed. 'Come on, Griff.'

Richard's clucking noises followed him across to the loose panel.

But then the plank swung up and Flora Slabber and her friends climbed through. When she saw Barnaby she blushed and started fingering the ribbons in her gold hair.

'What are you all doing out here?' she said coyly.

'Barnaby was going to go into the forest to look for the devil's list,' Richard called, 'but he's too scared.'

'You weren't going to really, were you?' Flora gasped.

Barnaby chuckled. 'It's just a stupid poacher's tale to try and impress his drunken friends.'

'Please don't.' She touched his arm, her liquid eyes filled with concern. Barnaby's heart quickened slightly: she definitely liked him. He couldn't help being flattered, despite the fact that close up her face was unattractively caked in white make-up. It would certainly be fun to make her fall for him, if only to drive the other boys wild with envy.

'Don't worry,' he grinned at her, 'I'll be fine.'

He stepped back from the plank and turned to Richard. 'Are you going to keep me company, then?'

'Ha!' Richard crowed. 'Don't think that I'm holding your hand!' but the forced laugh gave away his fear.

'Barnaby, please!' Flora whimpered, but without a backward glance he strode out across the field. A moment later he heard footsteps behind him. Richard fell into step beside him, carrying a lantern. The smirk had gone.

'I was only joking,' he muttered. 'Why don't you just hide behind the first line of trees for a bit?'

Because you'll tell everyone that's what I did, Barnaby almost said, annoyed that this option was now out of the question. Away from his audience Richard had lost all his confidence. Every now and then Barnaby glanced at him from the corner of his eye and he saw Richard chewing his lips.

They had been walking quickly and were almost a quarter of the way there when two ghostly figures swam up out of the gloom. Richard cried out and clutched Barnaby's arm. But then the moon slipped out from behind a cloud.

It was only the furrier's widow and her deaf son.

Richard bade them a good evening but Barnaby said nothing. The woman gave him the creeps. Whenever they were in the same place – in church or at the market where she sold berries and mushrooms from the forest – he always seemed to catch her looking at him. Her brightly coloured petticoats and the way she wove flowers into her grey hair were pathetic and faintly distasteful.

Her steps paused as they passed and Barnaby felt her eyes on him. He didn't return her gaze, nor that of the boy, whose dark looks reminded him unfavourably of Abel.

46

They came to the edge of the forest's shadow and Richard's footsteps faltered.

'It's all right,' Barnaby said. 'You don't have to come any further.'

Richard shifted from foot to foot and blinked rapidly at the trees.

'Right, well, you don't have to be in there long,' he said. 'Just to the midden heap and then straight back again.'

'Very well, Mother.'

Richard didn't smile. The lantern light had leached all the colour from his face.

Barnaby was about to step into the shadow when he heard a shout from behind. Griff was running across the field. Eventually he reached them and panted: 'Someone told your father, Barnaby. He's coming to fetch you back.'

Barnaby glanced back at the barn. More people had come out to watch. He could see their moving shadows in the pinpoints of lantern light. He was going to get a hiding for this.

'Take this.' He handed the lantern back to Griff. 'Otherwise he'll see it and come after me. The moon's strong enough without it.'

The two boys stared at him, open-mouthed.

'Right,' he grinned. 'See you soon.'

He stepped over the threshold of shadow.

It took a long time for his eyes to adjust enough to see anything at all. It was strange, walking blind, with just sounds to tell you that you were still in the real world. He could hear his feet crumpling the grass, the swish of his breeches rubbing together, his breath – still reassuringly steady – the rhythmic swilling of his blood in his ears. And

47

then there were the other sounds, the unpredictable sounds of the night: the distant cries of foxes, the murmur of the wind in the trees; a nightjar's strange whirring call, more like a cricket than a bird, and rustling everywhere, all around him. He even heard the whisper of a moth's wing as it passed close to his ear.

Eventually he was able to make out the lie of the land. Above him the stars seemed to multiply by the second, with new ones appearing and growing stronger until there was not the tiniest scrap of empty sky. He saw one, then another shooting star: it made an audible hiss as it whizzed by. Everything was clear and vivid and beautiful.

And then he looked straight ahead and saw the trees bearing down on him.

It was fatal to let his steps falter: if he gave his body any hint that he was afraid he'd crumble. He knew what it was like to be utterly drowned in terror. Until the age of nine he'd suffered from debilitating nightmares and would have to be carried from his bed, rigid and screaming, and rocked on his father's lap by the fire. His father and Agnes had believed it was the fairies tormenting him with horrific visions, trying to send him mad so that they could lure him back to them. In hindsight, being told that could only have made matters worse.

But he had learned to control his fear. His father had taught him how: to breathe deeply and loosen all his muscles one by one, to trick his body into thinking he wasn't scared at all. He followed the same routine now: rolling his shoulders and stretching his neck from side to side; balling his hands into fists and then stretching out the fingers; breathing deeply, in-two-three-four-five-six, out-two-three-four-five-six – tightening and relaxing every muscle he could without slowing his pace.

It worked, because the next time he looked up he was in the forest.

The sudden change of pressure made his ears pop and for a moment or two he was deaf as well as blind. Panic welled up inside him. He could hear only the crashing of his heart. He swayed. Was he falling? There was no way of telling, no marker to orientate himself by.

Then something struck him violently in the back and sent him reeling. The undergrowth swallowed him and for a while it was as if he was six again, lying rigid with terror on his sweat-soaked mattress. But the blow had un-popped his ears and as his reason returned he understood what had happened. He'd overbalanced and hit a tree trunk, that was all.

He sat up.

He could really do with a few slugs of Griff's foul-smelling mead. If only Richard could see him now, cowering in the undergrowth, his opinion of Barnaby as some sort of rival would evaporate.

The dark inside the forest was all-encompassing. He could see absolutely nothing: not even the white breast of the barn owl that just screeched demonically above his head and made him jump several inches from the ground.

He had a vague idea where the midden heap lay, but it was only ever Juliet that made the trip.

He set off in the direction he thought it lay: a little to the south-east – the direction the devil's wind blew from. A shaft of moonlight fell through the canopy to light the clearing beneath. He picked his way across to it and stood in the faint glow. Then he saw another clearing a little way off, the moonlight a little brighter there. Steeling himself, he waded through the darkness until he had reached it, then paused to get his bearings. He was fairly sure the heap lay to his left. There seemed to be another clearing further in that direction and he set off again.

He tripped a few times and had to make a detour around a huge knot of brambles he didn't see until they'd torn his face and arms. He could pretend they were wounds from demon claws. That would shut Richard up.

He stumbled on. The trees grew thicker and the birdsong died away, to be replaced by silence.

Something stung his leg through the stocking. Could a nettle do that?

To lift his spirits he began to hum. The frail thread of sound was immediately consumed by the silence. He stopped.

He'd been walking for a while now. Surely he was nearing the heap.

It was taking much longer than he'd expected to reach the next clearing, and now that he looked more closely the light didn't seem to be coming from above at all. It was as cold as moonlight but it pulsed and wavered like a candle flame in a breeze. Unnaturally. It was fairy light.

They had found him. They'd always wanted him back and now they had found him.

He dropped to a crouch in the undergrowth, turned and began to slither back the way he had come.

Twigs scraped his stomach and nettles scalded his exposed flesh.

The second clearing came into view again, the moonlight stronger now, a steady shaft slicing through the darkness. He would crawl around the circle of light so as not to be seen.

He was nearly there now, just a few more feet.

Suddenly the ground domed upwards, blocking his path.

There was no sense trying to run: the forest was theirs to enchant and distort however they wished. He had to face them: stand tall and demand to know what they wanted of him.

His mind whirred in panic and he closed his eyes and breathed deeply. There was a strong, sulphurous smell. The smell of enchantment.

Finally he opened his eyes and stood up.

'I am not afraid,' he said loudly and clearly.

Raising his hand to his eyes to protect them from the glare he waited for them to appear. Would they be tall like him, or tiny as children like they were in the stories? Somehow that would be worse. Would the other one be there: the one they had tried to replace him with? Hungry to return to its human family? He shivered. An icy clamminess crept across his skin. But hadn't Agnes said that in all probability it wasn't a live thing at all, just a lump of wood they had bewitched to seem like a human baby?

The canopy whispered. Dust motes tumbled through the cold white moonlight and he followed their trajectory, wondering whether they would transform into their fairy forms when they landed.

They did not.

And now he saw that the rising of the ground was not unnatural after all. It was just a little hill of earth, flattened

51

on top. And what was that rising up from a bumpy area protruding from the side – was it smoke? Steam?

Now that he thought about it there was something beneath the sulphurous smell: something unpleasant.

Shit.

It was the midden heap.

He laughed out loud.

Now he could make out cattle bones and broken crockery, a stocking, a rotting animal hide.

Then he caught his breath.

Lying on top was a small skeleton, picked clean by insects and vermin. A light breeze disturbed the few rags of skin that still hung to the frame. It had a strangely flattened skull and huge eye sockets. The spine was elongated, the arms too long, the legs too short. A strange, malformed thing: unlovable, inhuman.

Surely it could not be the changeling . . . Not after so long . . .

Then he let out a hoarse cry of relief.

It was a cat. Just a cat. A strip of red wool hung around its neck – loosely now, but possibly once tight enough to throttle it. He moved closer. Strung onto the wool were feathers, twists of iron wire, holed stones and what looked like animal teeth. These looked like the sorts of charms used by witches. Certainly the Widow Moone was always trying to hawk such bits of junk.

Hadn't the poacher thought he'd seen a cat at first, not a baby? Perhaps he had. Perhaps this was the sacrifice used to provide the blood for the devil's pen.

There might be some truth to the story after all.

He glanced nervously behind him, into the shadows.

The moonlight only stretched to the first line of trees. Beyond was unbroken darkness. Something in the darkness began to whisper. The whisper passed all around the clearing, spiralling closer and closer. He tensed up, waiting for whatever it was to burst from the trees upon him. But when it did it was only the wind, rushing up the slope, flapping rags and clacking the light bones of the chicken carcasses. It blew up his legs, billowed his shirt, then passed cold fingers through his hair.

And then something blew out of the ribcage of the cat to slap against his boot.

He picked it up.

It was a scrap of paper: yellowed and dog-eared. Just visible in the corner were a few clumsy markings in brown ink. He couldn't make them out. Perhaps one was an E, another an L or perhaps an R.

Then he froze. The devil's list had been written in blood: blood that would have turned brown as it dried.

He dropped it with a cry. At once it was caught by the wind and carried off into the darkness. He stared into the shadows, panting. There was no way he was going after it. Even if he came back without it he had surely done enough to impress Richard and set Flora's heart aflutter. He slithered down the side of the heap and stopped at the bottom. Then he turned in a slow circle.

He had lost his bearings.

He peered up through the gap in the canopy, but he was useless at navigating by the stars at the best of times and was now totally disorientated. He turned on the spot, trying to make out the lights of the barn through the closely packed branches. Eventually lights were appearing and vanishing all across his strained vision and he closed his eyes and rubbed them.

A rustling close by made him spin around.

A large fox was watching him from the other side of the midden heap. It was a grizzled, bony thing, with half an ear torn off. Its eyes glowed in the moonlight.

'Yah!' he shouted – a fox couldn't hurt him; it wouldn't dare try.

The fox gave a low bark and a split second later the bark was returned. Barnaby spun around. Another fox stood in the trees behind him, so thin he could make out the shadows of its ribs and spine.

He picked up a stick and swiped at this closer one. The fox skittered back but didn't depart. Then the other threw back its head and howled. It was an oddly human sound, almost a scream of anguish, but Barnaby understood its purpose.

It was a summoning.

Impossible to judge how close the answering howls were. And how many. How many would they need to be to feel confident enough to attack him? Four? Five?

The two on either side of him stood motionless, waiting.

Then suddenly, from the corner of his eye, he spotted something out of place in the haphazard fecundity of the forest.

A regular line of white spots.

Slowly, keeping both foxes in view all the way, he made his way to where the line began.

They looked like pearls.

He bent down and picked one up. It was cool and firm.

This was not chance, a will-o-the-wisp or his fevered imagination. These had been left here to mark a path. Was it a fairy trick to lure him to his doom? Or perhaps they were simply white pebbles or beads left to mark the way home by someone who had come to use the midden heap.

The trail stretched out into the darkness of the trees.

Rustling behind him made him turn. The foxes had climbed to the top of the midden heap and were staring after him with opaque, yellow eyes. Now both threw back their heads and howled, their fangs glimmering in the moonlight. Before they had closed their mouths and lowered their heads to resume the watch on their prey, Barnaby had sprinted off along the trail.

They were waiting for him at the edge of the trees. A line of lanterns, as if a search party was about to depart. There were screams when he burst from the shadows.

'What?' he said, steadying himself and grinning.

Griff bounded forward and hugged him, stinking of sweat, and then was wrenched away and his father's white face was an inch from his own nose, the lips quivering.

'What the hell do you . . .' he stuttered. Barnaby stared at him. He'd never seen his father in such a state.

'It's all right,' he said softly. 'I'm all right. It was just a dare, that's all.'

His father's bewildered eyes searched his own, then he took his son's face in his hands and pressed his cold clammy forehead to Barnaby's, which was warm and sweaty from the run through the trees.

'I thought I'd lost you again,' he muttered.

'Oh hush, you old piss-head,' Barnaby said softly, but he

55

let his father hold him until someone cleared their throat beside him.

It was Richard.

His face was almost as pasty as Henry's. Richard stretched out his hand. Barnaby shook it and for a long time Richard wouldn't let it go.

'You are no coward,' Richard said finally, then he turned and walked back across the field to where the barn still throbbed with music and rowdy laughter. The crowd had begun to disperse now, all except one woman. The furrier's widow. She was staring at him with that intensity that always made him so uncomfortable.

'Come on, Father,' he said, turning from her gaze. 'I don't want to miss the rest of the party.'

Back inside he was immediately surrounded by his friends.

'Did you find it?' Caleb said, his good eye now drooping with drunkenness.

He looked around the throng of wide-eyed boys and wondered where Flora had got to.

Finally he nodded. 'Just a corner, mind.'

'Where is it?' Richard said, back to his old belligerent self now that the shock was subsiding.

'Well, that's the oddest thing about it,' Barnaby said quietly. 'This wind suddenly blew up from nowhere and snatched it out of my hands and up into the trees.'

Caleb nodded slowly, 'An enchanted wind.'

'The devil's wind,' Griff said.

'Certainly smelled like it,' Barnaby said, but they were all too drunk to get the joke. All except Richard. 'Did you read the names?' he said.

'Huh?'

'The names on the parchment. Did you read them?'

'Umm. It was torn. I couldn't really see much.'

'Was the Widow Moone on it?' Caleb said.

'Er . . . yes. Yes, she was. That one I could read.'

'What about her sister from Gupton?' Griff said. 'Can't remember her name . . .'

'Er . . . I think there might have been another Moone. It was dark, you know, so . . .'

'Is that it?' Richard said.

Barnaby rounded on him. 'It was dark, the paper was ripped, and the wind blew it out of my hand. But feel free to go back and look for it yourself, if you like.'

Richard pressed his lips together.

'And was it written in blood?' Caleb said breathlessly.

Barnaby nodded.

There was a ripple of gasps.

'A blood list of the damned,' Griff whispered and even Barnaby shivered.

Then a gaggle of younger children tumbled into them and the spell was broken. The boldest child asked if it was true Barnaby had been visiting his fairy family in the forest. He told them that certainly it was and that the scratches on his leg were elf-shot. When Griff brought over a platter of pork crackling he refused, saying that he had feasted with his fairy friends on nectar and ambrosia, which turned out to be very filling. He told one of the younger girls that he would love to dance with her but he was worn out from the wild dancing on the fairy hill. The child gawped at him, then ran off and whispered to her mother who cast him a reproachful glance.

Though he was greatly enjoying the attention his eyelids started to droop. The tension of the forest had worn him out. He wobbled to his feet and, patting Griff's shoulder, made for the door.

Juliet was up when he arrived home. She greeted him at the door with a plate of cold ham and bread just baked for the morning.

'Your father's been back this last hour,' she said.

'That's because he's old and boring,' Barnaby said, tossing a hunk of bread into the air and catching it in his mouth. 'Can I have some warm milk?' He pushed past her and flopped down by the fire as she went out to the kitchen.

A few minutes later she returned with a cup. She'd flavoured it with cinnamon and brought a plate of cakes with it. Wonderful Juliet: she knew exactly what to do to make him happy. They had grown up together and he loved her like a sister, though she seemed considerably older than their mutual sixteen years.

'Was it fun?' she said, kneeling by the fire.

'You should have come.'

'There was too much to do here,' she sighed,

'In that case, sit down and have a rest,' he said, adding, 'Then I can use your plump lap as a cushion.'

She threw a half-burned twig at him but stretched out her legs, and with a deep sigh, he lay down and breathed in the familiar smell of her dress. He was glad to be home. The night's experience had taken more out of him than he'd imagined.

'What's the matter?' she said.

He looked up at her. Her eyes were the palest watery

58

blue, like an overcast sky. It was the first time he'd really studied her for a while. She looked tired.

'I went to the forest tonight,' he said.

She caught her breath. 'Who with?'

'Alone.'

'Barnaby!' she gasped. 'What were you thinking?'

'I was trying to impress Flora Slabber.'

'Oh.' Her eyes slid away from his.

'A witch coven was seen in the forest,' he went on. 'Dancing with the devil. There was supposed to be a list of the names of the witches, written in blood. I went looking for it.'

She stared at him.

He lowered his voice. 'And I found it.'

'You found the list?'

'Yes.'

'Who was on it?'

'Oh, you, me, Mother . . .'

She slapped him on the shoulder. 'Don't joke about such things.'

When she frowned she looked as old as his mother.

'Anyway,' he went on, 'you should be more concerned about the fact that I was very nearly lost and would have been eaten or frozen to death by the morning. There were lights that seemed to want to lead me deeper and deeper into the forest.'

Rather to his disappointment the anxiety in her face vanished.

'Marsh gas,' she said. 'And besides, if you'd been missing for longer than a minute your father would have had the whole village out looking for you.'

She got up, letting his head bump unceremoniously onto the floor. Picking up his plate she headed for the kitchen.

'Wait,' he said. 'What about these . . .?' He felt in his pocket for the pearl but it was gone.

'What?' she said.

'There was a path of pearls; it led me out of the forest. I picked one up but now it's gone and . . .'

'. . . And all that's left is a wet patch on your breeches.'

He looked down. She was right. There was a small damp circle where the corner of his pocket lay. He frowned.

She rested the plate on her hip, smirking. 'It couldn't conceivably have been berries, could it?'

Sure enough, right at the very bottom of his pocket, there was a slimy skin. He drew it out and they peered at it.

'Mistletoe,' she said.

'Well, I didn't think I was scared enough to piss myself.'

But she wasn't smiling any more.

'What?'

'Strange,' she said. 'The berries would have been taken by birds if they'd been laid in the day, so they must have been left tonight. As if someone knew you were coming and wanted to help you.'

There was silence for a moment, then Barnaby frowned.

'There's something else,' he said. 'When I went hunting the other day a huge black dog suddenly appeared. I thought it was going to tear my throat out. But then it was scared by some seeds flying in the wind and ran away.'

'What kind of a dog was it?' she said, her face troubled.

'An alaunt I think. I thought it must be one of the baron's hunting dogs.'

'Did it have a collar?'

'I didn't notice one. I suppose it might have. What's wrong?'

Her face was pale in the firelight. 'Lucifer often takes the form of a black dog ...'

Goosebumps sprang up on his arms.

'Have you upset anyone recently?' Juliet said.

'Only Abel.'

She gave a humourless laugh. 'Whatever you think of your brother, he is no friend of Beelzebub. No, I was thinking of witchcraft.' Her voice dropped to a whisper. 'Perhaps someone has performed maleficium on you.'

Barnaby sighed. Every time anyone in the village sickened or died Juliet was convinced it was caused by malevolent spells. Like most of the villagers she was a firm believer in witchcraft. She hung charms on her bed and always bashed in the shells of boiled eggs once the insides were scraped out, to prevent witches using them as boats. Frances had removed at least three witch-bottles from the chimney that Juliet had hidden up there to protect the household, scolding Juliet that their contents of hair, nail clippings, pins and urine were ludicrous and revolting. Once Juliet had even tried to cure a stye in Barnaby's eye by licking the eyes of a live frog and then licking the infection: for that Frances had almost dismissed her. Abel often accused Juliet of being a wicked pagan and threatened to report her to Father Nicholas. Barnaby was sure his mother was right when she said that cleanliness and faith in God would keep you far healthier than cat's urine and dried spiders, but he couldn't quite bring himself to ignore a magpie or to cross his knife and fork on his plate (although Abel deliberately did so to upset Juliet).

And tonight, while the fire whispered in the grate and beetles clicked in the thatch, he found it hard to scoff at her beliefs.

Instinctively he glanced across at the black square of the window. But it was cloudy now – too cloudy to see any flying shapes silhouetted against the moon.

'You were lucky to escape unharmed,' Juliet said. 'Something was protecting you. It seems that the spirits of the forest have not forgotten you.'

He looked at her uneasily, then quickly finished the milk and went up to bed. There were times he liked to be reminded of his origins, but not tonight.

3
Kingdoms of Darknes

He woke the next morning stiff and bruised from his fall in the forest. But no-one seemed to care about that. All they were interested in was that he had gone there alone. His normally level-headed mother screeched like a fishwife and after haranguing Barnaby she turned on her husband. Henry was too soft and indulgent with Barnaby, the boy was growing up spoiled and arrogant and needed to be disciplined with a firm hand or he would become unmanageable. While Abel smirked from the landing Barnaby just stared at her in astonishment. It was not like her to care so much about his comings and goings: usually she was far too busy coddling and fussing over his brother. If it had been Abel with a bruised backside, he would have been bedbound for a week with hot compresses and spiced honeyed wine.

It was an eternal mystery to him (and, Barnaby suspected, his father) how Abel occupied such a position in his mother's affections. Abel was self-pitying, humourless, spiteful and cowardly: a snivelling little toad, as Griff put it. And yet whenever he raised his long face from his Bible Frances was there with a beaming smile for him, listening politely as he spouted some verse obviously chosen for Barnaby ('*Pride goeth before destruction and a haughty spirit before a fall . . .*'). When his skinny legs hurt from kneeling on the cold church floor, his mother would massage them; if he got a tickle on his bird-chest she would rub beeswax and eucalyptus into it.

Barnaby, on the other hand, could do nothing right. If he been brave, it was reckless attention-seeking, if he was charming he wanted something, if Abel struck him he must have said something cruel, if he struck Abel he was a bully.

When one of Henry's associates brought back a pineapple from the Americas one Christmas, Frances allowed Abel to polish off the whole thing, for the sole reason that Barnaby had refused to eat his goose wing – and this was only because the previous year he had choked on one of the bones. Though he was only ten, Barnaby had forced himself not to weep at this gross injustice and, in the bitter darkness of that Christmas night, he vowed to harden his heart to his mother. From that day forth he had turned to the welcoming arms of his father. Henry had always seemed to have the measure of Abel and was as cool with his second son as Frances was with her first.

But a few days after Agnes's funeral something unexpected happened.

Barnaby and his father were breakfasting when his mother came down from Abel's room, sat down stiffly at the table and sighed unhappily.

'What's the matter, my love?' Henry said, looking up from his eggs.

She did not answer him but turned to Barnaby. 'Go and tell Juliet that she may tighten the bed-strings today.'

Without protest Barnaby got up and went out to the kitchen, leaving the door ajar. Juliet looked up from the sink and opened her mouth to speak but he put his finger to his lips and leaned in to listen at the gap.

Frances sighed again and ran her fingers through her hair.

'Oh I don't know,' she muttered. 'I just wonder whether Abel's interest in the Bible isn't becoming rather ... unhealthy.'

'How can the Bible be unhealthy?' his father spluttered, spattering the table with masticated egg white.

'I just don't like the message he takes from the texts,' Frances murmured. 'It is so harsh. So simplistic.'

'I shouldn't worry,' Henry said, patting her hand in a way that made her purse her lips. 'It's only a young boy's imagination.'

Frances seemed unsatisfied. 'I might ask Father Nicholas to speak to him.'

Barnaby thought about this as he munched his way through Juliet's plum jam tarts out on the back step. His mother really must be worried if she was prepared to speak to Father Nick. Was Abel's halo slipping a little in his mother's eyes?

The following morning, when Abel had gone to church for his daily prayer session, Barnaby persuaded Juliet to lend him the key to his brother's room, on the pretext of borrowing some linen.

He had not been into Abel's bedchamber for at least

three years, nor even seen inside, since their rooms had been moved to opposite ends of the house after Abel complained that Barnaby's snoring kept him awake.

Abel's was the only locked door in the house and for a split second, as he turned the key, Barnaby wondered if his brother had set a trap for interlopers. If so, it was bound to be the nastiest, most mutilating trap his vile little mind could imagine.

The door swung silently inwards revealing an interior as bare and white as a monk's cell. It smelled faintly of beeswax. He knew his brother was scrupulously clean, but there was not even the merest whisper of smelly feet or unwashed bedlinen. He walked across to the wardrobe and opened it. The clothes were arranged in order of colour: brown jackets at one end, white shirts at the other, separated by a large gap, as if Abel feared cross-contamination.

On the table beside the bed sat one of Abel's many Bibles. Barnaby glanced at the open page.

Now these are the judgments which thou shalt set before them. If thou buy an Hebrew servant, six years he shall serve: and in the seventh he shall go out free for nothing. If he came in by himself, he shall go out by himself: if he were married, then his wife shall go out with him. If his master have given him a wife, and she have born him sons or daughters; the wife and her children shall be her master's, and he shall go out by himself ...

So that was Abel's bedtime reading. What a strange person his brother was.

Sitting on the bed in that dry, cold little room, Barnaby felt a fleeting pity. What did Abel have in his life that gave him pleasure? Not hunting nor fishing, good food nor fine clothes, not friendship nor girls. There were no copies of the *Iliad* or *Odyssey* on the shelf beside the crucifix, no plays, no poetry. Even the Bible was a plain, brown thing without illuminations. Barnaby and Griff had spent a very educational afternoon poring over Father Nicholas's copy of Ovid's *Metamorphoses* that featured a graphic illustration of Leda being ravaged by the swan. Abel had to make do with the frontispiece of his Bible, which showed a dour King James in a feathered hat.

And then he realised. If Abel did possess such a thing, he wouldn't keep it on show for Juliet to stumble upon. After Griff had smuggled the priest's book out of the church library he had concealed it beneath his mattress. Barnaby leaned over and slid his hand under Abel's.

At first he felt nothing. Just the strings of the bed and a few loose strands of hay. He pushed his hand deeper and this time his fingers came into contact with some papers.

He smiled.

Crouching down beside the bed, he carefully drew them out.

They were dog-eared from use, some were torn, others water-damaged. At first he thought they might be erotic etchings done by some clumsy local artist – the first featured a gang of half-naked cavorting women – but then he read the title.

The Kingdom of Darknes

He looked more closely. Now he could make out the figure at the centre of the dancing women. Apart from the crescents of its slitted eyes it was entirely black; its bat-like wings raised above its head, claws spreading from the bony wing tips.

A line of text beneath read:

Exodus 22.18. Thou shalt not suffer a witch to live.

He tossed it onto the table. The next pamphlet was entitled *Signs and Wonders from Heaven*, and the image beneath made him snigger. It was an etching of a human being with the physical attributes of both a woman and a man, but with no arms or legs. A beatific smile lit its face. A chunk of text beneath read:

WITH A TRUE RELATION
of a Monster borne in Ratliffe Highway, at the sign of the three Arrows, Mistress Bullock the Midwife delivering thereof. Also shewing how a Cat kitned a Monster in Lombard Street in London. Also how the Divell came to Soffam to a Farmers house in the habit of a Gentlewoman. With divers other strange remarkable passages.

He didn't bother to open the pamphlet to discover these remarkable passages. Surely Abel didn't believe this horse shit.

The next did not have an amusing illustration, only a pompous title in an almost unreadably elaborate font:

The Discovery of Witches in Answer to Severall Queries Lately Delivered to the Judges of Asize for the County of Norfolk and now published By Matthew Hopkins, Witch-finder For The Benefit of the Whole Kingdom. London MDCXLV

Barnaby tossed it with the others.

The one beneath was particularly comical. In the centre was a grinning devil, surrounded by women who were kissing various parts of his hairy anatomy, while a ferret and a toad mated nearby and another woman suckled a fox. This apparently represented:

A TRUE RELATION

of the Confessions of eighteene Witches, who by confederacy with the Devill did not only cast away their soules and bodies, but made spoyle and havock of their neighbours goods and so were executed the 17 day of August 1644.

The list of names beneath seemed very long. He was surprised to see a vicar heading the first column: A 'Mr Lewes, parson of Branson'. He looked for him in the picture and finally saw him, his black cassock pulled up to his waist while devils poked his backside with pitchforks.

An amusing idea came into Barnaby's mind and he searched Abel's drawers until he found a scrap of writing lead wrapped in string. Beside the grinning devil surrounded by women he wrote: *Barnaby.* He gave the tortured priest buck teeth and a cloud of fart puffing out from his naked backside. Beside this figure he wrote: *Abel.*

After chuckling to himself for a few minutes he tucked the papers back under the mattress and let himself out of the room, feeling slightly giddy.

When Abel came down for dinner that evening his expression was thunderous.

The wine was poured. Henry threw back two glasses in

quick succession then began talking to Frances about the latest shipment of textiles from Arabia. Soon there was an animated discussion between them; now and again she gave a tinkling, almost girlish laugh. Barnaby smiled at the sight: it was rare to see his mother so animated, but then his eyes met his brother's.

'You are the devil,' Abel breathed.

Barnaby gave a quiet snort of laughter.

Abel's gaze did not falter.

'Even Satan doth transform himself into an angel of light.' he hissed.

Barnaby made a face at him.

'And the dragon stood before the woman which was ready to be delivered, for to devour her child as soon as it was born.'

'You're off your head.'

He concentrated on eating but his brother's stare seared the top of his head. His heart began to beat harder.

'Thine heart was lifted up because of thy beauty. Thou hast corrupted thy—' The sprout struck Abel on the nose, spattering his face with onion gravy.

'Barnaby!' his father bellowed.

His parents glared at him while Abel pressed his napkin to his eye and gave little whimpers of pain, which as far as Barnaby was concerned were entirely faked.

'My eyeball is scalded!' he wailed. Frances gave Henry a meaningful look before going to kneel down at Abel's side.

Henry glared at Barnaby.

'Father, I just couldn't stand—'

'ENOUGH!' Henry shouted, banging the flat of his hand on the table so hard the crockery rang. Then he stood up and, to Barnaby's horrified disbelief, undid his belt buckle.

'Father, what are you . . .?'

'It's time you learned that you cannot do exactly as you please, Barnaby.'

'Father, please, I didn't mean to hurt him . . .'

But Henry wrenched him out of his seat, dragging him through the kitchen, where Juliet stood staring in disbelief, and out to the stables.

The sun was just setting and even the deepest recesses of the yard were bathed in a honeyed glow, visible to anyone who was passing.

'No, Father!' Barnaby cried. 'Not here!'

Henry was breathing hard. A vein the width of a finger had sprung out on his forehead, pulsing with blue blood. The tip of the belt dangling at his side flicked this way and that as his clenched fist trembled.

'Unfasten your breeches.'

Barnaby stared at him. His father's stomach wobbled and his face was shiny with sweat. The muscles of his youth were drowned in fat and both his shoulders were so stiff with arthritis it would be simple for Barnaby to snatch the belt from him and toss it over the gate.

'Unfasten your breeches,' Henry said again.

They stared at each other. His father's faded blue eyes locked to Barnaby's bright ones; the grey curls and the blond caught the glow of the sunset.

Henry swallowed, then he glanced over at the kitchen window.

If Barnaby chose he could humiliate his father now in front of the whole household, and anyone who happened to be passing: show him that the old order had changed, teach him a lesson he wouldn't forget. It wouldn't take much – a kick to the old man's behind to send him reeling into the pig dung, a backhanded slap that would sting but leave no mark. With that he would assert his place in the household and no one would dare defy him again, including his foul brother.

Barnaby sensed faces at the window. Juliet was there, surely, and Abel wouldn't resist such a spectacle, though perhaps their mother would not choose to watch.

Henry blinked rapidly and slapped the belt against his open palm.

The sun had dropped lower in the sky even in those past few minutes. It threw Barnaby's shadow across the yard, broad and ten times his normal height, entirely covering his father.

He closed his eyes and breathed deeply, then he opened them and, in full view of the street and the faces at the window, he unfastened his breeches.

Barnaby lay awake listening to the sounds of the evening as it gave way to night. The streets became suddenly noisier as the inns threw out the last remaining customers. A drunk passed beneath his window, singing a love song punctuated by hiccoughs. Somewhere nearby two cats yowled like demons.

Carefully he shifted his position, rolling onto his stomach, then up onto his other hip, shuffling round so that he could still see out of the window. The whole of his lower back, his buttocks and the backs of his thighs throbbed. One or two of the lashes had broken the skin and the blood was now drying, so that every time he moved the scabs cracked and wept afresh.

He hadn't cried. For some reason, though no-one had passed by and the household had seen him cry often enough times, that fact was important. His father, however, had sniffed noisily throughout. It actually made matters worse since the tears had blinded him, and instead of striking his son's well-padded parts he had lashed the small of Barnaby's back and the muscles of his thighs, which hurt considerably more.

During the assault, which had probably lasted no longer than a minute, Barnaby's rage and humiliation and impotence had turned to a white-hot point of utter clarity. An idea had bloomed in his brain like ink in water.

He would get rid of Abel.

He rolled over onto his stomach and breathed in the thyme-scented pillow. How much happier the household would be with his brother gone. His mother would be able to see Barnaby's qualities for what they were, without them being refracted through the twisted mirror of Abel's jealousy. His father would not have to pretend impartiality any more, but could concentrate all his affection on the son he had patently always preferred. Griff and his friends would feel comfortable visiting the house without that black crow looming over them, judging them for having a second crumpet or laughing at a joke.

Eventually the throbbing of his injuries settled to a dull ache and finally he went to sleep with a smile on his face.

4
A New Maid

But the next day something happened that made Barnaby entirely forget his plan.

His mother hired a new servant.

This in itself was not anything unusual. They were a wealthy family with a reasonably large house and since their cook had died the previous spring it was high time Juliet had someone to share the load. But it wasn't a cook or laundrywoman who had been hired. It was another maid: a girl of fourteen with no particular skill and barely two years' experience. Experience that had been abruptly curtailed by her dismissal from her last position.

This bombshell was announced over breakfast.

'Dismissed for what?' Juliet asked tightly, frozen in the act of ladling porridge into her mistress's bowl.

'For stealing,' Henry said, looking meaningfully at his wife.

'Is that true, Mother?' Abel said sharply.

'It's true that this was the reason given by the Slabber family,' Frances began. Already Abel was opening his mouth, no doubt to deliver a pertinent passage from Isaiah about the evils of stealing, but Frances raised her voice to speak over him.

'But it is not the real reason.'

Abel frowned. 'What are you saying, Mother?'

'She is saying,' Henry interrupted, 'that our neighbours – highly respected upstanding members of our community who can trace their lineage back three hundred years – are liars.'

For a moment there was silence.

'Are you?' Barnaby said eventually.

Frances hesitated, then nodded.

'Mother!' Abel gasped.

'Well, they are,' Frances said. 'At least John Slabber himself is.'

'Explain to the boys why you believe this to be the case, my dear,' Henry said mildly.

Juliet had not moved a muscle, but stood behind her mistress's chair with a face of thunder.

'I believe it, because she told me so.'

'You believed a serving wench,' Abel began, 'over a respected—'

'. . . arrogant, lecherous bully,' Frances interrupted. 'From a long line of arrogant lecherous bullies.'

'Your mother doesn't know about his lechery first-hand, of course . . .' Henry murmured to Barnaby, who sniggered until his mother flashed them a withering glance.

'Only very rarely am I a bad judge of character,' she went on, briefly catching her husband's eye, 'and in this case, after speaking to the girl's family, I believe her to have been the victim of an injustice.'

'Yes, well, my dear, it's hardly surprising that Farmer Waters stood up for his daughter now, is it?'

Farmer Waters . . . Barnaby mused.

'Why else would they have dismissed her?' Juliet said. 'If she didn't steal, she must have been incompetent or lazy.'

Farmer Waters' daughter . . .

Oh no.

'That may be true, Juliet, but that wasn't the reason she was dismissed. Naomi told me herself – and was clearly mortified to do so – that John Slabber had made inappropriate advances toward her on several occasions. When she asked him to stop he struck her and when she went to his wife he accused her of stealing a side of beef. Few will believe her over the Slabbers, so if we do not give her a second chance the girl's prospects will be ruined.'

Brilliant. Just brilliant. Of all the nice, friendly girls in the village his mother had to go and choose a stuffy, pompous, humourless little . . .

'Well, I for one think you did the right thing, Mother,' Abel announced. 'It does not surprise me in the least that our thug of a butcher would behave in such a way.'

Barnaby spluttered into his porridge. Abel only hated John Slabber because the man had mercilessly ribbed him ever since he had burst into tears at the sight of a sheep's brain lying on the counter when they were boys.

Abel ignored him. 'I look forward to meeting such a righteous soul.'

'I don't,' Henry muttered, and Barnaby smirked. He

77

looked up to share the smirk with Juliet but Juliet was in no mood for humour.

'And may I enquire which jobs will be given to this new maid?'

Frances turned around and smiled up at her. 'Whatever you think yourself, Juliet,' she said. 'You know our family better than anyone. Naomi will work to you and do exactly what you say.'

'Hmf,' Juliet said, and went out to the kitchen.

Naomi Waters arrived the very same afternoon, with her wild curls tucked inside a starched bonnet. Barnaby kept out of her way, in case she thought he was looking at her inappropriately. But by the afternoon he was thirsty and went in search of Juliet. A glass of beer would be nice, and perhaps a slice of pork pie.

But Juliet wasn't there. Naomi was in the kitchen kneading dough.

'Ah,' he said, 'Miss Waters, may I trouble you for a beer and a slice of pie when you're ready?'

'Certainly,' she said, keeping her eyes on the dough.

He went back to his room and waited.

After a while he began idly kicking the iron studs in the floorboards. The thuds would surely carry downstairs and remind her what she was supposed to be doing.

But they didn't.

He went back downstairs. The bread dough was sitting in the sun on the windowsill beneath a cloth and Naomi had moved on to boning a chicken.

'That beer, please, Naomi, when you're ready,' he said, a little sharply.

'I won't be ready for a while,' she said, again without glancing at him. 'Would you mind getting it yourself?'

He stared at her.

She looked up at him. 'Juliet has instructed me to start preparing tonight's meal and if I don't get the chicken on to roast then it will not be done in time.'

'Um,' he said, 'um, Juliet would normally just, er, do the drink, and then get on with the er . . .'

'Oh,' Naomi said, wiping her brow. 'Well, she's in the yard if you want to ask her to do it.'

He swallowed hard and went back to his room.

A rhythmic thudding sound came from somewhere in the distance, as if someone was lopping branches in the forest. The afternoon sunlight was shining on the tacks in the floor, throwing discs of light onto the ceiling. He watched them lazily until they began to creep across the plaster. His eyelids were leaden. He closed them, just for a moment.

He was woken by someone shaking him by the shoulder.

'Wha!' he cried and promptly rolled off the bed.

'Dinner's ready,' Naomi said.

'Oh. Right. I'll be down in a minute,' he said, rubbing his elbow where it had struck the bed frame.

'It's on the table.'

She stared at him evenly.

He got up. 'For future reference, Miss Waters, Juliet usually gives me a little more warning, to ease me into wakefulness a little less rudely.'

'I didn't expect you to be asleep at six o'clock in the evening, Master Barnaby.'

He stared at her.

'I sleep when I choose,' he said.

She held his gaze. 'Evidently.'

He pushed past her in the direction of the door. 'Jesus,' he muttered, 'no wonder they fired you.'

'Enjoy your chicken,' she said.

The chicken was actually, though it pained him to admit it, considerably better than usual: moister, tastier, and with a crisp, browned skin flavoured with some herb he couldn't identify.

They were careful not to compliment the meal when Juliet was in the room but she could not have helped noticing that they all asked for seconds. Unlike Juliet, who was always rushing about in a panic at supper time, Naomi stayed to hear grace, bowing her neat little bonnet, from which a single curl had escaped, and clasping her red hands, to Abel's obvious approval.

'I thank the Lord for guiding your hands to produce such a fine meal,' he said as she cleared the plates afterwards.

'Oh, certainly,' she said, smiling. 'And may He breathe His spirit into the bread yeast too.'

Barnaby noticed that Frances was hiding a smile behind her hand.

The following morning he rose early and agreed to accompany his father to the cloth market in Grimston, to see how the merchants were faring with his imported wool and silk.

The journey was a long one and the road was bad, and after attempting to listen to his father describing the differing qualities of the various fabrics and how you could tell the difference, Barnaby finally vomited over the side of the cart and spent the remainder of the journey lying in the back with his jacket over his face.

His father and the driver spent their time discussing the latest wild story to circulate Grimston: that an enormous sea monster had been put on display at the market the previous week. 'Someone bought it and cooked it,' the driver said in hushed tones. 'And straightaway he were driven mad and drowned hisself in the river.'

'Extraordinary,' said his father, wide-eyed.

Grimston market was noisy and bustling and filled with bright colours and strong smells. The produce on sale was far more varied than at the market at home, and seemed to have originated from every corner of the globe. There were spices from India, silks from the East, China tea and fruit and vegetables Barnaby had never heard of including a bright scarlet fruit about the size of a plum. It was called a 'tomatoe', but was there purely for display as it was poisonous to eat. His father bought a huge wheel of cheese from Amsterdam and a flagon of malmsey wine. They paused at a stall selling trinkets and his father chose a silver locket for Frances. For a few pennies there were a selection of ribbons sewn with silver charms and Barnaby decided to buy one for Flora. He selected a pale blue gingham one with a tiny silver hare dangling from it. His father winked and goaded him all the way back to the cart, but Barnaby would not admit who it was for.

They lunched in one of the inns by the magistrate's court and his father ended up in conversation with a fellow Grimston merchant. It turned out that the man dealt in relics and holy charms. There was, the merchant claimed, a particularly good market for such items at the moment, with the witch fever that was gripping the county. The previous month he had made almost thirty pounds profit at a mass hanging in Norwich. For a moment Barnaby thought his father would buy some of the man's goods to sell on, but Henry changed his mind at the last minute, muttering that he didn't think his wife would approve. By the time they left the inn it was gone four o'clock.

The market had gone and some men were erecting a scaffold in the middle of the square.

The cart driver was not pleased and grumbled that the Beltane to Grimston road was notorious for robberies after dark. The breakneck speed he employed to avoid such a fate brought Barnaby's nausea rushing back and the first thing he did when they arrived home was stumble out to the kitchen for a cold drink, leaving his father to crow to Frances about how Barnaby had bought a gift for one of the village girls.

Juliet was sitting at the kitchen table crying over a pile of linen.

'What's the matter?' he said. 'Has something happened?'

She wiped her face on her apron and picked up one of the shirts.

'Look at this!'

'What?' he said. 'They look perfect. Much better than usual in fact.'

'Exactly,' she said, her voice trembling. '*She* did them.'

'Who? The Waters girl?'

Juliet nodded miserably.

Barnaby glanced behind him. He was pretty sure he had passed Naomi setting the fire in the room beyond while his parents discussed which of the village girls might be the intended recipient of the gift.

'She's nothing compared to you, Jules,' he said quietly, taking her hand. 'We couldn't live without you.'

'Nonsense!' Juliet snapped tearfully. 'She seems to be better than me at everything, and able to accomplish it twice as fast. When your mother realises, what reason will she have to keep me on?'

He sat down beside her and leaned across the table. 'Now, let's see . . .' He began counting on his hand. 'Your jam tarts are the best in the county. The chickens love you. You never complain. And you have very pretty hands,' he took them in his, 'which is more than can be said for *her*.'

As he jerked his head towards the doorway he thought he caught some movement but Juliet was weeping into her handkerchief again.

'Listen. I brought you a present from Grimston.'

Sniffing, she looked up from her handkerchief and he dangled the ribbon he'd bought for Flora before her red eyes. The leaping silver hare caught the evening sunlight and the reflections danced on her face.

'See how nice the colour looks against your hair.'

Juliet smiled but her hand stopped in the act of taking it and her eyes went to the doorway.

Naomi was standing there with the empty wood basket. She must have heard his parents discussing the gift and would know it had never been intended for Juliet. She would get back at them both by announcing it.

But she didn't.

'What a pretty thing,' she said softly. 'Shall I help you tie it?'

Juliet hesitated, then nodded.

Naomi set the basket down and came over. He held the ribbon out to her without meeting her gaze and she took it. Her cheek was pale and there was a flush on her neck. Had she heard what he said?

'You are so lucky to have such silky hair,' Naomi said as she tied the ribbon in a careful bow. 'Mine coils like pigs' tails.'

That night in bed Barnaby heard the girls giggling together down in the kitchen. He wasn't sure that he liked it.

On Sunday they all went to church. Although she'd never needed assistance in the past, Frances took Naomi's arm at the door and asked her to help her to her seat. Passing the Slabbers, Barnaby heard mutterings and Mistress Slabber even made the sign of the evil eye with her fingers. He held back so as not to be associated with Naomi and managed to catch Flora's eye. She blushed and smiled and he fervently wished he hadn't given away the ribbon.

As he sat down he heard Abel's nasal whine from the other end of the pew: 'What is that dreadful daubing, Mother? Father Nicholas should not have allowed the walls to have been so besmirched.'

'Actually, I think it's beautiful,' Naomi said.

'Yes,' said Frances. 'The work of a local lad, I believe.'

He followed their gazes. The wall on the far side of the church, which previously depicted cracked and flaking biblical scenes from the Norman era, had been whitewashed over, and there were the beginnings of a new mural. For now only the upper part of the wall had been painted: all billowing pink-edged clouds and vivid azure skies.

'You must talk to Father Nicholas, Mother,' Abel continued. 'The wall should be pure and unadorned. Anything else is apostasy.'

Frances sighed and looked down at her prayer book. Naomi pressed her lips together and turned her face to the lectern.

Settling in for the usual boring hour and a half, Barnaby glanced around the church, looking for Griff. To his intense discomfort he caught the eye of the furrier's widow. He looked away quickly and didn't turn around again, despite the fact that Flora was squirming and craning into his line of vision.

Abel was as awful as usual, bellowing out his responses to the prayers so loudly that half the church was staring at them. Eventually Barnaby did manage to catch Griff's eye and Griff made a rude gesture in Abel's direction that made Barnaby snort so loudly that Father Nicholas paused in his oratory to scowl at him.

It was only then that the plan came back to him: the plan to rid himself of Abel.

Barnaby lingered at the end, on the pretext of apologising to the old priest, and once the church had emptied made his way down one of the side aisles to the sacristy.

Father Nicholas was struggling to remove his chasuble. Sometimes his fingers were so stiff with arthritis he could not get the wafers out of the communion cup.

'Father,' Barnaby said, 'may I help you?'

'You may, Barnaby,' sighed the old man.

Barnaby went over and lifted the heavy garment over the

priest's head, leaving his sparse white hair standing up in wisps, then laid it on the back of a chair and went back to undo the cassock ties.

'I'm sorry for my rudeness during the service. Is there anything I can do for you to make it up?'

'Certainly you can,' Father Nicholas smiled. 'You can tell Barbara Howells that if she cannot keep her child quiet during mass then she must take him outside.'

'Ummm . . . Mistress Howells with the big dog?'

'That's right.'

'The one she sets on people she doesn't like?'

'Precisely.'

Barnaby took a deep breath. 'Very well, Father. But please be standing by to administer the last rites for me.'

Father Nicholas chuckled. 'It's all right, I'll accept a helping arm out to the porch.'

Barnaby linked his arm beneath the priest's and they began walking slowly down the central aisle of the church. Sunlight lanced through the side windows, throwing bars of light onto the flagstones.

'Actually, Father, I was hoping I might ask you something.'

'Hmm?'

'As I'm sure you know, Abel and I have not been getting on for some time.'

'Only since the day he was born,' the priest chuckled.

'Indeed, but recently it has got worse.'

Father Nicholas leaned conspiratorially into Barnaby's shoulder, his breath syrupy sweet with the dregs of the communion wine. 'Yes, well, unfortunately the second child was not as richly blessed as the first.'

'I feel for him every day, Father,' Barnaby said. 'And that's why I have been giving it some thought.' He had to work quickly: people were already massing at the door, waiting for the priest's attention.

'I don't know if you have noticed but Abel is extremely devout.'

'I had noticed.'

'He seems to have memorised the new Bible and regularly quotes from it.'

The priest snorted. 'His time would have been better spent studying the original Latin.'

'That's exactly what I thought, Father.' He slowed his steps even more and the dust motes caught in the shafts of light barely moved as they passed among them.

'He has the passion for the Lord's word, but not the education.'

He stopped and faced the priest, who squinted into the sunlight as he tried to make out Barnaby's face.

'What if he went away to study theology? In time might he not make a fine man of God?'

Father Nicholas shook his head. 'I fear not. I worry that his soul is twisted with envy and spite.'

'Yes, but away from my presence perhaps those meaner aspects would fade.'

The priest frowned and rubbed the patchy stubble on his chin.

'What do you want from me – a recommendation? I cannot in all conscience . . .'

'Not that, no. I just ask you to plant the seed in my father's head that this might be the answer to my brother's difficulties. Coming from me Abel will reject it out of hand. But I believe a spell away from home, immersed in his great love, religion, and safe from all the complications of family, would be very beneficial to Abel. After all, as second son it would be a natural career choice . . .'

Had he gone too far? No, the priest was thinking, his milky eyes hooded by his drooping eyelids. He was very old, surely older than Agnes. If he died there was a risk that Abel might end up back here as the parish priest, wielding more power even than Barnaby with all that he was to inherit. But it was a risk worth taking. Surely Abel's inadequacies would be obvious to all his tutors and if he *was* given a parish it would be some remote hamlet with a handful of decrepit parishioners and a church the size of a chicken shed.

Father Nicholas looked up at him, then reached a hand up and patted Barnaby's cheek. His fingers were so cold and gnarled it was like being brushed by the twigs of the ancient yew in the churchyard.

'You are a good boy and I will see what I can do for you.'

Barnaby managed to dampen his grin into a modest smile of gratitude.

'Thank you, Father. I'm in your debt.'

They reached the porch. The first person Barnaby saw was Naomi. She had gone to stand with her family by the churchyard wall. Her face was tipped up towards the sun as her brother foraged with a stick in the crevices of the crumbling wall. The sun had drawn a light sheen of perspiration out on her temples, making the skin glisten. It brought out the whorls of gold and honey and chestnut in her hair and gave her cheek a natural flush that contrasted with the powdered paleness of the finer girls. If she wasn't so spiky he might even have desired to speak to her.

'Right,' Barnaby said, rolling up his sleeves. 'A bargain is a bargain, and I will now go and discuss matters with Mistress Howells.'

The old man's laughter followed him as he made for the little group of his friends standing in the shadows of the yew tree.

But before he'd got there he spotted Flora, standing near the imposing tomb of the Woodcrofts. She was alone. He changed direction.

'Good morning Miss Slabber,' he said, leaning against the cold stone of the sarcophagus.

'Good morning, Master Nightingale.'

'You're looking very pretty, I must say.'

The lie slipped easily from his lips and he was certain it would please her since she had clearly worked very hard on her appearance this morning. Too hard perhaps: the excessive powder had cracked and flaked at the corners of her eyes and mouth, as if she had a nasty skin condition. Perhaps that was why she did not now return his winning smile.

'And you're looking rather scruffy,' she snapped. 'Doesn't your maid know how to use a flat iron?'

Ah, yes, of course. Flora probably considered their hiring Naomi as an insult to her family.

'No indeed. Nor much else I'm afraid.' He smiled even more winningly.

She gave a sharp little laugh, 'I cannot imagine why anyone would be so foolish as to employ such a creature.'

He caught his breath at the insult to his mother.

'Have you lost any silverware yet? If so you will probably find it at Grimston market.' Her mouth twisted into a sneer. 'Soon enough she'll be selling her own wares there.'

He took a step back. 'Flora, please. Don't speak that way.'

'What way? It's only the truth. Don't tell me you *like* her?' Flora spat the word as if it tasted bitter.

'No, not at all!' he cried, then, feeling guilty, added: 'Though she has done us no harm as yet.'

'Ha! How quickly she has wound you around those bony fingers of hers! Well, not all of us fall so easily into her web. Thieves and liars get their just desserts in the end.'

And with that she was off, marching across the graveyard, her velvet skirt whipping against the stones. Resting his head against the little stone dog at the feet of his ancestors, he considered how lucky it was that he hadn't acted on his initial attraction to Flora. The ugliness of her words had made her prettiness seem all the more counterfeit. He would have to be more careful with his flirtations now that the girls he grew up with were becoming of marriageable age, otherwise he might find himself in a real bind. Mr Slabber, for one, would not tolerate anyone playing with his precious daughter's feelings. He risked a glance at Flora's retreating back, and saw with relief that she was heading for a gaggle of her girlfriends, not to report him to her father.

His own father was deep in conversation with the priest so he went up to Juliet, who was talking to her grandmother, and wrapped his arm around her waist. 'Ah, Jules,' he murmured. 'If only I could marry you. It seems to me that the rest of female kind is entirely mad.'

She laughed and dropped her head onto his shoulder. Her hair smelled of ashes and the pungent aroma of the smokehouse.

A moment later his mother was calling them to go home. Juliet hurried away but her grandmother caught Barnaby by the arm, her beady eyes glinting beneath her black cap.

'Careful, pretty bird, or your song will break her heart.'

He snatched his arm away, unsure if he was being insulted, and went to join the others.

That night it was plain that something was afoot. Both boys were sent to bed early. They parted wordlessly at the top of the stairs and Abel went straight to his room and closed the door behind him. Barnaby, whose room was nearer the stairs, banged his door as if to shut it, then crept back out onto the landing and crouched in the shadows of the banisters.

His father was standing by the fire while Frances sat stiffly at the table. Her back was turned to Barnaby but the fury radiating from her was palpable.

'And how long have you two been plotting this?' she said finally.

Henry ran his fingers through his hair. 'I *told* you, I haven't been plotting anything. Father Nicholas approached *me* today after church. I'm only telling you what he said.'

Frances gave a hollow laugh. 'Don't make me laugh, Henry. This would be a dream come true for you. And Barnaby. I suppose he's in on it too . . .'

Henry's eyes flashed. 'It's nothing to do with Barnaby. Though I imagine he'd be more than happy with the arrangement, considering his mother seems almost unaware of his existence most of the time. Perhaps with Abel gone you might actually give him the time of day.'

Silence throbbed in the room like a wound.

Upstairs Barnaby's heart pounded. Perhaps he should not have spoken to Father Nicholas. He and Abel would only have to put up with one another for a couple more years. He himself could ask to be sent away to university, if only he could get to grips with his numbers.

When his father spoke again his voice was firm. 'There is nothing so unusual about a second son going into the priesthood, Frances. Abel cannot cling to your skirts for the rest of his life.'

She began to speak but Henry raised his voice over her. 'He's almost fifteen, and yet he has no friends of his own, no interest in girls, no hobbies besides the Bible. How else do you imagine he will make his way in the world? He has none of Barnaby's qualit—'

'Hush!' She glanced quickly up the stairs and Barnaby drew back into the shadows.

When he crept back his mother was standing, putting on her shawl. Henry watched her until finally she straightened and met his gaze: he blinked quickly and rocked onto his back foot.

Her last words were so quiet Barnaby wasn't even sure he had heard them correctly:

'You took my first son from me. You will not take my second.'

5
The Bracelet

The next morning Juliet woke him with a plate of cherry pancakes and a mug of warm milk sweetened with honey.

Except that it wasn't Juliet.

It wasn't even Naomi.

Sitting up, yawning, Barnaby caught a glimpse of skirts swooshing through the open door.

His mother's skirts.

Surprise cut the yawn short, leaving his mouth hanging open, and by the time he recollected himself and turned his attention to the pancakes they were quite cold.

'Today is the feast day of St Paul,' Abel announced when he went downstairs. The comment could only have been directed at Naomi, who was busy blacking the fireplace: Abel knew better than to involve Barnaby in his holiness and their parents were still upstairs.

'And whilst I agree with our good Protector,' Abel went on, 'that all idolatry is wicked, I feel the Holy Spirit moving me to pray.'

Juliet, who had appeared in the kitchen doorway with a tray of freshly polished silverware, rapidly retreated, but Naomi, who did not know better, continued with her work.

'Come,' Abel said, holding out his hand to her. 'Kneel with me.'

She took his hand and used it to pull herself up. Then she picked up her polish and her cloths and tucked them in her apron pockets.

'I'm sorry, Master Abel, but I'm too busy at present,' she said.

Barnaby looked up from his bowl of porridge. At the movement Abel's eyes flicked to the left: he knew Barnaby was watching.

'And what could be more important,' he said, 'than giving thanks to our good Lord?'

'Feeding the pigs,' she replied.

Barnaby choked on the porridge, spluttering oats and dried fruit across the table.

But his snort of laughter died as Abel grasped Naomi's arm and yanked her almost off her feet. He had not realised his brother was so strong; or perhaps that Naomi was so frail. She gasped in pain.

'You would mock the Lord?' Abel snarled, spittle flying from his lips.

'I need to feed the pigs now,' she said quietly, 'or they will not take another meal later and your father wants them fattened for slaughter. I will pray with you another time.'

The last word ended on a cry as the grip on her arm tightened.

'You are only worthy to pray with the swine,' he hissed.

But at the warning screech of Barnaby's chair legs against the flagstones he let her go and walked quickly out of the room.

The following morning Abel spoke to Naomi with barely concealed contempt and deliberately spilled his stewed berries over the white tablecloth as she passed them to him, leaving a large purple stain that would be almost impossible to remove.

Naomi lowered her eyes and apologised for her stupidity and Abel flashed a sneer of triumph around the table.

After breakfast Frances and Juliet went into the kitchen to discuss what was needed from the market that day, whilst Henry went upstairs to dress. Abel remained at the table, a sneering smile playing about his thin lips. Suspecting something was afoot, Barnaby lingered over his porridge. Sure enough, when Naomi came back to clear the dishes Abel said, 'When you've finished washing the plates, Naomi, I should like a bath. In my room.'

The bath was cast iron and large enough for a man to sit in with straight legs. It took twenty cauldrons full of water to fill it and the same to unfill it: twenty journeys up and down stairs with a full cauldron. In all Barnaby's life he could only think of three occasions when it had been used because it was so much work for Juliet, who would be given the rest of the day off: and those times it had been placed directly in front of the fire.

'I'm sorry, Abel, but Naomi is busy on my behalf today,' he said.

The smile slid from Abel's face.

'And what, pray, is she doing that cannot wait?'

Barnaby took a large spoonful of porridge, chewing slowly and thinking quickly.

'I've heard Naomi is an expert basket-weaver,' he said when he had swallowed the mouthful. 'I want her to show me some samples of her work. Perhaps it is something Father can sell in London.'

Henry was coming down the stairs.

'What's that? Basketwork? Hmm, there may be some call for it.'

'Very well, Father,' Barnaby said, trying very hard not to grin. 'I'll bring back some of the best examples and we can discuss whether or not they might be a viable proposition. Come, Naomi. If we go now you have all day to show me the various techniques.'

She blinked at him. 'There is willow and cane up at my father's house; if you would care to come there. Though the house is very rude and I fear you would not be comfortable.'

'I don't care. Come on.'

As he sprang up from the table and scooped his jacket from the back of his chair, Abel gave him a look of the purest loathing.

He whistled as they walked up the path, feeling more pleased with himself than he could ever remember. As soon as they were out of sight of the house he turned his steps towards Griff's place.

'Where are you going?' she said.

'You didn't really expect me to make you show me your *basket-weaving*? Now go and have fun with that brother of yours and meet me back here at dusk.'

'No . . . no,' Naomi frowned. 'You must come. Your father will be expecting to see something.'

He laughed again. 'Fear not, I shall simply tell him that you are a terrible basket-weaver and we should not make a penny out of you!'

Her frown deepened. 'I'm a good basket-weaver and if you won't come then I shall have to go back.'

He raised his eyebrows. 'And make my brother's bath?'

'If that is what's required.' She turned to go.

'He is so sour you can use the water for vinegar afterwards!' he called after her.

She turned and began walking back towards the house. With her wild hair imprisoned beneath the bonnet and the neat brown skirt his mother had given her she could have been anyone's maid: drab as puddle water. And yet he did not find her drab. In fact he found her utterly perplexing. How could she be so wilful and infuriating one minute, and so docile and obedient the next? She was more exasperating even than Flora. And yet he couldn't let her go back to be Abel's slave.

She was almost to the corner. He sighed heavily.

'Naomi!'

She turned, her back straight, chin lifted. 'What?'

'I *should* like to see some of your work. If you don't mind.'

She hesitated a moment then said, 'I don't mind,' and walked back to join him. As she drew beside him, then passed him, he chuckled to himself at her audacity, then fell into step beside her.

Soon they had reached the outskirts of the village. The wheat had grown much taller since he last came this way: it was waist-height now; emerald spears tipped with tight knots of grain lancing up towards the blue sky. He plucked a blade of grass, tucked it between his thumbs and blew hard. At the unholy screech crows erupted from the surrounding trees, like smuts from a collapsing fire. A field mouse scurried out from the protection of the grass and stopped dead in front of them. Naomi knelt and picked it up. It was almost completely round, with delicate shell-like ears and huge black eyes.

'Beautiful,' she said.

Then it bit her. While Barnaby would have been inclined to throw the thing across the field, she just set it gently down and it scurried off back into the greensward.

'I thought you farmers didn't like mice,' he said as they carried on.

'I'm not a farmer,' she said. 'I'm a maid, remember?'

'Well, I'm hoping you're a basket-weaver actually, or this will have been a wasted trip.'

'Not at all,' she said. 'It has saved you from the chore of sleeping.'

He opened his mouth but couldn't think of a response.

For once the witch tree was silent as they passed and she stopped to pluck a few green acorns from one of the lower branches.

'Don't,' he said instinctively.

'Why not?'

He laughed with embarrassment. 'The village girls say the spirit of the witch that was hanged here still haunts the place. She would not like you stealing her possessions.'

'I'm sure the poor old woman would not begrudge the piglets a little snack. Thank you, Madam!' she called up into the leaves, and they trembled a little as the wind breathed on them.

'Stop it,' he said.

She turned to face him. 'It's all right,' she said. 'There's no need to be afraid. I'm sure she was nothing but a poor mad old lady.'

'I'm not afraid.'

'We're all afraid of something.' She looked away from him and walked on.

'What are you afraid of?' he called after her.

She waited for him to catch up then said quietly, 'Your brother.'

He snorted. 'He wouldn't dare touch you, or he would have me to answer to. Plus he is feeble as a half-starved kitten.'

'It's not his body I fear,' she said.

They were halfway up the little path to the cottage when Mistress Waters came scurrying out, her face filled with consternation. 'Naomi! What have you done now?'

'Nothing, Mother,' she called back. 'Barnaby would like to see some of my basket-weaving.'

For a moment the woman's face brightened, then she frowned again. 'It's *Master* Barnaby.'

'Not at all, Mistress,' Barnaby called. 'Plain Barnaby is fine.' Then he grinned. 'Though Handsome Barnaby is even better.'

The woman blinked in surprise. 'Very well, Sir, whatever you wish.'

'Come on then, Handsome Barnaby,' Naomi said under her breath.

He followed her up the slope to the little stone cottage. It leaned markedly to the right, as if shying away from the forest on the other side of the lake. He himself wouldn't like to be so close to it.

The glass in the windows was so thick and undulating it was impossible to see through to the gloomy interior.

'Perhaps you would like to sit out in the sunshine,' Mistress Waters said, blocking the doorway with her body. 'I can bring you some caudell.'

The thought of warm, spiced egg yolks on a day like this made him feel nauseous. 'Is there anything colder?'

'We have no ice house and no cellar,' Naomi said quietly. 'So if the day is warm then the drink is warm.'

'If you can wait I can put a bottle of ale in the lake to cool . . .' Mistress Waters said.

'Actually, caudell will be lovely,' Barnaby said. 'It is not so hot after all.'

He waited on the wooden pew while Naomi went inside with her mother. The lake sparkled amicably today, inviting him in. Wavelets plashed musically against the bank as if giggling about their former misunderstanding. But he wasn't going in today, not for anything. Though the good opinion of a serving girl may not have mattered much he *was* her master after all, and his father had always told him that it was important to retain the respect of the servants. Though how Henry could imagine that Juliet still respected him, after the numerous occasions she had helped Frances undress him after nights of heavy drinking, was anyone's guess.

The little brother suddenly appeared with a stool, set it down in front of Barnaby, then sat on it and fixed him with a steely-eyed glare.

'Hello, young man,' Barnaby said. 'How are you?'

The boy said nothing, but shifted on the stool. Clearly the thing had been well made because it did not so much as squeak. The wooden legs were exquisitely carved with mice and field birds and the golden seat had been perfectly woven. Surely a peasant farmer could not afford such a quality piece.

Then he understood.

'Did your sister make that?'

The boy grinned. 'For me.'

'How much do you want for it?'

The boy thought hard. 'A penny.'

Barnaby guffawed and when Naomi emerged a moment later he told her how cheaply her labour of love had been lost.

'Oh it wasn't all my work,' she said, blushing. 'Father turned the wood for me. Here are some other things.'

She had brought an armful of baskets: some large enough to carry a week's worth of logs, others small and woven tightly enough to hold the most delicate of trinkets. There was not a single reed or stake of wicker out of place and in the centre of each base was a perfectly symmetrical five-pointed star.

'Why are you a maid exactly?' he said finally.

She smiled and shrugged. 'The wicker is too time consuming to gather in sufficient quantities and too expensive to buy. I do it for pleasure.'

'This is pleasurable? Doesn't it hurt your fingers?'

She held up her hands. 'They are not so delicate.'

It was true. Her fingers were stubby, the nails bitten to the quick, and the backs criss-crossed with scars.

'Now let me see yours.'

He glanced down at them then dug them into his pockets. There was no way she was going to see how shamefully soft and white they were.

101

'I think Father would be interested in these,' he said to change the subject.

'I couldn't produce them in enough quantities.'

'You could have help. What about your brother?'

'Benjamin? He's five. His fingers are soft as bulrushes.'

The boy had wandered off but glanced up at the mention of his name.

'We may be poor,' she went on, 'But we are not so desperate that we would cripple our children.'

Barnaby flushed. 'I did not mean ...'

'Perhaps *you* could assist me?' He was relieved to see that she was smiling again. 'Or are *your* fingers too soft?'

It seemed simple enough at the beginning. Naomi gave him a handful of sticks and a bodkin then showed him how to split them down the middle. He only wrecked a few and soon had enough to push the others through to make a cross shape, securing it with some fine, thread-like shoots.

He paused to smile smugly at her before starting on the spokes.

Here it all went wrong. The spokes would not stay an even distance from one another and kept bunching together; the thread snapped and had to be knotted to another length, which also snapped. She tried to help but he slapped her hand away and started weaving the willow strands in and out of the higgledy-piggledy spokes, fully aware that the basket was already doomed. But he was too clumsy and the jagged end of one of the spokes dug into his belly.

The sight of the blood soaking into the waistband

of his breeches made him feel faint. He closed his eyes and leaned back against the wall. Mistress Waters cried from the house, 'What's happened? Oh goodness, is he hurt?'

'I'm alright,' he murmured. 'Honestly.'

'Benjamin!' Naomi cried. 'Go and get some cobwebs from the wood shed.'

When the scampering footsteps returned, she wiped the wound gently with some damp material and pressed the soft gauze over the cut.

'There,' she said. 'It will be healed by tomorrow.'

He opened an eye. The cut was now covered in grey webbing and had started to itch already – a sure sign of healing.

'And wasn't it all worthwhile?' she said, holding up the wretchedly deformed basketwork.

He snatched it from her. 'It's mine and I shall finish it, or you will only berate me for giving up.'

More cack-handedly than ever he began thrusting the stalks through the yawning cracks in the weave.

'It would be perfect to hold something large,' she said. 'A pumpkin, perhaps.'

'Quiet. You're distracting me.'

'Benjamin!' she cried. 'Come and watch the master at work!'

A moment later the boy was peering over his shoulder, laughing as hard as his sister.

A shout from over by the lake made them all look up. Squinting into the low sun, Barnaby could make out three figures silhouetted against the glittering water.

'Your father has finally given up on your merchant's career, then?' a voice called.

It was Richard. His tone was gently teasing rather than the usual jeer, but Barnaby thrust away the basket and stood up.

'My maid was showing me some peasant crafts,' he called back. 'But I've had my fill of it if you are heading anywhere in particular.'

'Only to Griff's,' Richard answered. 'It's my aunt's birthday. There will be chicken and lamb and plum cake if the last one was anything to go by.'

'Excellent,' he said and, without looking back, went to join his friends.

'The sun has burned your face, Barnaby,' Richard said. 'You should be careful. The girls will not find you so handsome with a blistered nose.'

'My blistered nose will be infinitely more handsome than your great lump of dough,' he said with a grin, but he didn't feel like grinning.

He felt as low as a mongrel dog as he walked down the slope and away from the little crooked cottage. A stone whizzed passed his ear and a moment later he heard Naomi speak sharply, followed by a slap and the sound of Benjamin crying. He whistled to drown out it out.

He'd nothing to reproach himself for, Barnaby told himself later. Naomi was his maid, not his equal, and he had been perfectly courteous all day, had taken all the teasing about his basket in good humour, and had not even made her return to the house with him. Plus he had saved her from a fate worse than death – preparing Abel's bath. The girl had had an entire day off for heaven's sake!

And yet he couldn't shake the feeling that he had behaved badly.

When he got back that evening, full of devilled lamb kidneys and apple cake, all he wanted was a drink and his bed, but catching a glimpse of Naomi in the kitchen he decided to forgo the drink and went straight upstairs.

He was awoken next morning by a knock at the door. It was his mother.

'Have you see Abel's silver crucifix?' she said. 'He can't find it and is beside himself with worry.'

'No,' he said and turned over.

When he next awoke someone had filled his ewer with warm water and lavender and a bowl of cherries stood on his side table. He really hoped it had been Juliet. Peeling off the cobweb dressing in order to wash, he found that the wound had closed completely, leaving just a small red scar in the shape of a crescent moon. He remembered that Agnes had always said cobwebs had magical properties, but perhaps they were just sticky enough to keep cuts closed. Somehow he couldn't imagine Naomi believing in the supernatural abilities of a house spider.

The crucifix was still not found by the time he went downstairs and Abel was too distressed to leave his room.

Barnaby stepped over Juliet, who was on her hands and knees looking under the dresser, and sat down at the table.

He had no desire to help look for the necklace, which had been given to Abel on his last birthday, wrapped in a lawn shirt whose lace collar and cuffs had been painstakingly worked by Frances. Abel had dismissed it as showy and vulgar. That same year Barnaby had been given a florin to buy whatever he liked from Grimston market.

Naomi brought out some warm rolls and butter.

'Good morning, Master Barnaby,' she said evenly.

'Good morning,' he said, focusing his attention on splitting the roll.

'Naomi!' Juliet called from the floor. 'Your arms are longer than mine: is that something right at the back by the wall?'

Naomi got to her hands and knees beside Juliet.

'I think it's just a butt—' she began, but then something slipped from her apron pocket to clink on the flagstones.

Barnaby saw the bewildered look that passed between the girls before Naomi got up and announced that the crucifix had been found.

She had barely spoken before Abel emerged onto the landing.

'Ah,' he said. 'Where was it?'

Naomi swallowed and looked at Juliet.

'Under the dres—' Juliet began, but Naomi spoke over her, directing her words to Frances. 'It was in my apron pocket, Mistress. I don't know how.'

Abel gave a little gasp but Frances just frowned. 'How odd. Well, I think we're done, girls, if you could clear the table.'

'Odd indeed,' Abel said, coming down the stairs. 'How could it have got there?'

Naomi blinked rapidly, as if the sun was in her eyes.

'It might have fallen off your shelf, Master Abel,' Juliet said evenly. 'While Naomi was polishing the floor.'

Abel gave a derisive snort. 'That seems unlikely, don't you agree, Mother?'

'The important thing is that the chain was found,' Frances said with a strained smile. 'So get about your work, girls.'

With simultaneous *Yes'm*s Juliet and Naomi hurried to the kitchen.

That morning Barnaby was to have an introduction to the accounting ledger. A local man clerked for his father but Henry insisted that it was vital for a merchant to understand his own business and they duly traipsed over to the clerk's cottage which was, fortuitously, right around the corner from the Boar.

Barnaby nodded and *mmm*d as the clerk explained each column and row, the concepts of profit and loss and cash flow, and the necessity of obtaining receipts for all moneys paid and goods received. He tried to concentrate but his mind kept wandering to the brownish stain near the gutter of the ledger and wondering whether it was gravy or blood. The cut on his belly tingled and he thought how much he would prefer to be outside on that sunny pew again, using his hands to make something solidly useful, rather than his brain, which seemed to him as if it must be made of cold porridge. It was a mystery to him (and, he suspected, his parents) how a woman of his mother's education and a man with his father's natural quickness with figures could produce such a dolt of a son.

It was a great relief when they retired to the Boar and spent a pleasant hour or two drinking beer and listening to the barmaids gossiping about a witch coven that had just been uncovered in Stalyridge, a village a few miles away.

The witches had all been taken to Grimston for trial and would certainly hang. Barnaby wondered if their names had been on the list in the forest.

The following week a merchant colleague of his father visited the house. Barnaby made sure he was breakfasted and out of the way well before the man's arrival, in case he was asked his opinion on anything business-related.

He sat on the back step sharpening his hunting knives while Juliet washed the linen and Naomi churned butter. Mid-morning Juliet announced she had forgotten to pick up some lace she needed to repair one of Henry's collars and would pop into the village.

For some reason, when she left the atmosphere in the back yard changed. Barnaby's hands became clumsy and once or twice he nearly cut himself. For her part Naomi seemed to have forgotten how to use the churn and kept jerking the staff too hard so that the lid clattered up and down, frightening the chickens.

Having chattered happily away to one another all morning the conversation dried up and all Barnaby's attempts to restart it sounded, to his ear, either terminally dull or stupid. Once he said that a cloud drifting past the church spire looked like a rabbit's tail and then blushed furiously: all clouds looked like rabbits' tails. Fortunately Naomi just said, 'Hmm,' as if she hadn't really been listening.

It was a great relief to him, and perhaps also to Naomi by the way she leaped for the gate, when the Widow Moone came begging.

Soon the widow was enjoying a tankard of small beer and a large slice of pie at the kitchen table. The sun was now high in the sky and the way it flashed off the blades gave Barnaby a headache so he put away his rabbit-skinning knife, half done, and followed them into the kitchen. After helping himself to the pie, and pouring himself some of the better beer from the pantry, he sat down at the table opposite the widow. But watching, and listening to her eat, took away all his appetite.

She bolted the food like a starved dog, packing her mouth so full she could barely close it as she choked down huge hunks of pastry and meat.

'Slow down, Mistress,' Naomi said. 'There is plenty more.'

Barnaby fixed her with a disapproving glance – it was *their* pie, after all – but she turned back to the sink without glancing at him.

After the pie Naomi offered the widow some rhubarb crumble with the fresh cream from her own father's cows. Barnaby was about to protest about the cream, which he liked a great deal, when Abel came in. Crossing the threshold he came to an abrupt halt and drew in his breath.

'What is this creature doing in our house?' he demanded.

Naomi opened her mouth to reply but Barnaby spoke over her.

'We are giving alms to the poor, brother,' he said evenly. 'As the Bible commends us to.'

Abel ignored him and turned on Naomi. 'This woman is a witch!' he hissed back. 'Get her out!'

Naomi appeared not to hear him and stayed where she was, stirring ale over the fire.

Juliet entered through the back door, humming to herself. She stopped humming and visibly paled when she saw the Widow Moone at the table, slurping the thick yellow cream through her gappy teeth. After rapidly crossing herself Juliet curtsied and greeted the widow politely.

The widow did not reply: all her attention was focused on the finger she was using to wipe every last smear of cream from the side of the empty bowl.

'Juliet!' Abel hissed. 'Eject this woman from the house immediately!'

Juliet shook her head and breathed, 'Not I, Master Abel, I would not provoke her ire for anything, and you may have me beaten for it if you wish.'

Abel looked ready to snatch up the rolling pin there and then and take her up on her suggestion but instead he gritted his teeth and walked right up to the table.

'Depart, woman,' he declared. 'You have had your fill.'

The widow squinted up at him with one milky eye.

'Ah,' she said. ''Tis the Nightingale Runt.'

Abel's mouth open and closed. The widow leaned back in the chair.

'Instead of turfing me onto the streets, Runt,' she continued, making Abel wince, 'ye should be falling at my feet in gratitude.'

'Do not call him that, Mistress,' Naomi said quietly, 'Gather your belongings now: it's time you were off.'

The widow said nothing, only fixed her eyes on Abel, who had turned pale.

'Begone,' he managed finally, but his thin voice was drowned out by the simmering of the ale.

The widow rose from the table. Her skirts were as threadbare as fallen leaves in winter: no more than a filigree of brown lace. From her shawl hung strange trinkets: the skull of a mouse, a mermaid's purse with its curled horns woven into the wool, a desiccated sea horse, a hank of yellow hair plaited with red ribbon.

As she advanced around the table, Abel shrank back but seemed unable to unstick his feet from the flagstones. She passed Barnaby's chair and he was struck by foetid smells he couldn't recognise. His back felt wide and vulnerable as she moved behind him.

Juliet gasped as the widow took Abel by the shoulders and smiled into his fearful eyes.

'G . . . get your f . . . filthy hands off me,' he stuttered through stiff, white lips.

But the widow merely raised her hands to his cheeks and held his face.

'These filthy hands,' she said, her accent almost too strong to understand, 'eased your poor twisted guts, stopped you shitting green slime, and prevented your father from leaving you upon yon midden heap.'

Abel stared at her.

''Tis true,' she chuckled. 'He woulda sent you the way of t'other one were it not fer your poor ma, comin' to me in a lather askin' if I might find a way to bring you some comfort afore all the villagers ganged together to throw you in the lake.

' *"Not that Nightingale Runt screechin' again!"* they'd shout when you passed, hollering your guts out. Yer father could barely stand to be in the same room as you. He used to go out with that pretty brother of yours all day and only come back when you'd cried yourself out and your

111

poor mother was dead with exhaustion from rockin' and nursin' you.'

The bubbling of the ale grew louder and wisps of stream drifted from the pot to curl around the widow's wild hair.

'Lying bitch,' Abel whispered.

'Careful, Runt,' she said quietly. 'Or maybe I'll see fit to bring back them there gut twisters.'

Her hand made a sharp movement up by his hairline. Abel cried out and jerked his head free.

'There,' she said, holding up to the light the single dark hair she had plucked from his scalp. ''Tis all I need.'

For a moment everyone was still and silent. Barnaby could see Abel's heart throbbing beneath his thin shirt.

Then, with a laugh, she tossed the hair into the air. It danced for a moment in the updraughts from the fire, then drifted invisibly down onto the flagstones.

The widow turned back to Abel and grasped his shoulder once more, this time giving it a little shake.

'Be not so grave, Master Nightingale,' she said lightly. 'I were only a'teasin' you! Sally Moone's always been your friend, boy. Whatever your father and them others said, I knew there were nothin' wronger about you than there were about the last one.'

With that she patted his cheek, gathered up her meagre belongings and walked back out into the summer's afternoon. Halfway up the path a crow bobbed up to her and she spoke quietly to it before letting herself out of the gate and vanishing behind the wall.

The sudden hiss and billow of smoke made all of them cry out. The ale had boiled dry.

*

The next morning his mother noticed that one of her bracelets was missing: a pretty thing made from seed pearls imported from the Orient. As soon as the loss was announced the girls checked their pockets and Naomi was clearly relieved to find hers filled with nothing but crumbs.

A systematic search of the house began so Barnaby retired to his room to finish sharpening his rabbit-skinning knife. His father had more plans for him today but he had no intention of suffering more stultifying humiliation and would go and hunt coneys.

The cry made him jump so that the sharpening stone slipped and grazed his knuckle. He swore and stomped out of his room, certain it had come from Abel.

Sure enough his brother was standing on the landing, his face a mask of shock. He was pointing through the door of Juliet and Naomi's bedroom.

'What is it, my love?' his mother called anxiously up the stairs.

'Your b . . . b . . . bracelet!' Abel stuttered. 'I have found it!'

Barnaby went to stand next to him so that he could see into the room. Naomi's bed was nearest to the door. The bottom corner of her blanket had been lifted up and spread across the bed to reveal the shadowy space beneath. The bracelet was just visible, tucked behind one of the legs.

Frances stepped out onto the landing and came to join them.

They all stared at the bracelet.

Barnaby's eyes flicked to his brother, who was shaking his head wearily. Barnaby's lip curled, but before he could speak his mother called down the stairs, 'Naomi! Come up here, please!'

The shock on the maid's face when she arrived was only matched by the dawning horror of what the discovery meant. She had been dismissed for stealing before. Now all serving work would be impossible. If Frances chose to report her to the magistrate she could end up in prison. Possibly even hanged. But after telling the boys to go downstairs, Frances ushered Naomi into the bedroom and closed the door.

Barnaby lingered to listen.

The voices inside were low and even. No, Naomi was not unhappy with the work. Yes, she felt she was adequately paid – more than adequately. No, she had not taken Abel's crucifix and she had never seen the bracelet before this moment. No, she had no reason to believe Juliet felt any malice towards her: after a shaky start the two girls were now very friendly. Frances sighed. 'I do believe you, Naomi,' she said, 'and I hope these two incidents are merely unfortunate coincidences. Please be more careful from now on: check your pockets and keep your room tidy, and perhaps we can avoid any more unpleasantness.'

'Yes, Madam,' Naomi said miserably. 'Thank you, Madam.'

Barnaby hopped lightly down the stairs and was sitting at the table when Naomi came down. Her cheeks were flushed and she kept her head bent as she crossed the parlour into the kitchen. Abel's glittering eyes followed her all the way.

'Barnaby was listening at the door,' he said as their mother descended.

*

114

The next few days passed without incident, but the following Sunday Abel developed stomach cramps after breakfast and was too ill to go to church. His mother fussed over him so much they were late leaving the house, but they had not gone far before Barnaby doubled over and cried out in pain.

Juliet flew to his side. 'What is it?'

'It cannot be the oysters,' Naomi said quickly. 'They were alive until the very moment they went into the pie.'

'Oysters in July are always a risk,' Juliet said, looking at her with reproach. 'I'll take him home, Madam.'

'No, no,' Barnaby said, straightening up with a wince. 'It's not far. I can manage alone.'

He crept the few steps back to the corner and round it, then straightened up and strode quickly to the house, ducking beneath the line of the hedge to approach from the far side, so that he was only visible from the kitchen.

The kitchen door was ajar and he squeezed through so as not to disturb the creaky hinges.

The house was still and silent. Perhaps Abel's sickness had not been faked after all: perhaps he was asleep.

A creak from one of the floorboards suggested he was upstairs at least, but not in his bed. It had come from somewhere above the kitchen; his parents' room perhaps. Now there was a scuffling sort of sound, as if papers or clothes were being moved about.

Barnaby slipped out of the kitchen and, keeping close to the wall, made his way across the parlour. Stockinged feet padded overhead. There was more rustling and then the footsteps padded back into his parents' room again. He crept to the bottom of the stairs. More rummaging sounds;

the clink of metal against metal. Then Abel came out of the room, his nightshirt drooping off his narrow shoulders, his greasy brown hair uncombed and sticking up in spikes. He was carrying something: something that flashed in the dusty sunlight filtering through the window at the end of the landing.

Abel went straight into the room adjacent to his parents': Juliet and Naomi's bedchamber. Barnaby ran lightly up the stairs and along the landing, glancing into his parents' room as he passed. The chest that sat at the foot of their bed was wide open. This was where they kept all their most precious items, including a silk tapestry from India, silver plates, and two German mazers rimmed with silver that had been given to them on their wedding day.

Outside Naomi's door he stopped and, pressing his back against the wall, cautiously peered in.

Naomi's trunk, pathetic in comparison to his parents' fine maplewood and leather one, lay open on the floor. All her things had been tossed out: a nightdress, some undergarments, a shawl, a Bible and a wooden doll.

Abel was bending over the trunk, tucking something inside, and didn't notice Barnaby step into the doorway. He set about gathering up the items he had tossed out, carefully refolding them and placing them back inside the trunk.

'Feeling better?' Barnaby said.

Abel started, then spun around.

'Why are you not at church?'

'I must have caught your malady. What are you doing with Naomi's things?'

Abel's mouth opened. His sly black eyes flicked sideways and then back to Barnaby's face.

'I decided to take the opportunity to search her room,' he said. 'To make sure she had not stolen any other items.'

'And what did you find?'

'I shall discuss it with our parents upon their return.'

'No. You will discuss it with me, now.' Barnaby took a step into the room. 'What did you find?'

Abel did not reply and as the two boys stared at one another Barnaby felt a red wall of fury descend across his vision.

'What did you find, toad?'

Still Abel said nothing.

Barnaby entered the room and Abel scuttled backwards, coming up sharp against Juliet's bed. Barnaby walked forwards to stand over him.

'I know you, you sly dog!'

'And I know you!' Abel spat. 'Son of the Beast! Spawn of Satan! Would that you had never been returned by the demons that suckled you! Would that you—'

Barnaby punched him in the face.

'THOU SHALT NOT NOT BEAR FALSE WITNESS AGAINST THY NEIGHBOUR, ABEL!' He struck him again and a ribbon of blood flew out of Abel's nose to spatter Juliet's sheets. 'THOU SHALT NOT BEAR FALSE WITNESS!'

The last blow knocked Abel onto the floor and he sobbed in the spreading pool of blood.

'Come!' Barnaby snarled, hauling him to his feet. 'The village shall know your baseness!'

'NO!' Abel shrieked. 'Let me go!'

He continued shrieking as Barnaby dragged him out of the room, and thrashed so much going down the stairs that halfway down Barnaby let him go and he tumbled the rest of the way.

They lurched along the dusty road to the church, leaving a snail trail of Abel's bloody snot and tears. After a few minutes the tower rose up in front of them and when its shadow fell across him Abel gave a howl of despair.

The service had finished and the congregation were milling around the churchyard. His mother was standing by Mistress Waters and at Abel's cry her head snapped up.

'Nearly there,' Barnaby panted. 'And you're lucky: the church was nearly full today.'

With one last burst of effort he slung Abel's arm further over his shoulder and pushed on.

But his mother and father were now hurrying across to the lychgate.

'We must hurry, Abel,' Barnaby said through gritted teeth, 'if we are to have our audience.'

Abel squinted up through puffed eyes. *'And now art thou cursed from the earth,'* he burbled, *'which has opened her mouth to receive thy brother's blood from thy hand!'*

But having dragged Abel's dead weight so far, Barnaby had reached the limit of his endurance and when Abel dug his heels into the dust and resisted all efforts to go further Barnaby gave in and waited as his parents hurried towards them.

'What's happened?' Frances shrieked. 'Is he dying?'

But Barnaby didn't reply at once. He waited for Juliet and Naomi, who were now hurrying through the lychgate, eyes and mouths wide.

'Barnaby!' his father cried, close enough to see Abel's injuries. 'What have you done?'

Still Barnaby waited, until the girls and his parents were before him, shocked and afraid. Naomi looked up at him with clear green eyes and for a moment he could not tear himself from her gaze. Then he turned to his mother and gave a grim smile.

'Here is your thief,' he said, and threw Abel down in the dust.

6
The Gift

It was agreed that Abel should go away to study after all.

Father Nicholas sent letters of recommendation to the dean of Emmanuel College in Cambridge, and Abel was accepted to study theology.

The days before his departure crawled by. Letters had to be sent to the College, replies received, accommodation and transportation arranged, effects packed.

Naomi had been given some time off, ostensibly to help her parents on the farm, but Barnaby suspected it was to keep her out of Abel's way. He missed her calm efficient presence and the quality of her cooking. He missed the way she never bothered picking up his clothes from his bedroom floor and the fact that she always found time to put a sprig of buttercups in the window but never to warm his cup of milk.

The morning after her last day Barnaby found a package with his name on it outside his bedroom door. He took it into his room and opened it on the bed. It was a beautiful corn doll with a pale green ribbon around its neck. A note with it read: *thanc yoow.*

He turned the doll over. Then he smiled. He recognised the clumsy star shape in the centre of the base. Naomi had turned the wretched thing he had begun on the pew outside the cottage into something perfect and beautiful. He set it on the windowsill, looking out across the fields to the lake and the forest behind. The ribbon glowed in the sunlight: the pale green of summer grass, or of the lake bed on a burningly hot day, or of Naomi's eyes when she raised her head from kneading the bread.

In the fields surrounding the forest scythe blades flashed in the sunlight.

Another few weeks and she would be back.

August arrived and the weather turned unseasonably cold. Frances was frantically knitting undergarments for Abel, having heard rumours that there would be no glass in the windows of the classrooms, nor any heating of any kind. The students apparently were forced to sit on long bare planks without backs, with another plank set before them for a desk. Abel could not bear any discussion of the matter. He crept about pale and silent and thinner than ever, seemingly unable to muster the energy even to quote the scriptures.

Eventually the morning of the departure dawned. Barnaby came down for breakfast to find his mother already weeping, his father stony-faced and his brother submitting listlessly to Juliet's attempts to dress him. He breakfasted quickly, gulping down the porridge so fast it gave him hiccoughs. This was not the sort of atmosphere to linger in. And besides, even though Abel was a monster and deserved his banishment, Barnaby couldn't helping feeling guilty that all the present unhappiness in the house had been caused by himself. And it would only get worse as the hour of Abel's departure drew nearer.

'I'm going out,' he said, but no-one seemed to notice.

He headed over to Griff's, and found him in the fields. Griff suggested trying the cider that had been brewing now for several weeks and they retired to the brew-shed. The stuff was revolting but they drank determinedly until their bellies writhed and they were forced to run to the privy. Then they moved on to Griff's father's wine cellar.

They emerged, blinking, into the daylight to find that it had been raining. The air had a fresh smell and the dust had been washed from the windows of the houses, making them glitter in the sunlight. Barnaby had lost track of time, assuming it must be well into the afternoon, and so safe to return home, but when he rounded the corner he saw a coach standing outside the house. Abel's trunk was being loaded onto it. Abel himself stood limply, staring at the ground while his mother fussed and murmured, dabbing her eyes with a handkerchief. Henry stood beside her, stiff and unsmiling.

'He won't be going yet awhile,' Griff whispered. 'Looks like the horses are still at the blacksmith's for new shoes,'

'Good,' Barnaby whispered back. 'They'll be all the swifter to carry him away.' His tongue was fat and slow from the cider and when they crept forwards along the line of cottages his steps wobbled.

They sidled past the little group and had made it to the door before his mother called after them, her voice thick: 'Aren't you going to see your brother off?'

'Of course,' Barnaby said, enunciating carefully. 'I was just—'

Griff interjected, 'He was just going to fetch his farewell gift.'

His mother blinked in surprise.

'That's kind,' she said. 'But hurry now, the horses will be back soon.'

The boys went inside and closed the door, pausing on the other side of it and leaning on one another's shoulders to muffle the sound of their laughter.

'So, what's your gift going to be?' Griff whispered when they had recovered themselves.

'I suppose I could give him father's razor for his tonsure,' Barnaby said.

Griff grinned. 'I've got a better idea.' He leaned forwards and whispered in Barnaby's ear. A smile spread across Barnaby's face. They stumbled upstairs.

When they went back outside, the horses were harnessed to the coach and Abel was climbing the steps. The sun was low in the sky now and the interior of the coach was dark and forbidding. It was a shabby old thing. Here and there the leather had peeled away from the frame and the wood beneath was rotten and splintered. Griff whispered that Abel would be lucky to make Salisbury before it collapsed beneath him.

Abel ducked his head and the darkness swallowed him. A moment later his pale face reappeared at the window. There was no glass, so if he wanted to keep out draughts when the coach picked up speed he would have to button down the curtains and sit in darkness.

Henry stepped forward and said something to his son:

123

Abel nodded. Then Henry held out his arm to help his wife over the churned mud at the edge of the road. Leaning into the coach Frances spoke inaudibly, then reached inside and embraced her youngest son for some minutes. Barnaby looked away.

When she stepped back the coach driver gave a flick of the reins, clicked his tongue and the horses began to move.

'Go on, then,' Griff hissed. 'Give it him.'

Barnaby stumbled forwards, carrying a small package wrapped in a sheet of his father's writing paper and bound with one of Juliet's hair ribbons.

'What's that?' his brother said thickly.

'A . . . a parting gift,' Barnaby said.

'I want nothing from you.'

Barnaby tossed the packet onto the seat beside him.

'The very best of luck, brother,' Barnaby said, then he stepped back and let the coach trundle on.

Griff caught up with him. 'Did he open it?'

'No.'

'What? So, you didn't get to see his face. What's the point in that? Come on! If we cut around the back of the Boar we can catch him up before he reaches the edge of the village!' He set off at a run.

Barnaby hesitated a moment, then set off after his friend.

The market was just clearing as they emerged onto the part of the square that joined the main road out of the village, and there were plenty of people still trying to get bargains from the traders as they dismantled their stalls. They dodged the old women and children scavenging squashed fruit from beneath the wheels of the stalls. One of the traders tossed an apple into the air, but before it could land in a young mother's outstretched basket Griff plucked it from the air, leaving them arguing who would pay for the loss.

As they passed the final stall Barnaby collided with a woman. It was the furrier's widow. He almost knocked her basket of mistletoe from her hands, but managed to catch it in time and made sure she had a firm grasp on it before he ran on.

'There!' cried Griff.

The coach was still trundling along at a pace they could easily match. Griff put on a burst of speed and was the first to catch up with it.

'Hey, Abel!' he called. 'Did you open the present?'

There must have been an answer from inside because then Griff said breathlessly, 'Ah, don't be like that about it, open it, go on!'

Griff was tiring now. Strong as he was, his heavy limbs and great muscular shoulders from the plough weighed him down. As Barnaby caught up with the coach Griff fell back a little.

'Open it, Abel!' Griff called, but Barnaby was beginning to hope Abel would just throw it out into the mud. Now that he was sobering up he was starting to regret the gift. Jogging alongside the coach he held out his hand. 'Give it back then, if you don't want it.'

Abel's eyes narrowed, then he took the package from the seat beside him and began unpicking the ribbon. A strand of Juliet's strawberry-blonde hair was caught in the knot and as it loosened the strand was caught by the wind and snatched away. The paper fell open to reveal a folded pile of white linen.

Abel lifted it out and unfurled it into a long strip.

'What is it?'

Barnaby was about to take it from him when Griff put on a burst of speed and caught up with the coach.

'Do you like it?' Griff panted.

'What is it?' Abel said again.

Griff started laughing.

Abel frowned down at the linen.

'Give it here,' Barnaby said and made a snatch for it with his free hand, but Griff caught hold of it and held him back.

'You want to know what it is?' Griff cried. 'It's one of Juliet's breast bindings!'

Abel blinked rapidly as he tried to understand. Then disgust contorted his features. He dropped the linen as if it were a burning rag about to set the whole coach alight. It landed in his lap and he gave a shrill scream, batting and plucking at the thing until finally he managed to send it flying out of the window.

The garment snagged on a splinter of wood and caught there, streaming out as the coach picked up speed, like the ribbons of a wedding.

The boys skidded to a halt.

'It's a breast binding, you fool!' Griff howled in delight. 'The last chance you will ever get to touch one!'

He screamed with laughter as the coach wheels rumbled out of the village.

Barnaby forced himself to laugh as loudly as Griff: the harsh sounds bouncing off the walls of the houses and rebounding on them until there were legions triumphing in Abel's humiliation. And then he really was laughing, tears of relief that streamed down his face. Abel was gone, hopefully for good, barring a few visits home at Christmas and Easter. Barnaby never had to encounter that grim spectre in the hallway, face it over supper or block out the hissed prayers and curses. His father's guilt would fade and his mother might even begin to soften towards him.

There was a movement to his left.

Someone said his name.

He turned.

The furrier's widow struck him hard on the side of his head, knocking him onto his back in the mud.

For a moment there was absolute silence. Even the market traders stopped what they were doing to stare.

The widow stood before him, her chest heaving. Barnaby was so shocked he could only blink at her as she raised a shaking finger and pointed it into his face.

'SHAME ON YOU!'

Then she turned, picked up her basket and hurried back through the crowd of shocked onlookers.

7
Farmer Nightingale

It rained for the rest of the summer. Barnaby fidgeted in the house, hunted coneys and played dice with Griff when he wasn't busy on the farm. Juliet befriended a crow. It came every morning for bread soaked in milk, tapping on the kitchen window and scaring Barnaby half to death. Once, when she was too busy to make the milk straight away, the bird hopped across the kitchen table and began tapping the milk jug with its beak. This astounded Barnaby. He started trying to train the bird; spending hours attempting to get it to bring him things in return for hazelnuts. The bird seemed to catch on very quickly, preferring shiny objects like cutlery and buttons and coins. Once, when the Widow Moone had turned up selling her crazy charms, he had got it to fly over, drop a coin into her basket and return with a clove-studded apple. The widow had cackled and said it was a clever little devil that she could use herself.

On one of the few fine mornings he was sitting on the back step, shuffling three cups around on the slate beside him while the crow looked on, its beady eyes fixed on the cup under which he had hidden a hazelnut. He shuffled them faster, swishing them in and out of one another, bluffing and double bluffing, while the bird's head darted this way and that.

A disturbance in the sunlight of the path made him look up. His hand stopped moving.

Her hair was loose again. It had grown longer since the last time he had seen it free from the prison of the bonnet, and rippled as she walked, flashing bronze and copper and honey and chestnut.

A stabbing pain in his hand reminded him that the bird was waiting for its reward. It stopped pecking him as soon as he looked down and jabbed its beak on one of the cups. Barnaby raised it to reveal the hazelnut, and the bird hopped away, satisfied.

'Good morning, Master Nightingale,' Naomi said, stopping a few feet away.

'Good morning, Miss Waters,' he said, squinting up into the sunlight.

'Is Juliet at home?'

'No, but I am.' He stood up and leaned on the doorframe. 'I don't suppose you feel like making me some warm milk?'

She smiled. 'Of course. Right away.'

He waited for her on the step, throwing nuts for the crow and feeling mightily pleased with himself. Though she'd pretended it was Juliet she was here to see, Naomi's cheeks were definitely red when they spoke and her eyes had sparkled. He'd always prided himself on his ability to see when a girl liked him: they usually did.

But when Naomi returned with the milk – cold and unspiced – she said, 'When will Juliet be back?'

He frowned. 'No idea. You'll have to wait.'

'I haven't got time.'

Her cheeks were still red, but now he saw that her shoulders were too, and her forearms. She was sunburned, not blushing.

'I needed to tell her something.'

'You'll have to come back tomorrow then.' He concentrated on throwing the nuts, without looking up.

'It's important.'

He didn't answer. His good mood had evaporated and he aimed the next nut at the crow's flank. It flapped off, squawking in outrage.

'Do you think you could pass the message on to her?'

He shrugged. He knew he was being a pig but couldn't seem to help it. *For goodness' sake,* he told himself, *she's only a servant: what does it matter what she thinks of you?*

'There's something wrong with the wheat,' Naomi went on. 'Black rot in the grain. It happens when there's been too much rain. People say it doesn't matter, that it tastes the same, but it makes you sick. Badly. If you eat too much of it it can kill you. Barnaby? Are you listening?'

'Poison in the wheat,' he intoned. 'I'll tell her. You can run on home now.'

Though he didn't look up, he felt her stiffen beside him. Then she turned and walked quickly down the path. The crow was nowhere to be seen so he went back inside to oil his bow.

On her return, after Barnaby had passed on the message, Juliet discovered a few specks of black in the latest batch of

130

flour and decided there was to be no more bread until it was back to its normal appearance. Barnaby's father was annoyed but Frances conceded that it was up to Juliet, so long as she provided an alternative. They managed on potatoes and rye after this, but the crow was unimpressed with this change of diet and, to Barnaby's disappointment, stopped visiting.

The only thing to look forward to was apple harvest time, when he usually helped gather in Griff's father's crop.

But the bad weather ruined the harvests. The wheat rotted in the fields and the tree fruits were wizened and blighted.

Barnaby went round to Griff's anyway and they managed to find a way of amusing themselves by pelting one another with the rotten fruit. Once Griff managed to strike him full in the chest with a slimy plum, leaving a huge crimson stain on his shirt.

On the way home he ran into Naomi. He was shocked at how exhausted she looked. Her hands were covered with blisters, puffed and milky like the eyes in a roasted lamb's head.

Her head was bent, so he stood in front of her to block her path. She looked up and gasped. Her hand flew to his chest. 'What have you done?'

Surprised, he glanced down. It was only the plum stain. 'Griff and I were having a battle with his father's fruit.'

Her face darkened and she drew away from him. He realised that he had made her feel a fool. To change the subject he gestured at her blistered hands.

'But those are genuine injuries.'

'From the sickle,' she said coldly. 'It's harvest time. As you might know if you actually did any work.'

He opened his mouth to speak but she had already marched past him and away down the lane to her house.

As the sun rose the next morning he was waiting by the Waters' strips of land, armed with a sickle he had borrowed from Griff. To his great good fortune the day had dawned dry and clear and his heart leaped as two figures approached, silhouetted against the low red sun. But the slighter figure was not Naomi, after all, but some spotty youth he didn't recognise.

Farmer Waters stopped dead when he saw Barnaby.

'Eh-up, Master Nightingale. Is there a problem? I haven't touched any of your father's strips if that's what you're—'

'Not at all, Mister Waters,' Barnaby interrupted. 'I only thought I might be able to help you with the last of the harvesting.'

Waters stared. Then he scratched his head and shifted uneasily from foot to foot. 'Ah, well, that's very kind of you but, as you can see, I have help and I'm afraid it's all I can do to pay my nephew a decent wage.'

'I wouldn't require payment.'

'No?'

The sun was rising quickly now and a shaft suddenly shot over the farmer's head and straight into Barnaby's eyes, making him wince and stammer.

'I . . . er . . . I saw Naomi yesterday and—'

'What's she been telling you?' Waters cut in. 'That I can't manage me own land? She's no right to go—'

'She said no such thing!' Barnaby said hastily. 'I saw her hands, that's all, and th ... thought I might be able to spare her any more suffering.'

Farmer Waters looked at Barnaby thoughtfully.

'Well, in that case,' he said eventually, 'you're most welcome.'

If Barnaby had regretted his offer when he saw Naomi would not be present, he regretted it even more once the work began. The ground was waterlogged and tramping across to the uncut strips they were soon up to their knees in cold sludge. The wetness made the sickle even harder to control: like a horse, it seemed intuitively to know that there was an inexperienced hand controlling it, and it bucked and twisted and once nearly sliced into his ankle. By contrast Waters and his nephew moved in a slow and fluid rhythm, and the corn laid itself down before them with whispering sighs. To Barnaby's eyes it didn't seem as gold or as tall as it ought to have been and there were strange black excrescences, like rats' droppings, where the grain should have been. By mid-morning he was extremely grateful Naomi wasn't around. His corn lay in ugly tangles and he was only halfway down his first strip when the other two had finished their fifth and paused for breakfast. They shouted over at him to join them but he could not bear the humiliation and soldiered on, though the palms of his hands were raw.

As the sun rose higher the other two men stripped off their shirts and Barnaby was surprised to see the impressive muscles of the spotty youth: far more clearly defined than his own since there was less flesh to cover them. He was staring at the boy's back, rippling as he picked up another huge armful of corn, when there was a shout.

His heart sank.

The other two straightened and wiped the sweat from their brows. Waters' nephew walked to meet Naomi as she approached, carrying a large ceramic jug and two cups. She began to say something and then stopped abruptly. Barnaby bent his head and carried on working, trying to keep the sickle steady.

'Ale, Barnaby!' Waters shouted.

With a deep breath he laid down the sickle and tramped over to the others. Waters and the boy were sharing one of the cups and Naomi handed him the second without looking at him. As she poured the ale she slopped it a little and the cool liquid soothed his burning hand.

'Master Nightingale came to help us,' Waters said.

Stop now, Barnaby thought, *don't say any more, don't say what a useless farmer I would make.*

'That was very good of him,' Naomi said, fussing with the beaded handkerchief that covered the jug.

To Barnaby's horror he saw that the youth was smirking and glancing across at Barnaby's half-finished strip, clearly itching to say something that would belittle him in front of Naomi. The thin lips parted, but Barnaby drowned him out.

'The ale is lovely! Did you brew it yourselves?'

'Aye,' Waters said and launched into a lecture about the best grain mix and the excellence of his yeast, which had been in the family for several generations.

Barnaby nodded as if he fully understood. At home it was the servants that drank ale, the family stuck to wine, or beer if it was hot. He glanced at Naomi and she rolled her eyes. The boy was now scowling.

'Patrick,' she said, going up to him and touching his arm in a familiar, almost intimate gesture, 'Mother wants to know if you will dine with us.'

'If you've enough,' Patrick said gruffly.

'Is Mother back from Stalyridge then?' Waters said to his daughter. 'How's Aunty?'

'Not good,' Naomi said, glancing at Barnaby. 'The blood's still coming, day and night. She's got it into her head that it's witchcraft and she won't be better until the old women hang. She wanted Mother to go to the aldermen and report it as maleficium but I told her not to.'

'If they be witches,' Patrick said, ''tis right to speak up against them.'

Naomi scowled at him. 'Or perhaps Aunty Catherine just has the same sickness that took our grandmother.'

'Don't get involved, girl,' Waters said to his daughter. 'It doesn't do to be seen to be protecting them. Now then ...' To Barnaby's dismay he handed the mug back to his daughter and picked up his sickle. 'Let's try and finish before nightfall.'

Barnaby's heart dropped to his boots as he returned his mug, picked up his sickle and trudged back to his forlorn strip. He realised too late that she must now know how poorly he had performed. Risking a glance over his shoulder he saw she was smiling. He blushed furiously, then turned back and continued with his inept labours.

They did finish before nightfall, thanks mainly to Patrick, who seemed impervious to pain or exhaustion. Even as the sun sank behind the forest he was still swiping the blade with the same vigour he had displayed at dawn.

It was only Naomi's appearance with more ale and an

135

invitation for Barnaby to join them at supper that finally ended the day's exertions. They drank in silence as the shadows turned indigo. As the air cooled, the fragrance of moist, cut corn mingled with the wild garlic and honeysuckle of the hedgerows. Bats darted overhead making the clouds of midges swirl in panic.

He would have liked to accompany them, if only to annoy Patrick. But his hands were swollen and bleeding, his legs were jelly, and all he wanted to do was collapse in his bed.

'Thank you, Mister Waters,' he said, finishing his cup. 'For suffering my clumsy efforts. I hope I was some help.'

'Certainly you were, Master Nightingale!' the farmer gushed. 'But don't go telling your father that I'm the one responsible for all them blisters!' He laughed and Barnaby quickly thrust his hands into his pockets.

'Certainly not,' Barnaby said. 'I shall say they were caused by too much dicing at the Boar.'

Waters laughed and even Patrick lifted his lip to show a brown tooth.

'Goodnight, Farmer Waters,' he said with a bow. 'Patrick . . . Naomi.'

He did not linger to see her reaction but as he walked away, trying to stride rather than hobble, her voice drifted after him with a soft chuckle, 'Goodnight, Farmer Nightingale.'

The journey home felt ten times longer than usual and occasionally he had to lean on a wall for rest. He finally wobbled through the door as the clock struck ten.

'Barnaby!' his father cried, rising from his chair by the fire. 'Where have you been all day? We were worried.'

You might have been, Barnaby thought. His mother was at the table, engrossed with another of his brother's letters. She did not raise her head at his entrance.

Letters had come from Abel twice weekly at first, but they soon tailed off to once a week, then once a fortnight, and this was the first missive since early September.

Juliet appeared in the doorway with a plate of mutton and a mug of wine.

'Alleluia!' Barnaby cried, throwing himself down in a chair and stretching his hands to receive the meal. 'You are my own, true darling!'

The first bite of mutton was the most divine morsel that had ever passed his lips.

'It seems the Lord Protector himself came to speak to them,' his mother said without raising her head from the letter. 'Abel says he was very wise and devout.'

'And a traitor,' his father muttered.

'He says that Mister Cromwell described how far steeped in sin is our society and that the reformation had not gone far enough to strip away the excesses of Catholicism.'

'Really,' said Henry drily. Barnaby licked mutton fat off his fingers as noisily as possible.

She read a little longer, then gave a fretful sigh: 'He says he hopes to become an instrument of purification: Oh Henry ...' She put the letter down and took off her glasses. 'I do hope he's not being led along the wrong path.'

'I'm sure he's fine,' Henry said, batting his hand. 'Just settling in, that's all. They'll set him straight soon enough.'

Frances sighed again and tucked the letter back in its envelope. 'I'm going to tell him to come home for Barnaby's birthday so we can make sure he's all right.'

Barnaby shot his father a panicked look. The party was always the high point of his year and this year, his sixteenth and therefore special, promised to be even better than usual. It was to be held in the church. The pews were to be pushed back and a hog spit placed before the altar. A considerable amount of alcohol had been ordered, and Lord Pembroke had provided five sheep and ten chickens (mainly, Barnaby's father said, in gratitude to the village for not turning against him and his Catholic family after Cromwell's victory over the King). Abel's dour presence would ruin the whole evening.

'I'm sure that's not necessary,' Henry said. 'You need to give him the chance to make his own way in life.'

Frances gave a non-committal murmur.

Barnaby tossed back the dregs of the wine, belched and struggled up, unable to repress a groan.

'What's the matter with you?' his father said. 'Not coming down with something, are you?'

'I'm fine,' he croaked. Then, using his father's shoulder for purchase, he pivoted himself towards the staircase and, with intakes of breath and little squeaks of discomfort, made his way up to bed. If this was an honest day's work, he thought as he mounted the stairs like a geriatric, then you could keep it.

The next day he was walking stiffly over to Griff's when he met Flora Slabber returning from the market. Though she did not seem so pretty as the last time he saw her it pleased him to see her blush deeply when she saw him, and he fell into step beside her.

'What have you bought?' he asked.

'Just a few cakes for me and Mama, and some material for a dress. Mama says I shall have a new one for your birthday party. I chose blue velvet because the colour works so well with my hair.'

'Yes,' Barnaby said, 'I'm sure it does.'

They passed the apothecary. Sitting by the wall outside was the cart belonging to the furrier's widow. He recognised it by the bright paintings that adorned the side: of flowers and wild animals and strange creatures half hidden in the long grass. The widow had taken to wheeling it around the village even on non-market days, trying to sell her wild berries and mushrooms. Today it was brimful of rosemary. Flora inhaled deeply. 'Oh I love that smell,' she said.

He went over to the cart and snapped off a sturdy twig, then came and tucked it behind her ear, making her giggle. They continued along the street arm in arm.

He felt a bit guilty for stealing from such a poor woman but pushed it from his mind. Not only had she attacked him in front of the entire village, but she was also behind with her rent, though his father hadn't yet turfed her out of the hovel she'd built on their land. Whenever Barnaby remembered that awful afternoon, floundering in the mud surrounded by the crowing of the villagers, he was flooded with shame and fury.

But before they had gone much further there was a strange cry behind them. It sounded as if a drunk was calling his name but when he turned he saw the widow's deaf son jogging to meet them. He was a dark and swarthy youth but muscular and well-built, with quick black eyes.

'Masser Nighthingale,' he said, stopping in front of them, 'I am glad I saw you.'

Barnaby straightened and lifted his chin, embarrassed to hear the sound of his name so mangled in front of Flora.

'What can I do for you?' he said loudly.

'My mother is sick,' the boy said in his strange thick tongue. 'And I do not possess her knowledge of the forest. We owe your father two months' rent. I have received a commission to paint the church but until I get paid in a month's time we cannot pay you. I am sorry.' He spoke slowly and seemed to be enunciating his words very carefully, but plainly he wasn't stupid. His bright black eyes held Barnaby's and Barnaby blinked. For one so afflicted the boy was certainly bold. Barnaby could feel Flora waiting for his response.

'What's your name?' he said imperiously.

'Luke Armitage.'

'Well, Mr Armitage, your mother is almost two months behind and I think that is lenience enough.'

Flora leaned across and whispered to him, 'He is reading your speech from the movement of your lips.'

Sure enough, Luke was staring at his mouth. He brought his hand up to cough into it, then left it there as if quite naturally rubbing his jaw. Sure enough the boy's brow furrowed.

'I shall expect the rent by Monday.'

'What did you say?' the boy said.

'MONDAY,' Barnaby said loudly.

The boy nodded curtly, then turned and walked back to his cart.

Flora's titter was like the squealing of the widow's cart's wheels as the deaf boy made his way home. Barnaby's conscience pricked him and he almost went after Luke to tell him he could take another week. But it had started to rain. Flora grabbed his arm and they hurried on.

8
The Party

It seemed to take forever to arrive but at last the day of Barnaby's birthday party dawned, clear and bright and chilly. It was the first really cold day of the year and the air was soon fragrant with peat and woodsmoke. The roads out of the village were treacherous with ice and Henry said how lucky they were that the wine had arrived the previous day or the carts may not have got through.

The only possible event that could mar the day was Abel's arrival, but as the afternoon wore on with no sign of him, Barnaby dared to hope that the roads were too bad for him to travel. It wasn't as if his brother would actually *want* to come; he had been summoned by Frances.

As the shadows deepened and the lamps were lit Barnaby went to his room to put on his party clothes. On the bed was the new outfit his father had ordered from France. Barnaby had chosen the cut and fabric, and the few adornments (fine without being fussy), but seeing it for the first time made him draw in his breath.

The doublet of embroidered, glazed linen glittered like gold in the candlelight. Slashed to a high waistband, it revealed the white lawn shirt beneath, with its mother-of-pearl buttons. The breeches were dove-grey velvet, tied at the knees with black ribbons, and the black boots were so polished they reflected his own face back at him.

He began to strip off, whistling to himself. Juliet came in while he was pulling on the shirt. In her hand was a small package.

'It was lying on the step this morning,' she said softly.

She held it out for him but he didn't take it.

He knew what it would contain. Beneath the wrapping of white linen there would be a bunch of forest flowers: forget-me-nots and buttercups, pansies, cornflowers, goldenrods and mouse-ears, occasionally a delicate briar rose. Too fragile to last more than an hour or so without water, they would already be drooping, the edges of the petals browning and curling.

The bundle would be tied with a strip of blue cloth embroidered with roses. These roses had been stitched, clumsily, by his mother when she was barely sixteen. Stitched onto a swaddling cloth to wrap her firstborn son. It must have been painstaking work: hundreds of tiny pink flowers with yellow seed heads and a whisper of green at the base. It was the most loving thing she had ever done for him. But it hadn't been for him; not really. It had been for the child that was taken away. They had wrapped the changeling in it when they left the creature on the midden heap, and when Barnaby was returned he was wrapped in a coarse blanket that smelled of dung.

This dreadful ritual, of returning the swaddling, strip by

strip, binding those mean little flowers, had been enacted every birthday morning for as long as he could remember. Henry seemed to take an odd pride in it – that his son was so adored by the fairy realm – but it always upset his mother, so that over the past few years Juliet had been careful to find and hide it before anyone else could discover it.

'I don't want it,' Barnaby said. 'Put it in the fire.'

Her eyes widened. 'Oh no, no. You must not insult them like that! It is their gift to you.'

'It's not. It's just some spiteful villager mocking me.'

For years he'd thought it was Abel – though the trick seemed too clever for his brother's mean little mind – but now Abel was gone.

'I mean it. Take it away.' He went back to fastening the buttons of his shirt, but the arrival of the package had put him out of sorts and his fingers were trembling.

Juliet hesitated, then, muttering unhappily, tucked it into the pocket of her apron.

'Come,' she said. 'Let me help you.'

As she bent her head to fasten the tiny round pearl buttons of the cuffs he noticed that her hair was greasy and she smelled faintly of stale sweat. Naomi had still not returned to work, her brother having fallen sick a few weeks previously, and after getting used to having help, Juliet seemed to find being on her own again doubly hard. Barnaby had sent various provisions up to the Waters' farm – dried fruits imported from Turkey, loaves of rye bread, cakes made with apples from Griff's orchard. Now he felt guilty for making Juliet do all that extra baking.

'What are you wearing tonight?' he said.

'This probably,' she said. 'I'll be helping out with the food so whatever I wear will get greasy and spoiled.' She went over to refresh the fire.

He thought for a moment, then pulled out one of the ribbons woven into his cuffs, and went over to where she was kneeling.

She jumped as his fingers touched her hair.

'Stay still,' he murmured, then he gathered up a section and tied it with the ribbon.

'But what about your jacket?' she said, looking up at him. The crackling flames of the kindling had burned her cheek a deep scarlet.

'Only my father would notice, and I don't care how handsome *he* finds me.'

As she stood and brushed the ash from her apron he remained where he was, gazing at his reflection in the mirror above the fireplace. His hair had grown long and the loose curls rested on his shoulders, which appeared broader thanks to the cut of the jacket. He ran his fingers through it, careful not to snag a fingernail on the birthmark at the nape of his neck, which always bled so easily. His face was losing its childhood plumpness. He kept expecting to see the narrowing of the jaw and the arch of the nose that ran through the Nightingale line, but so far they had not materialised. In fact his jaw appeared to be squaring and widening, and his nose was as straight as it had always been. Presumably this was from his mother's family, though he couldn't think of any good-looking Woodcrofts. Perhaps such features only became acceptable when mixed with those of the Nightingales.

Juliet began fussing with his collar, trying to fasten the top button, but he stopped her hand, he did not wish to feel constricted tonight, especially since there would be considerable quantities of food and drink passing down his throat. He was about to drop his hand, but then he happened to glance into her face.

The adoration in her eyes was like the sudden headrush of strong liquor. Without pausing for thought he bent forwards and kissed her.

He had grown so much taller over recent months that when he pulled away she was low enough to lean her head against his chest.

He couldn't think of anything to say and stood swaying there slightly as her chest rose and fell against his belly.

'Never let me go,' she said softly. 'Not even when you marry. I want to be with you always.' She looked up at him. 'Promise.'

His voice was as high as a child when he spoke. 'I promise.'

When she left he sat down heavily on the bed and stared at the distorted reflection of his face in the polished toes of his boot. It sickened him. He had been so intoxicated by her adoration that he had acted thoughtlessly. He loved Juliet like a sister and to make her believe that he had stronger feelings for her was base and cruel. He *did* possess those feelings, the time had come to accept the fact, but they were not for Juliet, and they were not for Flora.

Eventually he got up and, rather subdued, made his way downstairs.

His parents were sitting by the fire, speaking in low voices, and both looked up when they heard his feet on the stairs. At once his father's face flushed with pride. The old man looked ridiculous, in some absurd conical hat with an ostrich feather that waggled in the up-draughts from the fire. His belly was too large for his gaudy doublet and he had undone the last buttons, which only drew attention to the problem. Barnaby was so busy taking in this mortifying ensemble that it was several minutes before he felt his mother's eyes on him. He was surprised to see her expression of warmth and, yes, almost affection.

She rose and came over to him and he saw she was wearing the brooch his father had helped him choose for her five Christmases ago, before he had given up trying to please her. It glittered in the firelight, like a tiny flame of love in her breast.

He bent to receive her light kiss on his cheek.

'Any woman would be proud to call you her son,' she said as she drew away, smiling.

Then his father was at his side and leading him to the door.

'Aren't you coming, Mother?' he said, turning back.

She was still smiling, but more wistfully now. 'I'll wait for Abel a while.'

'Oh. Goodbye, then.'

As Henry opened the door a gust of snow struck their faces.

It was an unpleasant journey. The sleet found its way inside their shirts and shoes and several times they almost slipped on their backsides. But the sight of the church dispelled any despondency.

Its windows glittered and lanterns hung from every nook and crevice in the walls. Garlands of scarlet and pink amaryllis hung around the necks of the gargoyles protruding from the porch and more lanterns clustered in the yew tree. A couple of farm children decked out in their Sunday best chased one another between the rapidly whitening gravestones. Barnaby hurried forwards, drawn on by the spicy perfume coming from a copper pan steaming on a brazier just inside the doors.

A girl poured a cup of mulled wine for each of them and they passed through the porch. Henry turned and grinned at Barnaby, slapping him gently on the back. 'Happy birthday, son.'

Barnaby grinned back and pushed open the door.

It was so bright inside he had to squint. Lanterns hung from every beam and candles crowded every surface not already occupied by cups and flagons and bottles. There was noise, and warmth, and the mouth-watering smell of roasting pork. When the fiddler saw him he struck up a fast jig and soon they were surrounded by dancing.

Grinning and greeting his tenants, his father led him through the crush and up the central aisle. They mounted the altar steps to cries of congratulation and the raising of wine glasses.

The altar cloth had been replaced by a linen tablecoth, upon which stood pewter plates and wooden bowls. There was sugar cake and gingerbread, lemon posset and trifle, breads and wafers with slipcoat cheese and quince jelly, a whole baked salmon, a pottage of veal.

To line his stomach Barnaby began with bread and

cheese, nibbling when he could whilst his father led him around a crowd of portly red-faced men he didn't recognise. He shook their hands and made pleasantries while his father introduced him as the Nightingale with whom they would soon be doing much of their business.

Then he saw Naomi. She was standing with her mother by a table that had been laid out for the villagers. There were fewer meat and sweet dishes here: only tongue hash and herbed giblets, one or two fruit fools, and the rest vegetables. Naomi was bending down to feed her brother spoonfuls of pie, most of which was ending up on his smart white smock. He looked thin but his cheeks were pink and his eyes bright.

'Don't you agree, Master Nightingale?'

One of his father's business colleagues was speaking to him.

'I feel much as you do,' Barnaby said, nodding sagely. This seemed to satisfy the man, who waggled a chicken wing at him and mumbled, 'Sensible lad.'

The chicken must have gone down the wrong way because now he started coughing. The coughs soon became gasps for air and the merchant's face turned purple.

'Are you all right, Wat?' his father said, banging the man's hulking back and trying to understand his choked grunts. The merchant's eyes were bulging now and there was fear in them.

'Barnaby!' his father shouted. 'Go and fetch some farmhands, we must knock out the blockage!'

But before Barnaby had gone more than two paces the merchant gave a sudden violent cough and a glob of masticated meat sailed across the apse to spatter the newly limewashed walls.

The man's colleagues gathered around him as his face lightened from puce to pink to its original sallow yellow. He was handed a drink, and another chicken wing, which made him laugh so much he began coughing again. Barnaby took this as his cue to escape, pocketing a few choice morsels from the table as he did so.

As he descended the steps he caught sight of Griff, waving frantically from the other side of the nave and gesticulating towards the backs of Flora and another girl, who were giggling and whispering nearby. He held up a finger – *one minute* – then made his way over to the villagers' table. Kneeling down beside the boy – Benjamin, was it? – he drew a sugared plum from his pocket. Benjamin's eyes widened. The sugar sparkled in the candlelight, as if it was a ruby.

'Now, then,' Barnaby said, 'I believe that only hale and hearty boys are allowed sugared plums, not puling sickly ones. Isn't that right, Naomi?'

She smiled down at him, her eyes shining.

'Oh, yes, Barnaby, sick children can only have gruel and watered milk.'

'I am quite well!' Benjamin cried. 'Ask Mother!'

'Is he?' Barnaby said to Naomi.

She pretended to think for a minute, while Benjamin's eyes grew larger and anxious, then finally she nodded. The plum was handed over and the boy sank his teeth into it with utter savagery.

'I'm glad he's better,' Barnaby said, standing. 'We were all worried.'

'Thank you for all the things you sent,' she said.

'Benjamin looked forward so much to Juliet's visits. I'm sure he made himself remain sick for longer so as to keep them coming!'

'Will you be back to work soon?' he said. Naomi's smile faded. 'Of course. You may tell your parents I will return tomorrow if they wish.'

'No, no,' he said hastily. 'They did not tell me to ask you, I just . . .'

But she was no longer listening. Someone was summoning her to take round trays of sausages and she began picking her way through the crowd to the food table without a backward glance.

There was a tugging at his sleeve. 'Got any more?' Benjamin said.

Barnaby handed over the last of the treats from his pocket and went over to join Griff, who had managed to commandeer an entire cauldron of fruit punch.

Some time later – he didn't know how long – Abel was there.

Griff pointed him out, standing beside Frances as she spoke to one of the yeomen's wives. At the sight of him Barnaby's hand jerked and he spilled wine all over his gold doublet.

Abel was dressed in the garb of a priest, but without those patches of colour provided by the chasuble or cassock. He was so black it was as if a part of the church had been cut out, through to the night beyond.

His hair was now very short, emphasising his knobbly skull and the hard lines of his face, so drawn it was almost skeletal. He was glaring around the church.

Instinctively Barnaby ducked behind Griff.

'You'll have to take him seriously now, Barnes,' Griff muttered.

'Yes,' Barnaby murmured, peering over Griff's shoulder. 'I think that's the effect he was trying to achieve.'

The yeoman's wife moved away and as soon as she had gone Abel gripped his mother's arm and dragged her to him. He too had grown taller in the past six months and now loomed over her.

They could not hear him over the fiddle music but his face was twisted in anger. Barnaby pushed Griff aside, intending to go to his mother's aid, but Griff held him. 'He's bitterly jealous. Don't make it worse. Come on, Flora and Mary are waiting for us.'

He allowed himself to be led to where the girls were giggling in the shadows. Griff at once pulled Mary into an embrace but Barnaby wanted to go home. He'd had too much to eat and too much to drink, he'd offended Naomi, and now his brother was here. But there was no chance of escape. Some ceremony had been planned for him so he'd just have to wait. And it could be a long one because his father was currently busy honeying up to some rich landowner from Devon.

'Does the birthday boy want a kiss?' Flora whispered in his ear, making him jump.

He presented a cheek but she turned his face and kissed him full on the mouth. Her lips were hard and insistent, like the beak of a chicken, and her breath had been soured with too many sweet things. As subtly as possible he eased himself away. Flora's eyes snapped open.

'What's the matter?'

'Sorry,' he said. 'I feel a bit sick.'

She frowned and opened her mouth to speak, but just then the altar bell rang. Gradually the church fell silent. His father was standing at the lectern, although Barnaby wondered how he'd made it up the stairs because it was obvious that Henry was extremely drunk.

'Ladies and gentlemen,' he began sloppily. 'Friends, tenants and colleagues, I welcome you to the sixteenth birthday celebration of my son and heir, Barnaby Nightingale!'

There was applause and cheering.

'As many of you know, Barnaby's babyhood had its share of drama and we only just managed to hang on to him!'

Laughter filled the room.

'But,' his father's face softened and Barnaby squeezed his eyes shut in preparation for what was bound to be mortifying, 'we thank God and the saints every day that he was brought safely back to us. He has since become the son every man dreams of.'

Murmurs of assent, *aaaahs* came from the women.

Barnaby peeled open one eye to look at his mother but she was not looking at her husband: her attention was fixed elsewhere and she seemed anxious. Barnaby followed her line of vision to where Abel stood. The spit had been set up by the font in order that people might wash the grease from their hands, and Abel was standing beside it. As Barnaby watched he leaned over the blackened carcass of the pig and dipped his fingers into the holy water. After withdrawing them he crossed himself then stared down at his fingers, rubbing the tips together with a look of disgust, before wiping them dry on his black gown.

'As is Nightingale family tradition,' his father droned on,

153

'to mark his coming of age the eldest son receives his own signet ring with the family crest, and the sword with which Great-Great-Great – I forget how many, for which I'll blame the baron's fine wine! – Grandfather Percival Nightingale fought beside the Black Prince.'

There was more applause.

'Come, Barnaby, and receive what is due to you.'

His father spread his arms and the applause grew louder as Barnaby made his way to the front of the church. For years he had looked forward to this moment but now it just felt excruciating. It certainly didn't have the solemnity he'd imagined it would. His father was drunk, Barnaby was minus his doublet thanks to the wine stain, and as he passed through the red-faced villagers he could hear someone being sick.

'Come on, Barnes!' his father cried. 'There's drinking to be done!'

He mounted the stairs of the lectern and his father pulled him into an embrace that stank of beer and sweat. Releasing him, Henry fumbled in his pocket, drawing out a button and a cork before eventually chancing across the ring, then he held Barnaby's hand high enough for the congregation to see, and slid it onto his little finger. At first it wouldn't go, and in those moments during which his father pushed Barnaby marked how much taller and broader than his father he had become. Taller and broader than all the Nightingales present, in fact.

The ring finally shunted into place. Next his father bent down and picked up the sword. It was a disappointment: the narrow blade notched and rusted, the hilt bare and worn. Nevertheless he stood straight-backed as his father took the hand with the too-tight signet ring and closed the fingers around the hilt before jerking Barnaby's arm above his head, in the process nearly taking his own eye out with the rusted tip.

'My son!' he roared and there was prolonged, drunken appreciation.

Barnaby forced himself to smile and nod graciously around the room.

Only one face did not reciprocate. Abel glared at him.

And then Abel took a step back, straight into the spit. Immediately the whole edifice collapsed, and the remains of the animal clattered to the floor. The applause was cut short.

Abel took a step forwards.

'Peace!' Henry cried over the din. 'There is plenty more food to go round.'

Abel held Barnaby's gaze for a split second then his bird's chest swelled and his thin lips parted and he roared, 'Blasphemy!'

For a moment there was absolute silence, then Henry broke it.

'Abel, please!' he called from the lectern, his voice reedy in comparison to his son's.

'This! . . .' Abel swept an arm around the church, taking in the plates strewing the floor, the overturned flagons and bottles, the mouths hanging open, spilling food onto the floor. 'All of this is the work of the devil!'

Still nobody spoke. Barnaby's heart pounded to the rhythm of his brother's footsteps as Abel stalked up the aisle.

'With the brilliance of his countenance Lucifer has

blinded you to this wickedness. The desecration of the House of God! The fouling of His altar, the besmirching of His holy water, the gluttony, the lust, the—'

'Shut up!' Barnaby shouted. He stumbled down the lectern steps.

Abel raised his arm and pointed at his brother. 'And this is he! Son of the Morning!'

Somebody tried to stop Barnaby, plucking at his sleeve as he passed, but he carried on down the aisle, breaking into a run as Abel's voice rose still higher:

'For thou hast said in thine heart, I will ascend into heaven. I will exalt my throne above the stars of God: I will sit also upon the mount of the congregation, in the sides of the north. I will ascend above the clouds: I will be like the most High!'

Barnaby's head swirled with fury. He was barely three steps from his brother. He clenched his fist into rock, then drew back his arm, so far that his whole body twisted. This time he would kill Abel.

But then something happened.

His brother's ghastly voice became suddenly muffled as a black curtain fell across his face.

Abel pivoted round, struggling to uncover his face. Someone had tossed his own cassock over his head and now everyone in the church could see his braies. He was so painfully thin that they hung off his hips, revealing the crack of his backside, and they were stained yellow at the seam. His spider-thin legs descended into a pair of holed grey hose held up with suspenders and boots that were far too big for him.

The church exploded into laughter.

156

Barnaby froze. Behind him he could hear his father splutter with mirth as he tried to speak.

Then someone sprang forward and wrapped a scarf around Abel's neck, tying it quickly at the back to secure the cassock over his head, leaving him to fumble with the knot as the place echoed with screams of delight. Children shrieked as he blundered towards them.

After rebounding off pews and pillars and laughing villagers who thrust him away as if it was a game of blind man's buff, he eventually swerved towards Barnaby.

Somewhere he could hear his mother wailing, as the rest of the room bayed like a pack of hounds.

Abel was close enough that Barnaby could hear his shrill curses, interspersed with sobs.

He raised his arms and Abel blundered into them.

For a moment they stood locked together. Abel's bony chest shuddered against Barnaby's. Barnaby let his arms close gently on his brother's shoulders. He was surprised to find his anger had evaporated. The whole evening had been a disaster and this was a fitting way for it to end. Abel had lost any chance of one day holding a position of respect in the village: from this day forth he would be a laughing stock.

Abel must have sensed who held him for he began to struggle.

'Stand still,' Barnaby muttered into his ear, 'and I will untie you, brother.'

Abel froze. Then he muttered, 'You are no brother of mine, you are the devil's brother.'

And then Abel tore himself free with such force he tumbled head-over-heels across the back of a pew and landed on his backside amidst the burning pools of pig fat. He struggled to get up but his hands could get no purchase, and he screamed as the hot grease burned him. He began fumbling with the cassock and eventually managed to tear it off his head, then he stared wildly around him, his face scarlet, the tufts of his shorn hair sticking out at ridiculous angles. Barnaby walked across to him and stretched out a hand to help him up.

Abel spat at him.

'One day you will get what's coming to you,' Abel hissed.

Enough, Barnaby thought. The compassion he had felt a moment before evaporated.

'True enough I am not your brother,' he said quietly. 'I am the Prince of Fairyland and these,' he swept an arm around the room, 'are my loving subjects. Where are yours, Abel? Where is one who loves and admires you? Even our mother is ashamed of you. Take comfort in your grubby pamphlets and your Bible stories for they will be your only companions for the rest of your sorry life. You are just where you belong: slithering at my feet.'

The laughter was dying now. The fiddler had struck up once more. Someone called for another drink. Barnaby turned and walked away and the crowd opened to receive him.

9
Ice

A few days after the party winter fell like a hammer.

The remaining leaves dropped from the trees so quickly that in less than a week the branches were bare and black and birds fell dead from their roosts overnight. Many farmers hadn't even begun bringing their cattle in and, on their morning rounds, discovered some of the younger animals had died from the shock of it. The old ones stood huddled together in the fields, barely discernible in clouds of their smoky breath.

A traveller on the road to Grimston was discovered, stiff as dry leather, crouching by the blackened embers of a fire.

Barnaby woke to the crunch of Juliet's feet on the grass as she brought in the washing.

He was surprised to find himself fully clothed, then dimly remembered blundering about the room several times in the night as he grew colder and colder.

He had no intention of stripping off again to wash in the steaming bowl of water she had left. The steam was no indication that the water was hot: the air in the room was so cold that ice had formed on the inside of the window. He got up and went over to it, watching her through the intricate lacy patterns of ice on the pane. She moved stiffly, folding the laundry as if it were made of wood.

Behind her the forest was a huge black fist threatening the sky. He shivered a little at a thin breeze creeping between the glass and the frame.

The crow was back, pecking for worms, and occasionally she would turn her head to speak to it. The creature must have sensed his presence for its head suddenly jerked up and it regarded him with an eye that was, even from this distance, disconcertingly human. Its dour black garb and judgemental gaze reminded him of Abel and he had a sudden desire to break its wings.

He turned away, rubbing his face. The mirror above the wash bowl was misted but when he wiped it clear he wished he hadn't. His face had a greyish tinge and there were shadows beneath his eyes he had never noticed before. Even his teeth looked yellow in the watery sunlight.

Though he had slept late again the sleep was fitful and plagued with anxious dreams. Abel was gone; never to return in all probability. Leaving the party directly after his humiliation he had passed the night at the Boar and taken himself straight back to Cambridge the following day, without even collecting his things from the house. Other than unpleasant reruns of the incident in his dreams, Barnaby didn't care: he was more furious at the way Naomi had behaved afterwards.

After all that Abel had put her through she had actually helped him up from the pig fat, and tried to get the worst

160

of the filth off him, while he snarled and slapped at her hands, finally pushing her over and ruining her dress. All the while she'd been throwing Barnaby black glances, as if it was *he* who had behaved badly! Though she had returned to work, they were barely speaking.

In a foul mood he opened the door and walked out onto the landing. All was silent downstairs. Even though Abel had gone, his oppressive presence lingered in the house, congealing the air. His mother seemed constantly on the verge of tears and his father shuffled about as if he had aged ten years.

Barnaby went downstairs loudly enough for Juliet to hear him, and sure enough he had barely sat down before she emerged from the kitchen with a bowl of porridge scattered with dried berries. He grunted that he should like a drink too and she disappeared again.

He was halfway through his breakfast when there was a knock at the back door. Juliet came in from the kitchen.

'One of your tenants is here,' she said. 'Your father has gone out already. Is your mother down yet?'

'No. Who is it?'

'Goodwife Armitage.'

Barnaby stopped picking the berry skins from his teeth. 'The furrier's widow?'

Juliet nodded, then added quickly, 'The poor old woman doesn't look well. She says she has been sick and—'

He didn't let her finish. Pushing back his chair, he stood up and stalked in the direction of the kitchen. The memory of her attack still stung every time he thought about it. Clearly she was here about the rent: her son had never returned with what was owed. This was his chance to pay her back for the humiliation she had caused him.

The door was slightly ajar and he saw her at the table, her bony shoulders hunched over a bowl that Naomi was ladling steaming porridge into. This was too much. He glared at her but she didn't even glance at him.

The widow was about the same age as his mother, although far, far thinner. So thin that the sunlight shone red through the papery skin of the hand that held the spoon. Her hair was prematurely grey but the sun caught the odd gold strand, so perhaps she had once been blonde. Her dress was decorated with scraps of ribbon and lace, a silver charm and some shell buttons. With her broad, straight jaw and fine nose she might once have been handsome, but now she just looked haggard and ill.

'Goodwife Armitage,' he said, stepping over the threshold.

The spoon stopped halfway to her mouth and she raised her head and stared at him with misty blue eyes. The intensity of her gaze was such that he couldn't think what to say. Eventually she lowered the spoon back into the bowl.

'Master Nightingale,' she said softly. 'I had hoped to speak with your father.'

'Yes, well, he's not here, and besides I handle much of the family business these days, so you may speak to me.'

He put his hands on his hips, then felt self-conscious and lowered them to his sides, then he put them in his pockets. The way she was looking at him made him feel most uncomfortable.

'I've come to discuss the rent,' she said.

He snorted, then felt silly and changed the snort into a cough.

'I'm afraid we are very behind. I believe Luke told you that I have been poorly and unable to go gathering in the forest. He hopes to—'

'We can't wait forever,' Barnaby snapped. 'You must deliver what you owe by the end of the week or find somewhere else to live.'

Crouching in the hearth, Naomi took a sharp intake of breath, but the widow's eyes remained soft.

'You are young to be so unforgiving,' the widow said.

'It is not that I am unforgiving,' he said haughtily. 'But if I allow you such a dispensation then all the other tenants will want it and then where should we be?'

'Surrounded by happy and grateful tenants, I should expect.' She was holding back a smile, as if she was teasing him. In front of Naomi.

He took a deep breath and opened his mouth to repeat his directive that she must pay, but she spoke first.

'You live in a sumptuous home, Master Waters,' she said. 'You are surrounded by beautiful things and,' her eyes shifted to Naomi, 'kind servants. And yet you seem troubled. Luke and I have little and yet we muddle along in perfect contentment. Are you not happy with your lot?'

He snorted. 'On the contrary I am extremely happy. My life is better than anyone's.'

'And do you appreciate it?'

'Of course I do,' he snapped. 'I thank God every day for it.'

She raised her eyebrows. 'Really?'

'Well, as often as I have time,' he spluttered. 'I am very

occupied in learning my father's business as I shall soon take over it.'

She nodded, with that same slow smile. 'And what do you think God would ask you in return for these blessings?'

He blinked at her, confused.

'Well, that . . . that I express my thanks in worship, of course!'

He could hear that his voice was becoming shrill.

'But what of your deeds, Master Nightingale?' she went on quietly. 'If you have the world's goods and see your brother in need, yet shut your heart against him, how will God's love abide in you?'

It was here that she made her mistake. To parrot the Bible, as Abel always had, merely angered him.

'You have heard my decision,' he said coldly.

'You will learn,' she said, holding his gaze with her faded eyes. 'When you have suffered yourself, you will learn.'

'And what suffering am I to go through?' he jeered. 'Perhaps a mouse will nibble my calfskin gloves or my wine at dinner will be corked.'

As soon as he said it he felt bad and wished Naomi hadn't been there to hear him.

'I'm sorry, Goodwife,' he said more gently. 'But we are all struggling to get by in these hard times.'

The lie sounded as hollow as it was and clearly she was not fooled. All he wanted to do now was duck out from under that gaze of hers and so he gabbled a farewell and made for the door. Hopefully she would ignore what he'd said anyway and he could just leave it to his father to deal with.

At the door he turned back. She was struggling up from

the chair like a woman twenty years older. His impulse was to go over but Naomi got there first, throwing him a look of reproach as she helped the old woman shuffle to the door. It was strange: he couldn't imagine this frail, soft-tempered creature could be the same woman that had attacked him in front of the whole village.

'Might I ask you, Goodwife,' he said, 'why you felt the need to strike me that day by the square?'

He expected her to lower her gaze, to mumble apologies or denials, but she did not.

'Your behaviour was wrong,' she said simply. 'You needed to be corrected.'

He opened his mouth to reply – *who did she think she was to tell him what to do?* – but in the end he said nothing. She was sick, probably dying. What satisfaction could he possibly gain from berating her?

'Your son is painting the church, I hear,' he said. 'Is he doing a good job?'

Her face broke into a smile.

'He is a fine boy,' she said. 'I am proud of him.'

A stab of jealousy made him head for the door but before he could leave the kitchen she called him by his first name. He turned to see she was reaching a hand out across the table to him.

'Bless you child,' she said faintly. 'May you find happiness.'

He stared at her hand for a moment, then turned and left the kitchen without another word. His appetite for the rest of his breakfast had gone and, snatching his coat from the stand by the door, he went out into the bright morning.

The whole village was white, with the frost on the ground

165

and the chimney smoke in the air. Nearby someone was weeping: it sounded eerily close, as if the heavy air had somehow compressed the village. His knees creaked as he walked quickly away from the house and the chill air stung his throat. It was uncomfortable being outside. With nowhere else to go he made for Griff's place.

'Did you hear about the Hocket girl?' Griff muttered as they crouched by a fire which was, by Rawbood standards, feeble.

'Dead?' Barnaby hazarded.

Griff nodded, the flames dancing in his wide eyes. 'Bent over backwards, her head touching her toes, screaming that the devil had come for her.'

'Jesus,' Barnaby breathed.

'They're saying it's witchcraft, of course, and Mistress Hocket's accused the Widow Moone.'

'There's a surprise,' Barnaby said drily. 'The widow's mad as a bag of cats.'

'Apparently there was some altercation between her and the Hocket girl. The widow tried to put a flower in her hair and the girl threw her off, calling her a dirty old woman. Goodwife Hocket says the widow gave the girl a malevolent look and muttered something under her breath, and the day after she fell sick.'

'Horseshit,' Barnaby said. 'According to Na— our maid, the sickness is caused by poisoned wheat. We've been eating potatoes and oats these past three weeks because of it. I'm so sick of the stuff that frankly I'm prepared to take my chances with the witches.'

His laughter was cut short by the appearance of Mistress Rawbood, wringing a cloth between her hands.

'Barnaby Nightingale!' she gasped. 'Do not invoke demons in my house, even in jest!'

'Sorry, Mistress,' Barnaby said. 'I did not mean to offend.'

'Yes ... well ...' Griff's mother blinked rapidly then disappeared back into the kitchen.

'Mother believes the Widow Moone is a witch,' Griff breathed when she had gone. 'And last month she had a run-in with her: the old woman came here begging for our vegetable peelings and Mother said no, so now she thinks we're all doomed.'

Barnaby chuckled quietly but Griff's smile seemed a little strained.

He leaned over to put another log on the fire but Griff stayed his hand.

'Father says we must be careful,' he mumbled. 'The harvest was so bad we have little to sell. The store of wood we have will have to last all winter.'

This time Barnaby laughed out loud.

'For goodness' sake!' he cried. 'If you lack anything just tell me! We will have plenty to spare.'

'Let's hope so,' Griff said. 'These will be lean times all round.'

The days crawled by. It was too cold to do anything except hunker down by the fire, and Christmas was still weeks away. Naomi and Juliet worked their fingers to the bone, struggling through with colds and chilblains and aching backs from constantly chopping logs and lugging them around. When Barnaby wasn't stuck looking over figures with his father he helped them out, and the atmosphere between himself and Naomi eased.

Remembering what Griff had said, one day he offered to take some logs over to their families. Juliet's lived nearby and the errand was soon run, but the trudge up to the Waters' farm with the larger of the sacks on his back drained all the strength from him and once he was out of sight of the cottage he crouched down on his haunches and rested his head on his knees.

He didn't know how long he stayed like that but after a while he noticed that he was shivering. Raising his head he saw that the sun was half gone behind the forest. He needed to get home before the chill of night bit.

He was passing the church when a figure emerged and stepped into his path. He tried to sidestep but the boy moved to block his progress. It was the deaf boy, holding a brush that dripped yellow paint onto the snow. This was the last thing Barnaby needed. By now he was extremely cold and had started to feel unwell. The boy was glaring at him.

He said something in a harsh tone, but his voice was so thick and flat Barnaby couldn't make out his words.

'W ... what?' Barnaby said, teeth chattering. 'I c ... can't understand you.'

The boy took a breath and repeated himself, slower and more carefully.

'You told my mother to get the rent and so she went to the forest to collect berries and holly to sell and she came back sick and next day she died. You killed her.'

Barnaby's lip curled. 'I didn't kill your damn m ... mother,' he snapped, his teeth chattering. 'It's not my fault if you weren't m ... man enough to support her.'

'I told you to wait,' the boy spat. 'Until I was paid. Now I am.'

He drew out a bag from his pocket and threw it to the ground. It landed in the snow with a heavy thunk.

'There,' he said. 'May it bring you nothing but sorrow.'

He went back into the church and slammed the heavy door.

So, the blue-eyed woman with the strands of golden hair was dead. It was no more his fault than the starvation of a pauper was the fault of the baker. Nevertheless, despite the cold, it was some moments before Barnaby could bear to bend down and pick the money up, and when he did so it felt like a bag of lead. The blessing she had given him whispered in his head like wind stirring dead leaves. His eyes blurred with tears and he knelt on the snowy ground and prayed for forgiveness.

'Good God, son, you're blue!' his father cried as Barnaby struggled to close the door against the wind. 'I don't feel well,' Barnaby said. 'I'm going to bed.'

He lay staring up at the ceiling, unable to stop shivering despite the roaring fire in the grate and the huge weight of the blankets.

The widow was dead. Naomi had fed her warm porridge by the fire, but he had sent her out to die in the cold.

The blankets were suffocating and he tried to push them off, only to discover he had no strength in his arms. He tried to get up but only managed to roll off the bed, landing heavily on his belly on the floor. His neck was so stiff he couldn't move his head, could only stare at the chamber pot beneath the bed. The vivid greens and purples of its painted grapevine were so bright they hurt his eyes. He tried to call out but he had no voice. The pot blurred. The vine uncoiled and stretched its tendrils out to engulf him.

10
Fire

He woke in bed. The room was dimly lit by a single candle and Naomi sleeping beside his bed.

He was freezing cold and his mouth was dry as paper.

'Naomi,' he croaked and she started awake. 'I'm thirsty.'

She reached forward and touched his forehead with the back of her hand. She gave a laugh that was almost a sob, then composed herself and drew her shawl around her shoulders. 'I must go out and fetch your mother.'

'Where is she?'

'Abel's back,' she said.

'What?'

'He has come with another man, a Mr Hopkins, and two women. They are staying together at the Boar. He would not stay here. Not with sickness in the house.'

'Sickness? Whose sickness?'

She stared at him. 'Yours.'

'What do you mean? I'm fine.'

He sat up and, apart from a little muzzy-headedness, he truly felt perfectly well.

As she leaned over to pull the blankets around his bare shoulders he noticed the dark rings around her eyes. The fingertips that brushed his flesh were ice-cold and he saw there was no fire in the grate.

'Why have you been sitting here in the cold?' he said.

'You've been at death's door for a week,' she said, taking the candle over to the fireplace and lighting the kindling. 'Burning hot all over, even with no fire and the windows open to let in the snow. Juliet and I have been taking turns to watch you.'

He sat up and rolled his stiff shoulders.

'Your father has been beside himself. So many have fallen sick and died, we feared you would go the same way.'

She went to the window and closed it, then stood staring out into the blackness.

'I try to tell them it's the poisoned wheat but they won't listen. They just make their charms and tuck their bottles of piss up the chimneys and think that will keep them safe from attack from poor old ladies who have lost their wits.'

'What do you mean?'

'Witches. The Hockets were the first, accusing the Widow Moone of murdering their daughter, and now anyone whose cow has died or whose child has a fever thinks they've been attacked by diabolical forces. The poor old crone's freezing to death in the dungeon of the manor house, then she will be transported to the gaol at Grimston. If she lives to the trial it will be a miracle.'

Her drawn face was reflected in the black pane.

'What evidence is there against her?' he said.

171

'Nothing but the claims of her accusers.'

'No magistrate would convict on that, surely.'

But before she could answer, something struck the window-pane in front of her face. She screamed and sprang back. He tried to get out of bed but his legs collapsed beneath him. The thing struck again and he scrambled along the floor on his knees to reach her. But then she was laughing.

'It's all right,' she said. 'It's only Lolly, Juliet's crow! She must have been neglecting him while we tended you. I'll give him some milk.'

She reached up to open the window again but Barnaby cried out for her to stop. It might have been the story of the old women's plight but he was overcome with a sense of dread at the great black wings and beady eyes of the bird.

She helped him up and steadied him as he tried to stand. The bonnet was back on but a single chestnut curl peeped from beneath the lace. He hooked his finger around it and pulled it down to bob above her eye.

'That's better,' he said.

She stepped away from him too quickly and he fell back onto the bed. But before he could scold her for it she was out of the door, her hurried footsteps clattering down the stairs.

When his parents returned he was comfortably ensconced by the fire, full of hot, honeyed porridge and spiced cider.

They were speaking in low tones as they came through the door but stopped immediately when they saw him. His father gave a strangled cry and flew over to the chair, enfolding Barnaby in an icy embrace. He smelled of whisky.

'You're better!' he cried, slapping his cold hands on Barnaby's forehead and chest before Barnaby swatted him away. He turned to his wife: 'He's quite well, my love!'

His mother walked a few steps into the room then stopped. Her chest rose and fell rapidly. 'Girls!' she cried hoarsely. 'Why did you not fetch us back?'

Juliet emerged from the kitchen, beaming. 'His Royal Highness would not let us. He wanted it to be a surprise.'

His mother came across to him, bent down, and kissed him on the crown of his head. Her hand rested on his shoulder, and before he could stop himself he had reached up and grasped it. For a moment their fingers were entwined, then she withdrew hers, walked over to the other chair and sank down, her head in her hands. Behind her head was the dark stain that had been there as long as Barnaby could remember. As a child it had seemed to change shape: one day it was something as innocent as a bird's wing or a teardrop, but at other times it became a narrowed eye or a claw. Juliet would occasionally try to clean it off, but to no avail.

'Are you well, Madam?' Juliet said.

'Quite well, Juliet, thank you,' Frances said through a tangle of hair, and the maid vanished.

His father was babbling on: how long had he been awake and what had he eaten and had he pissed yet? Barnaby ignored him.

'Mother?' he said.

When she looked up her face was ashen.

'What is it?'

173

'Never mind, Frances,' his father said quickly. 'Don't strain the boy.'

'Tell me, Mother,' Barnaby said. 'Is my brother sick?'

'No, no; he is perfectly well!' Henry said loudly.

'Only in his body,' Frances said.

Barnaby waited for his father to refute this but Henry seemed to wilt, sinking down on the arm of the chair, his back bowed like an old man.

'What do you mean?' Barnaby said.

Frances raised her head and stared into the fire. Barnaby had got Juliet to build it up to a roaring white-hot inferno, and the glare stripped Frances's face of its lines and shadows. It was one of those times when Barnaby saw what she must have looked like when she was young: a strange little elf whose thoughts did not flow smooth and easy like his and his father's, but who seemed to see a deeper and more troubling reality.

'Your brother has made an acquaintance with a man named Hopkins,' she said eventually.

'Yes,' Barnaby said, frowning, 'I heard. And they have brought two girls with them, I hear. Perhaps he has chosen marriage instead of the priesthood.' He attempted a grin, but if this was the case then his inheritance would have to be shared equally with Abel.

Frances did not smile.

'It seems,' she began, and she seemed to age before his eyes, 'that this man Hopkins has come to Beltane Ridge for a reason.'

'What reason?' Barnaby said, and even as he spoke he knew he was not wholly better because the cold had already crept back into his bones.

174

Frances said, 'Mr Hopkins calls himself "The Witch-finder General".'

Barnaby laughed, glancing at his father, but the older man's clear blue eyes were fixed on his wife. When his mother spoke again her voice was as cold as the flecks of ice on his father's sleeve. 'Mr Hopkins is here to kill witches.'

11
Water

The whole village had turned out for the show. A three-inch layer of ice on the lake had to be broken before they could begin and several of the younger men had been delegated for the job, including Patrick, who had stripped to his waist in the bitter cold, to display a back covered in purple spots. Naomi glowered at him as he hammered away at the ice with a wooden mallet.

They had all come up together, but while Barnaby and his parents and Juliet remained on the near side of the lake, Naomi had gone across to the other side where the Widow Moone stood tethered to her guard. The Hockets glared at her, but the widow seemed to have no idea of their attention, nor anyone else's. She muttered to herself and occasionally tried to turn and speak to some invisible presence behind her. Once when she did this the gaoler slapped her across the face. Naomi flew at him shouting and he raised his hand again. He would have inflicted the same correction upon her but for a sharp reprimand from

Barnaby's father, who had gone to stand with the mayor and Father Nicholas. She settled back into silence but a moment later reached out and took one of the old lady's hands. The widow didn't seem to notice.

Barnaby marvelled at this show of support: when witch-craft accusations flew about like plague spores it was dangerous to take the side of the accused. Especially since Naomi did not know the widow any better than they did. And yet it was also brave. He couldn't imagine himself having the courage.

Soon the men had managed to open up a jagged patch of water and the mayor stepped forward to address the crowd.

Behind him stood Abel and his friend, Matthew Hop-kins, and the two women Barnaby had taken to be their mistresses. He saw now how wrong he had been. They were very fat, and old enough to be Abel's grandmothers. Abel looked better than Barnaby had ever seen him. He had filled out and his face was flushed as he listened to the mayor's words. Because of the wind Barnaby could hear very little from where he was standing but on the bank opposite Naomi's face was set with fury. The speech ended and the guard had set about binding the Widow Moone's waist with a long stretch of rope when Naomi attacked him. The big man threw her off into the mud, to laughter from the crowd, and some hisses of disapproval. She struggled up and turned on the mayor.

'You approve of this nonsense?' she shouted. 'You consider this a wise course of action, Mayor Strudwick?'

The men ignored her and the widow was dragged towards the edge of the water. All eyes were on her as it

177

finally seemed to dawn on her what she was about to undergo. Then Barnaby happened to glance at his brother. Abel's attention, and that of his friend Mr Hopkins, were focused not on the Widow Moone, but beyond her struggling figure, to Naomi.

Abel said something and Mr Hopkins listened. Abel said something else: Mr Hopkins thought for a moment, then he nodded. Hopkins turned his attention back to the widow, but before Abel did likewise his black eyes swept across the crowd until they met Barnaby's. The two brothers locked gazes for the merest second. Then Abel smiled.

Barnaby's blood ran cold and for a moment he was frozen to the spot.

Then he turned and began pushing through the villagers behind him. They grumbled and pressed together, unwilling to give up their view even for a moment to let him pass. He forced them violently aside, breaking through the line to the clear ground behind, his heart banging. Abel had changed, that was certain. Gone was the wretched air of defeat that made people so despise him. But there was one thing that would never change. His loathing of Barnaby. He would do anything to get back at his brother: even if it meant harming others.

Barnaby skirted the perimeter of the lake, catching an occasional glimpse between the press of bodies. One end of the rope around the widow's waist was held by the guard, but the other had been passed to someone on the opposite bank and they were drawing it tight, pulling her inexorably into the water.

Naomi stood close to the water's edge. Her brother was there now too, clutching her and crying, and she patted him absently, her gaze fixed on the widow, whose wails had become hysterical shrieks as the water swallowed her.

'Swim the witch!' someone nearby shouted, and soon the cry was taken up by others.

'Swim the witch! Swim the witch! Swim the witch!'

It found its rhythm, like the beat of a funeral drum, and the widow's wails could barely be heard over it.

'Naomi!' he bellowed. 'Come away!' but she could not hear him.

The widow was flailing in the water now, her mouth a gaping black O as she went under and came up and went under again, veering between sinking and floating, like weighing scales finding their balance. The men at either edge of the rope strained and skidded on the slimy mud. And then a cry went up: 'She floats!'

A gasp rippled through the crowd.

Barnaby was transfixed. It was true. The Widow Moone's entire upper torso was bobbing above the water as if she was made of cork. The water had rejected her. It was a sure sign of witchcraft. The old woman herself had gone limp and her head lolled forwards, curtaining her face with clumps of matted black hair.

And then there was a cry as one of the rope-holders slipped onto his backside. For a moment the rope slackened and the widow plummeted up to her neck in water, but the man swiftly righted himself and she bobbed to the surface again.

Then another cry went up. 'This is deception! They are pulling the ropes taut deliberately to make sure she floats!'

It was Naomi.

179

'Tell them to slacken the ropes and we shall see the truth!'

What the hell was she thinking? The faces that had turned towards her were uniformly hostile.

The rope-bearers shouted angrily that she was lying and the crowd took up their anger with jeers and thrown clods of mud that spattered her dress.

The mayor called for silence. Abel and his new friend were now standing beside the old man, and while Hopkins's face was an expressionless mask Abel's fury was easy to read. He spoke something in the other man's ear and Hopkins glanced sharply at Naomi again.

Barnaby set off at a run. Even as he did so he could hear a woman screech that Naomi must be one of the widow's accomplices. The drab colours of the peasants' clothes merged into one brownish-green smear as he tore through the reed beds and leaped the tussocks. A cheer went up but he did not stop to find out its cause. The lake was much broader than he remembered and it took agonisingly long minutes to skirt around to the opposite side. Once there his way was blocked by an even greater crowd.

He thrust through them, cursing them under his breath at first, and then out loud, deliberately elbowing soft parts and kicking feet out from under their owners.

Finally he burst out into the open. At first he wondered why they had not crowded this part of the bank too. Then he saw the cause. The widow's motionless body was being hauled from the water. Weed trailed from her boots and the sulphurous stink of rotting mud made those near the front cover their mouths. Others crossed themselves and made the sign to ward off the evil eye.

Naomi was on the other side, her eyes locked onto the

scene by the water's edge. One of the rope-bearers slapped the widow's face and she groaned. The wretched sight of her vomiting up lake water a moment later dispelled the crowd's fear and soon they were chatting amongst themselves about whether or not she would be burned, and how long it would take her to die.

'Naomi, come away! It's not safe!' he cried. But he had to call her name three times before she looked up and when she did it was as if she did not recognise him. And then, for the briefest of moments, her eyes lit up.

'Talk to your father!' she cried over the hubbub. 'Get this nonsense stopped!'

He nodded. She held his gaze a moment, then turned and was gone.

That evening, in need of something to calm his nerves, Barnaby called on Griff and persuaded him out to the Boar. It wasn't the best idea since he might very possibly bump into his brother. But if Abel were to venture into such an ungodly place he would certainly stick to the dull, silent dining room with its smoke-blackened oil paintings, not the spit-and-sawdust bar which would be full of drunken villagers celebrating the day's excitement. Though Barnaby didn't feel much like socialising tonight. When he got home from the lake he did as he had promised and spoke to his father, but was shocked by his reaction: he had never seen Henry so angry.

When Barnaby told him that Naomi thought the rope-bearers had pulled it tight to keep the widow from sinking, his father threw down the pen he had been using to mark his accounts.

'I heard what the idiot girl said!' he roared. 'And it was as good as accusing the mayor!'

'Well, it did seem as if—' Barnaby began, but his father shouted over him.

'I will not be drawn into this! The old woman has been accused by upright people of the village, she has confessed her crime, and she has failed the swimming test.'

'She confessed?' Barnaby said.

'Indeed! To Abel's friend, Mr Hopkins. That is, I believe his job – to extract confessions from witches.'

'Let's hope he will soon be on his way then,' Frances said from the doorway.

'Of course he will,' Henry snapped. 'The witch has been discovered and will be punished. He has done his job.'

'Let's hope so,' his mother repeated faintly.

When Naomi finally appeared back at the house she was sent home in disgrace for the remainder of the weekend.

But the atmosphere in the Boar was lively enough to cheer him up. In fact it was positively carnival as the drinkers compared recent misfortunes that had befallen them and discussed whether or not the Widow Moone had been responsible.

'I had a boil come up on my backside a couple of weeks ago,' Griff said thoughtfully over their first pint of ale. 'Perhaps it was because of Mother refusing her the vegetable scraps.'

'I should think it more like you caught it from Mary behind the smokers' shed,' Barnaby said, starting to feel better.

They drank steadily and after an hour or so Barnaby headed to the yard to relieve himself. He picked his way

182

through the smoky, crowded room and out into the cold night air. Usually he preferred to pee up against the stable wall rather than use the privy, but tonight his spot was taken by an amorous couple who clearly did not mind the sharp tang of ammonia that rose up from the sawdust beneath their feet.

Reluctantly he turned his steps towards the far side of the courtyard, taking a deep breath before kicking open the rickety door and stepping gingerly into the gloom.

The sawdust squelched beneath his feet. The dampness seeped into the leather of his shoes and he prayed the soles would not leak. God knows what was festering down there. The board was so rotted that no-one dared sit on it any more for fear of falling into the cess-pit below, the smell of which was so deadly you had to keep the door open.

Keeping as far as possible from the ragged hole in the wood, Barnaby took aim and peed quickly. He was rearranging his clothes when he heard voices outside.

It was Abel.

'Your reward will be in heaven but in the meantime . . .'

There was a soft clink, as of coins being passed hand to hand.

'Thank you, Abel. But it was only my bound duty as a Christian.'

'It was, Flora, it was.'

Flora.

As quietly as possible Barnaby moved to peer through the crack in the door. Directly opposite, above the entrance to the dining room, there were three floors of guest accommodation. Standing on the first-floor balcony were Abel and Flora. Something in her palm flashed in the lantern light as she tucked it into her skirts.

'And you will not tell it was I?'

'By no means,' Abel said. 'We would not wish to expose you to the risk of injury.'

'You believe she is dangerous, then?'

'All witches are dangerous, Flora.'

'Well, goodnight, then.'

Abel gave an obsequious bow as she turned and made her rather hurried way down the stairs to the courtyard. As she passed the privy door and was lost to the sight of those above, her smile drained away and she wiped her fingers on her dress.

Afterwards Abel stood for a long time in the shadows, utterly still. Even though Barnaby was lit only by a sliver of grimy lantern light, he felt as exposed as if he were standing in a shaft of noonday sun. After a few minutes Abel walked back up the landing towards a door to one of the guest rooms. As he did so his face briefly passed into the lantern light and his smile made every hair on Barnaby's body rise up.

12
Bile

The next morning at church, although neither Abel nor his new friend were present, prayers were said for Mr Hopkins: that he might be guided to root out all that was rotten in the village. There were lots of intercessions for the sick and dying; far more than usual. Barnaby's attention wandered.

The church seemed more cheerful somehow and he remembered that the deaf boy had finished his frescoes. He was not a bad artist, Barnaby mused as he peeped out from behind his clasped hands. The folds of the disciples' garments and whorls of their beards were so realistic you might grasp them in your hand. This eastern wall dealt with New Testament stories and the colours here were the bright blues and golds of day. The western wall depicted Old Testament scenes and here the mood was darker: Adam and Eve trudged through barren wastes, Shadrach, Meshach and Abednego were thrown into the fiery furnace, Elijah prayed by the widow's dead child, Lucifer was hurled from heaven.

Barnaby did a double take.

The falling angel looked nothing like the demons Barnaby had seen in books or paintings. It wasn't black and hairy, or even scaly like a serpent. It was a man; peach-fleshed and perfectly formed. He tumbled head first, his yellow hair streaming out behind him. White light radiated from his body but his face was stained red by the scarlet flames that licked up from the base of the painting, waiting to receive him. Barnaby turned in his seat and bent his head sideways to try and make out more clearly the features of the Lucifer figure.

He froze. His mouth dropped open. He looked around the church for the artist and saw him a few rows back, his dark eyes glinting with amusement as they gazed back at him.

After the service the deaf boy was waiting for him in the graveyard. As Barnaby stumbled over the hummocky graves, the boy's back straightened and his eyes glittered.

'What's that supposed to mean, you bastard?' Barnaby shouted as soon as he was close enough. There was a sudden silence from the congregation that milled around the porch behind him.

The deaf boy didn't move or speak, but just watched his approach.

'Answer me!'

He twisted his ankle clambering over the final grave and righted himself, cursing. The deaf boy dropped onto his back foot and raised loose fists.

'Really?' Barnaby yelled. 'You want to take me on?'

He was within a few feet of him when the boy finally spoke.

'You are a dog.'

186

'What?'

'You act like a lord, but you are nothing.'

'I'm better than you'll ever be!'

But the boy didn't say more. In fact he clamped his mouth shut, blushed furiously and raised his fists. As they circled one another there were shouts from the parishioners: his father's voice was becoming rapidly louder and closer. Realising that they didn't have long the two boys launched themselves at one another.

Barnaby landed two good punches to the boy's face and the boy got one in on Barnaby's nose and a crippling knee to the groin before they were pulled apart. Barnaby struggled to be released, though only half-heartedly, but the deaf boy allowed himself to be led away without a backward glance.

Barnaby stamped home cursing and threatening dire retribution, to Juliet and his father's sympathetic murmurs and his mother's tight-lipped disapproval, and they were almost at the gate before they saw the diminutive figure hunched against the cold. It was Benjamin. His face was as white as the frost that covered the road.

'Mister Nightingale!' he cried when he saw them, running forwards. 'Can you come straight away?'

'What is it, child?' Frances said gently. 'Is Naomi sick?'

'Not yet, though she will be if they carry on.'

'They? Who?'

'Your son, Sir, and his friend Mister Aitkins.'

'Hopkins.'

'They say Naomi has been accused of witchery and they must find out if it's true.'

Barnaby's heart stopped.

*

187

He, Benjamin and Henry passed quickly through the village, grim-faced and silent. They had come at dawn, the boy said, with a letter from the mayor, which they claimed allowed them to carry out all necessary investigations. They demanded to speak to Naomi alone and then afterwards Abel left to fetch the 'searchers'. Benjamin did not know what this meant, only that his sister had gone so pale he thought she might faint.

'What are these searchers?' Barnaby had asked his father, but Henry didn't know.

The little cottage was partly shrouded in mist from the lake and the path up to it had been churned to mud by the feet of the excited crowd from the widow's swimming. The place was in darkness except for an upper window, which shone bright butter-yellow.

They hurried to the front door, wide open despite the bitter cold, and followed a trail of muddy footprints into the house.

Waters and his wife were huddled together by a dead fire, their faces turned to the ceiling. Benjamin ran over and pressed himself into his mother's arms. Waters looked up at Barnaby and his father. 'The searchers have come. With ropes.'

Barnaby ran to the staircase and scrambled up, until he came to the door at the top. It was locked. Behind it he could hear a man's voice.

'Abel?' he shouted, hammering on the wood. 'Are you in there?'

The voice stopped abruptly. He thought he could hear whispering, then there was a tremulous cry, 'Barnaby? Is that you?'

'Naomi!'

Swift footsteps approached the door.

'Master Nightingale.'

It was a voice he did not recognise, soft and insidious.

'Let me in!'

'I'm afraid that's not possible. I have been instructed by the authorities to interrogate Miss Waters on suspicion of witchcraft.'

'Well, you may do so in the presence of her father and employers.'

The man, Hopkins, chuckled. 'That is not the way it is done.'

Barnaby kicked the door and the hinges splintered. One more and the thing would come off. He swung back his foot.

'If I am not allowed to continue my work unmolested,' Hopkins said smoothly, 'then the interrogation will have to take place in the county gaol.'

Downstairs Naomi's mother mewed a pathetic *no*.

Barnaby leaned forward and pressed his lips to the gap between the door and the jamb. Warm air trickled from inside the room.

'Abel, you piece of shit,' he snarled. 'Get out here, now.'

'Yes, Abel.' Barnaby was surprised to find his father beside him. 'Come out here and explain your involvement in this wretched business.'

'I will not!' Abel said shrilly, but after some reassuring mumbles it was Hopkins who spoke again.

'Mister Nightingale. Your son is assisting me in my endeavours and, as he is now an employee of the government, I'm afraid the calls of family must come second.'

He gave a breathy chuckle that made Barnaby gouge his fingernails into his palms.

'We are all anxious to get this over and done with, and your interference only prolongs Miss Waters' discomfort.'

'Discomfort?' Barnaby shouted. 'What are you doing to her?'

He went to kick the door again but his father held him back and Farmer Waters came scrambling up the stairs to drag them back down.

They waited in silence in the cold, low room. The only sounds were the buzz of Hopkins's voice followed by Naomi's higher-pitched replies, hour after hour, until Barnaby's feet and hands were numb with cold. The room grew dark and Mistress Waters lit a single tallow candle.

The loud thud as the bolt was drawn back on the door above made them all start violently. Light spilled from the covered staircase onto the flagstones and they all sprang up, but then the bolt scraped once more and the light on the flagstones went out.

A moment later Matthew Hopkins stepped into the room.

Barnaby had not paid him much attention at the lake the previous day but now he saw he was a young man, perhaps only in his twenties, with a short dark beard and elaborately curled hair. Hopkins had attempted to make himself more imposing with a black satin doublet trimmed with gold and the bucket-topped black boots of a magistrate, but he was still thin and narrow-shouldered and his yellow face ran with sweat.

Barnaby absorbed all of this in the split second it took to pull back his fist. But at Hopkins' cry of surprise another man came barrelling down the stairs, launched himself across the room and came crashing down on him. Barnaby's head struck the wall and he dropped like a stone.

A moment later the polished black boots appeared in his wavering vision.

'Any man,' Hopkins said coldly, 'who seeks to obstruct me in my duties will be dealt with most severely.'

Barnaby could do nothing but slump against the wall waiting for his sight to clear. His father was remonstrating with Hopkins, who placated him silkily. Then he heard his brother's voice, sharp and nasal, employing a tone he had never before used with their father.

'Go home, Sir, and leave us to our business.'

'Oh, and what *business* is it of yours, boy?' his father snapped. 'What qualifies you to torment these women?'

'Experience of the world, Mister Nightingale,' Hopkins interrupted. 'Piety, purity of heart and the gift to see wickedness in all its forms.'

'Nothing at all, then,' Barnaby croaked.

But then Waters stepped forward, his head bowed. 'Might I ask if you have finished with my daughter.'

'Almost,' Hopkins said kindly. 'She has confessed to nothing but now there is just the matter of the searching.'

'The what?'

'My women must now search her for the devil's markings.'

'She has none!' Mistress Waters cried. 'I have known her body from birth and it is pure and unblemished!'

'Then that is in her favour,' Hopkins smiled, bowing slightly. 'We will be back later. In the meantime I leave you in the care of Master Leech, in case you are the subject of any . . . attacks.'

The huge man who had knocked Barnaby to the floor stepped forward.

'Attacks?' Waters echoed.

'Indeed. The villagers are afraid, and fear, I am sad to say, so often drives people to violence. I bid you good day.'

As they swept across the room to the open door Barnaby stuck out his foot to trip his brother, but his reactions were still dull from the blow to the head and Abel hopped deftly over him. His brother's high-pitched giggle trailed back to him as the two men walked away down the path and vanished into the mist.

Barnaby struggled up and staggered to the bottom of the staircase but Leech moved quicker, blocking his path.

'I only wish to speak to her. I will not try to enter.'

Leech stared at him, dead-eyed. The man stank of sweat and a crust of yellow warts disfigured the right side of his face.

Barnaby tried to push past him. In a movement that was surprisingly swift for such a lump of a human, he was thrust back into the arms of his father.

'Go home, gentlemen,' Waters said. 'Please.'

The look of desperation in the farmer's face deflated Barnaby's will to fight.

'It will go better for Naomi if we let them do what they have to and make no trouble.'

A chill, grey dawn was breaking as they left the cottage and their breath billowed before them. The mist was slowly clearing now, coiling upwards in wisps like fingers stretching for the sky. Barnaby walked across to the water's edge, the grass crunching beneath his feet. The hole in the ice made by the widow had healed and the only sign that anything had happened was the ridged mud on the shore. Embedded in it were hazelnut shells: remnants of the snacks of the crowd as they enjoyed her suffering.

'What I should like to know,' his father said quietly behind him, 'is who accused her.'

Barnaby turned and stared at him. Above his father's head a huge ribbon of starlings swirled across the white sky, contorting into mysterious shapes and patterns.

'Barnaby?' his father said. 'What is it?'

But Barnaby ignored him and set off at a run down the path to the village.

The maid opened the door, patting her bonnet and smiling demurely when she saw who it was.

'Is Flora there?'

'Well, yes, certainly,' the girl said. 'But she is alone and I don't think it would be seemly to—'

He barged past her into the cottage. It was only slightly larger than the Waters place but far more luxurious, with glass in all the windows and heavy tapestries to keep out the drafts. The light cast by the wall sconces bounced off the silverware to make the room sparkle.

'Flora!' he bellowed.

The maid's feet pattered up the stairs and he heard the surprised screech of a chair in a room above.

'FLORA!'

The maid reappeared and hurried down the stairs. 'Miss Slabber will be down presently.' She scuttled away through a door but her footsteps skidded to a halt on the other side and there was a rustle of skirts pressed against wood.

A minute or so later Flora came out onto the landing

193

and stepped daintily down the stairs. She had rouged her cheeks unnecessarily since an angry scarlet blush was creeping up from her neck.

'Barnaby,' she said.

She paused on the final step and seemed reluctant to come further.

'Naomi Waters has been accused of witchcraft,' he said.

Her pretty lips pursed. The maid's bonnet whispered against the door.

'That is . . .' she began then stopped. Her fingers fluttered at her side. She must have dressed hurriedly because her bodice had not been buttoned properly and there was a small gape at the side, like an open mouth.

'Was it you?'

Her eyes narrowed. 'What makes you say that?'

'I saw you take money from my brother.'

The blush seeped away and her blue eyes turned to ice.

She stepped off the stair and brushed past him in a haze of scent. Going to stand in the centre of the room she folded her arms and tilted her chin up.

'It is my belief that she is a witch.'

He breathed in slowly and out before speaking again. 'Why?'

'She has performed maleficium against us because of the manner in which she was dismissed.'

'And how has this *maleficium* manifested itself?' Barnaby said. 'You look perfectly healthy to me.'

Flora lifted her chin defiantly. 'She made Pockets sick.'

'Pockets?'

'My cat.'

Bile surged into Barnaby's throat. 'Have you considered,' he said evenly, 'that perhaps it was not witchcraft but just a rotten mouse?'

'It was not only the business with Pockets.'

'There were other such calamities?' He smiled icily.

She bit her lip. The flush remained only on her chest, which rose and fell in irregular stutters.

'Look ...' she began, then stopped and took a deep breath. 'Look at what she has done to you.'

He stared at her. 'What?'

She winced, as if she was looking into the sun. 'Even as ugly and drab and viperish as she is, she has bewitched you into liking her.'

'What?' he laughed. 'She is my maid, of course I like her.'

'More than me?'

'At this moment, yes: considerably more!'

They stared at each other and his laughter died. One of the candles must have gone out because the room had grown duller somehow. The pinkness of Flora's cheek had greyed and her hair was the colour of dry grass.

There was whispering behind the door followed by a muffled giggle: evidently the maid had been joined by others.

'Perhaps,' Flora said softly, 'you should take more care of others' feelings.'

He had gone too far. If he was not more careful she would never back down.

'You're right. I'm sorry. I didn't mean to upset you.'

'Yes, you did,' she hissed.

There were soft thuds on the stairs and he looked up to

see a black-and-white cat staring at him with large green eyes.

'Is that Pockets?' he said pleasantly. 'I'm glad he's well.'

It didn't work. Her eyes were cold as she bent and rubbed her fingertips together until the cat padded across to her and wound itself between her legs.

'Please, Flora,' he said. 'Take the accusation back. Or they will burn her.'

'No,' she said coldly. 'They will hang her.'

His chest constricted. He had wrecked his chance to save Naomi. Whatever happened next would be his fault. He struggled to keep his voice steady as he spoke. 'I am sorry to have barged in. I bid you goodnight.'

He walked to the door and reached blindly for the handle.

'Wait.'

He stopped. A thin, icy wind crept through the keyhole.

'Perhaps your callous behaviour is not caused by witch-craft . . .'

He waited, not daring to breathe.

'But just the fickleness of a silly, selfish boy.'

'You know, Flora,' he said, without turning, 'you have always understood me so well.'

'You liked me before,' she said quietly.

'I did,' he said.

'Perhaps you would again.'

He swallowed and then said, 'I'm sure of it.'

Her motionless figure was reflected in the glass. 'Those are just words.'

'How can I prove it to you?'

'The way any lover proves his devotion.'

He began to understand.

'My father will be in this evening if you wish to speak to him.'

He opened his mouth but his voice would not come. He watched in the glass as she bent to pick up Pockets and rub its sly face against her own. She murmured something and its purr reverberated in the silence.

'Shall I tell him you will be calling?' she said lightly. 'That you wish to ask him something?'

He raised his hand to lean against the door.

'Yes,' he said. 'Please do.'

'Very well,' she said, 'I will write to Mister Hopkins straight away.'

'Thank you. Goodnight, Flora.'

'Goodnight,' she said, then added softly, 'my love.'

He opened the door, stepped outside, closed it behind him, walked a few paces, then retched on the snow-crusted ground.

The village had woken properly by now and the square was criss-crossed with footprints. It was too cold to linger and no-one stopped to speak to him as he tramped home. The vomit had splashed his breeches and shoes and he'd inadvertently wiped his mouth with his sleeve, so now he stank and would have to change his clothes. Passing the church he almost bumped into the deaf boy, muffled to the eyebrows, carrying a basket full of paint tubes. They both looked away and the boy deliberately bumped his elbow as they passed one another.

The house was as warm as a bread oven and all the lanterns were lit. When she saw the state of him Juliet insisted on his having a bath, which she dragged to the fire and eventually filled. As he watched her traipsing back and forth to the kitchen with the cauldron, he grew sleepier and sleepier. The flickering firelight made his shadow on the floor grow and shrink and quaver, as if it were as insubstantial as the flames themselves.

Eventually the bath was ready and after Juliet had stripped him he stepped into it and lay back. The water was blood-warm and she laid a cloth over him so that his bent knees wouldn't get cold.

It would all be over soon. The outcome of the nonsensical search was irrelevant now that Flora was to retract her accusation. She would do it, of that he was certain, so long as he fulfilled his part of the bargain. But what a bargain. There might yet be a way out of it. Perhaps if he grew very fat and didn't wash, or perhaps if he feigned madness and grubbed about with the pigs in the mud. The thought made him smile, and then the pigs took on the features of Abel and Hopkins and Leech and when they opened their mouths to speak they purred like Pockets.

He was woken by an icy blast followed by the slam of the door and sat up with a cry. The bath water was cold and his limbs were stiff and goosebumped. Then his father sprang into his line of vision, wafting cold air from his cloak and spattering Barnaby with particles of snow.

'She is saved!'

Frances appeared beside him, pink-cheeked and smiling. 'The accusation has been retracted.'

Barnaby stood quickly, sloshing water all over the floor. 'Already?'

'Hopkins received the letter not half an hour ago. He will be bringing all this nonsense to an end as we speak.'

Barnaby exhaled. *So soon.*

Wrapping the towel around him, he stepped out of the bath and began rubbing himself vigorously to warm up.

'Perhaps we can persuade the Hockets to retract their accusation of the Widow Moone,' Frances was saying as she removed her hat and cloak. 'And then that beastly man can go back where he came from.'

'With Abel preferably,' Barnaby said, fastening the towel around his waist.

His mother's lips pursed. 'I think perhaps Abel should remain here, don't you, Henry?'

'Oh certainly,' Henry said. 'I shall take pleasure in knocking some sense back into him.'

'Hmm,' Frances said faintly, adjusting her bonnet.

'What o'clock is it?' Barnaby said, stepping into the clean clothes Juliet had left out for him.

'Late afternoon,' his father said. 'And none of us even breakfasted yet. Juliet!'

'I won't eat directly,' Barnaby said. 'There's something I must do.'

'Oh, very well,' his father said. His mother looked at him quizzically.

'Nothing important,' he said, concentrating on the buttons of his shirt cuff. 'I won't be long, and then I might go up to the Waters place and see how Naomi is.'

'Wait till the morning,' his mother said. 'Give her some peace and quiet to recover.'

The door was snatched open before the echoes from his rap had died away.

Flora stood before the fire in a bright yellow satin dress

trimmed with fur. Her parents flanked her and Pockets sat primly at her feet with a smug look in his reptilian eyes.

'Master Nightingale!' her father cried.

'Mister Slabber,' Barnaby said with a bow.

The butcher clapped his hands. 'Wine, Sara!'

Though the whole ordeal could not have taken more than ten minutes from start to finish, by the time he emerged from the house he felt as if he had run a hundred miles.

He had never seen three happier people. Even the damned cat kept jumping on him and digging its claws into his thighs.

There was no need to rush things, so the marriage would take place in the year each of them became eighteen. It would have to be a summer wedding, of course, since Flora did so suit light, summery colours (pretend exasperation from Flora; a slap on her father's wrist). Her little hand was as perfect as a doll's in his. There was no reddening or roughness of the skin and the nails were long and unchipped. She smelled like sugared fruit. Hours seemed to pass before someone remarked that the snow had begun again. Barnaby saw his chance and got up to leave, promising that his father would be round in the morning to seal the arrangement. He produced a ring he had taken from his mother's jewellery box and slid it onto her finger. It was too big. When they kissed goodbye her lips were hard and eager.

The snow became heavier and heavier until he was walking blind, and by the time he got home it had piled up so high on the front step he could barely open the door. He told his father what he had done and gave no explanation.

His mother was furious. He accepted her remonstrations in silence then, once he had secured his father's promise to visit the Slabber house in the morning, he went to bed.

For a while he lay awake and stared at the ceiling. Would Naomi guess why he had done what he had done? Would she be sorry to lose him to another? Had she ever felt about him the way he did about her? It had never seemed so, and yet he had tethered himself to a girl he felt nothing for to save her. Perhaps Flora had been right all along. Perhaps she had bewitched him.

To regret his actions would be a base and cowardly thing to do and he really tried not to. But it was clear to him that there would be no getting out of this. If he dared try and break the arrangement, Flora's father would have him in court. A nasty little thought insinuated itself into his mind that perhaps she would die in childbirth. He was disgusted with himself. All the pride over his noble act turned to shame and foreboding. Tugging the blanket over his head, he put his fingers in his ears to block out the soft whispers of snow against his window.

13
Milk

Barnaby was woken by Juliet, with hot milk and fresh scones with damson jam. He had slept deeply and felt refreshed and altogether more optimistic about his situation. She stoked the fire and laid out his clothes while he yawned and stretched and finally swung his legs over the side of the bed. The floor was too cold to walk on without stockings so she got him some from the drawer and then opened the curtains. The sudden glare made him wince. The entire countryside was blanketed with snow. Each cottage was iced like a cake and only smears of grey from the chimneys broke up the uniform white. Through the ice-crusted panes he could just make out the shadow of the forest. Nothing was moving. The village must still be in their beds.

'Why did you wake me up so early?'

'It's past nine.'

But something *was* moving: a cart inched slowly up the hill in the direction of the lake – although the lake itself had been swallowed up by the endless white.

He dressed, went downstairs and breakfasted by the fire. Today, he noticed, the mark on the chair-back looked exactly like a bloodstain. His mother was not speaking to him but his father gave him the odd wink and occasionally rolled his eyes at her back.

'Well,' Henry said, finally, 'I shall make my way to the Slabber residence.'

Frances stopped eating but did not look up from her plate. Then as his father pushed out his chair she said, 'Are you really sure that this is what you want, Barnaby?'

It was easier to reply since she did not look at him.

'Quite sure, Mother.'

'You will not break the engagement.'

'No.'

'Whatever Flora is . . .' Frances tailed off. 'She doesn't deserve that.'

After a moment she picked up her fork and resumed eating.

For a moment he was tempted to tell her the real reason for his engagement: she of all people would understand, might even admire him for it. But then again, those high principles might make her tell the Slabbers the truth and he couldn't risk Flora going back on her word.

He walked with his father to the market square then the two parted ways and Barnaby made for the path that led up to the lake. As he climbed he was engulfed in fog and though his boots were thick-soled and waxed they were soon heavy with moisture. The snow was a foot deep in places and trekking through it was so exhausting he considered turning back several times.

Eventually he stopped and let his breath billow around

him to mingle with the fog. He was far enough up the path to make out the blurred shadow of the forest to the east but the Waters place was still hidden behind the brow of the hill.

The ground began to shudder beneath his feet and he heard the faint thunder of horses' hooves up ahead. The cart he had seen earlier, possibly. Where had it been going? There was nothing up there but the lake and the Waters place.

But the fog and snow had made the cart sound far more distant than it was and, before he knew what was happening, the white veil of fog tore and the huge black shape was bearing down on him. He cried out and threw up his arms, making the horse rear, then he managed to scramble into the ditch as the driver roared and cracked his whip as he struggled to keep control of the vehicle. Eventually the animal was sufficiently subdued for the driver to lean from his seat and hurl abuse at Barnaby. Too shocked to reply, Barnaby just crouched in the stagnant water until the driver whipped up the horse and the cart trundled on into the fog.

But not before he had seen its occupant, her face grey, her eyes staring from matted knots of hair.

'NAOMI!' he bellowed, but his voice echoed back off the shroud of fog that enveloped him.

The Boar's stables were almost fully occupied. The weather had forced the drinkers from the previous evening to stay the night, and conditions hadn't improved enough for them to leave yet. Barnaby saddled up the lightest, youngest-looking bay mare and led her out of the yard, grateful that her footsteps were muffled by the snow. On the way out he peered up at the higher floors, tempted to storm up there and confront his brother, but if he wanted to catch up with the cart he would have to leave now.

It must be heading to the gaol in Grimston. On a good day the journey by cart took under two hours; today it might take until sundown and Barnaby would be swifter on horseback. Mounting the mare, he passed through the streets to the market square then steered her onto the road that led out of the village. Untrodden drifts lay in swathes as far as the eye could see and it took long minutes to plough through them to reach the crossroads. A few flakes of snow fell against the horse's caramel brown flank, melting immediately at the heat of effort that radiated from her. Would she make it? If on the Grimston road she became too exhausted to continue she would certainly die; Barnaby too. It was ten miles until the next village.

But as they continued, Barnaby found that if they kept to the black, sludgy tracks made by other vehicles they could maintain a pretty good speed. By midday they had passed the last village before Grimston and the horse showed no signs of tiring. The high sun had burned off the fog and the tracks became little streams of dirty water. They settled into a comfortable pace.

Flora had retracted her accusation of witchcraft, so was Naomi's arrest for some other reason? Perhaps she had struck one of Hopkins's women as they 'searched' her. He smiled grimly. It was no more than they deserved. Perhaps she had lashed out at Hopkins himself. If so he hoped she had caused some injury. He would make sure she got the best lawyer and pay any fine that was imposed. Or . . . his smile faded, had Flora withdrawn the retraction as soon as she was sure of their engagement? He wouldn't put it past her.

The snow was heavier now, eddying around the mare's nostrils as she puffed and snorted. She was tiring. His own legs, wet from ditch-water, had gone numb, his hands on the reins were stiff and aching.

The sinking sun was in his eyes now, flashing red between the trunks of the trees. It would soon be dark. He squeezed the mare's flank but she had no more left in her.

A few minutes later the sun vanished and the road plunged into shadow. At first there were just rustlings and the last calls of the day-birds, but soon more eerie sounds came out of the blackness: distant screams, a low chirruping that sounded like a chuckle, the sudden snap of a branch close by. He gave the mare a cruel kick, muttering sharply to her, but she only whinnied with pain.

Then something sprang from the trees to his left. The mare reared up but he managed to hang on, his heart galloping. Had the forest spirits come for him at last?

But it was only a man. A man with a knife. He made a lunge for the reins but Barnaby easily kicked him back, sending him stumbling down the snowy bank into the trees. Then the horse wheeled sideways: a second man had her bridle. Kicking out at this accomplice, Barnaby lost his balance and fell heavily onto his back; the snow not thick enough to prevent him jarring his head against a rock. A moment later the man's knife was at his throat and rough hands were fumbling at his belt. His money pouch was expertly sliced off and after a final kick to Barnaby's head for good measure, the men were gone.

Once the dizziness had subsided he rolled onto his front and levered himself up onto all fours. His lip was split and blood spots splattered the snow, scarlet against the white. Or not quite white. Night had deepened and now the snow was just the lightest shade of the greys and blacks that loomed all around him.

He staggered to his feet, clicking his tongue for the mare, who had probably been spooked and bolted.

But it was worse than he could have imagined.

Hoofprints vanished in a straight line up the track: she had not bolted, the men had taken her. And now he was alone in the forest as night closed in, with no horse, no money, wet clothes and a five-mile walk to Grimston.

He sank down onto his haunches in despair – if only he had told his parents where he was bound – but a howl from the forest jolted him up again. If he was to die, better it be from cold than from being torn apart by wild animals. After rubbing his thighs to get the blood flowing again he started walking.

By the time the snow really started falling he was too far gone to care. Walking had become something mechanical, detached from the fading point of his own consciousness: his legs were someone else's; his arms dangled by his sides as if broken; his eyelashes were so crusted with snow that he walked blind, ricocheting off trees and tripping in potholes. The next time he fell he could not get up again. The world reeled, the shades of grey and black twisting together, spinning faster and faster, like the spool of a spinning wheel. But then he noticed that one of the strands was orange. He tried to focus on it but it spiralled away from him. He squeezed his eyes shut, pressing his thumbs into his sockets until the spinning receded. For the briefest of moments when he opened them again he had a clear view of the path ahead. The orange glow radiated from the windows of an inn not three hundred paces ahead – he must have reached the outskirts of Grimston – but it might as well have been three million.

The snow was as soft and warm between his fingers as his own duckdown quilt. He felt so light he might take off at any moment and float towards the inn. The image of himself drifting through the night sky as bewildered bats and owls flew past made him giggle. Giggling and trembling like a drunk, he barely noticed as he crawled inside the semicircle of amber light. Then the door swung open and he was enveloped in a warm fug of tobacco smoke and sweat and beer.

He shuffled over the threshold and fainted.

It wasn't so bad in the end. A day spent shivering by the fire while the landlady plied him with broth and potato cakes. As she said, he was lucky not to have been more badly injured and the road was known to be a terrible spot for banditry and what did he think he was doing out there in the dead of night? On his way to visit friends in the town, he said, and she seemed satisfied. It transpired that her husband had done business with his father and they were prepared to wait for payment for his board and lodgings until he returned home, and even to loan him a few shillings for his onward journey, though they made him stay one more night to make ensure he was fully recovered, despite his protestations.

So, the following morning he bade them farewell and limped the short distance into the town, still bruised from the fall.

The gaol was easy enough to find: squashed like a black insect under the fine white shoe of the magistrate's court. The people who climbed the steps of the court seemed not to see the waxen faces that stared from the barred windows beneath them and were deaf to their cries for food or water, although they did hold handkerchiefs to their noses to try and block out the smell. Melting snow ran off the streets to dribble between the bars and Barnaby could feel the deadly cold emanating from the place from ten feet away.

Suddenly he was afraid. How could she have survived a minute down there?

Ignoring the pain from his bruised hip he set off at a run around the building and eventually came to the entrance to the gaol.

The gaoler received his meagre bribe wearily and led Barnaby down a flight of stairs that vanished into the gloom.

'How is she: Miss Waters?' Barnaby asked him.

The gaoler shrugged. 'Alive.'

As they reached the bottom and began walking past the cells Barnaby realised he should be grateful even for this small mercy. In the first cell were three men: one lay in the black puddles on the floor, his breath coming in irregular rattles, while a second huddled in the corner muttering something that might have been a prayer. The third had been rolled back against the far wall and was obviously dead. Evidently the corpse had been there a while and Barnaby covered his nose and mouth with his sleeve.

In the cell opposite, three old women crouched on the floor, indistinguishable from one another with their filthy rags and wild hair.

'Your friend's lucky,' the gaoler said. 'As of this morning she has some company.'

Barnaby said nothing.

'Although not so lucky for the company!' the gaoler added with a wheezy laugh.

At the sound of his voice one of the old ladies stirred. The lantern light caught the glitter of an eye she fixed on Barnaby through matted hair. She clawed her way up the wall to stand, then began hobbling over to the bars.

Barnaby quickened his steps.

'An apple for luck, pretty!' she called in a cracked voice, stretching a skeletal hand through the bars.

He hurried past.

None of the cells was empty, and each inhabitant looked as wretched and half dead as the next. Occasionally he saw a bucket, but it seemed that most of the prisoners were forced to relieve themselves against the walls, and a channel running down the middle of the tunnel was filled with brown, stinking liquid. The gaoler must have followed his gaze for he leaned over conspiratorially and whispered, 'Thems as pays gets the buckets.'

Whoever had been shouting from the windows had given up now and the silence deepened the further they went. Occasionally he would hear laboured breathing or the scrabble of rodents but there was no weeping or moaning nor any talking amongst the prisoners.

And then he did hear a voice, one that was achingly familiar, and clear and beautiful as a lullaby. He set off at a run. The gaoler struggled to keep up and when Barnaby reached the cell the voice was coming from, he couldn't make out anything in the darkness, not even the pale circle of a face.

Naomi was speaking tenderly to the other occupant of the cell. She broke into a quiet song and he pressed his forehead against the iron bars and waited for her to finish. She was alive. And she could still find enough hope to sing.

The gaoler caught up and shone his lantern into the cell.

There were two wooden pallets, one on each side. Naomi crouched in the puddles beside one of them, upon which lay a motionless figure. They had shorn off all her curls.

'Naomi,' he said when the lullaby ended.

She turned and raised her hand to shield her eyes from the light, then slowly let it drop.

'Barnaby?' she said.

'Yes.'

She rose unsteadily and came across to him.

Her face was gaunt, and there were bruises on her cheeks, but she attempted a smile.

'She is not well,' she said, nodding to the figure on the pallet.

He frowned. 'I have not come to see her. I have come to see you.'

A shadow of confusion passed across her face.

'Get on with it,' the gaoler said. 'It stinks down here.'

Barnaby spun round. 'Piss off,' he spat. 'Or you will get no more from me.'

211

The gaoler sighed and turned to go. Barnaby snatched the lantern from him and waited until the old man's back had disappeared into the gloom. Then he hung it from a hook on the wall and turned back to Naomi. Reaching through the bars, he took one of the hands that dangled limply at her sides.

'What happened?' he said. 'The accusation was withdrawn. Why did they take you?'

She averted her eyes from his.

'Did they make you confess? If so it can only have been through torture and will not stand in court ...'

'It wasn't that,' she said, and her voice lowered to a whisper. 'The searchers said ... they said they had found a ... a teat from which I suckled the devils' imps.'

He stared at her.

She withdrew her hand from his and pulled the sleeve of her dress up to the elbow. On the white skin of her inner arm was a mole. It was not quite round, and had rippled edges like a flower.

'They said it had an infernal shape.'

She rolled down her sleeve.

'But it's just a mole,' he said.

She pressed her lips together and nodded.

'Is that all?'

She took a deep breath. 'When they had found it they said they must wait for the imp to come for its milk, and so they tied me to the chair and I was so tired I fell asleep and when I woke up there was a cat in the room; I had never seen it before, and the cat came over and started rubbing itself around my legs. They said it was the imp I sent to do my infernal bidding.'

Anger tightened his chest. 'Such as?'

'Making the snow come early, blighting the crops . . .'

'What, you alone?'

'They said I was a member of a coven. That there were more of us. That's when they went after Juliet.'

It was as if all the air had been sucked out of his lungs.

'What?' he managed finally.

Naomi half-turned to reveal the figure on the pallet and his heart stood still. How could he have missed her? Right there in front of him, not two feet away, were the familiar patched soles of her shoes. He had seen them so often from the comfort of his bed while she knelt to stoke the fire or polish the floor. He knew every contour of every crack and each careful mend of the hem of her dress.

'They were crueller to her than to me,' Naomi said. 'She was delirious when they brought her in this morning.'

'This morning?' he echoed stupidly.

'She has a fever. She needs water but he will not give me any.'

In the shadows just out of range of the lantern something moved. He leaned forwards until the cold damp metal bars were against his cheeks.

'Juliet?' he called softly. 'Wake up. It's me, Barney.'

The figure made no sound.

He took Naomi's hand again and squeezed it.

'I will get you out of here, I swear. Look after Juliet and try to stay strong.'

She swallowed, nodded, then slipped her hand from his and went back to kneel beside Juliet's pallet. He unhooked the lantern and returned the way he had come. On the way past, the old woman who had called to him earlier reached through the bars at him. Nestling in the crook of her elbow, like a grotesque tick, was a black lump with purple lines emanating from it. He had never seen such a thing. If anything was an imp's teat then surely it was this monstrous thing. Surely any sane magistrate would tell the difference. He shrank from her clutches and hurried back to where the gaoler squatted, warming his hands over a couple of stubby candles.

In the end he gave the man all the money the landlady had loaned him, and his own coat, on the promise that Naomi and Juliet would be well fed and watered, and provided with blankets and candles.

Then he trudged back up to the fresh air. He felt guilty as he drank in its ice-cold freshness, sweetened with the scent of bonfire smoke. Somewhere nearby meat was roasting. He wished he had saved some money to buy the girls a meat pie or some chops but it was too late now. The only thing to do was to try and find someone willing to take him back to Beltane.

The first inn he came to was full of maudlin drunks, perhaps those who had just been fleeced at the court, and he moved on. The second place was much larger with a wide yard filled with horses and vehicles. The atmosphere inside was bustling and efficient. Young boys and girls came flying out of the kitchen carrying plates of food stacked three to an arm. Trying not to be mown down, Barnaby made his way across to the bar.

It took several minutes before he was able to attract the landlord's attention.

'I'm looking for a lift back to Beltane Ridge!' he shouted

over the hubbub. 'Payment on arrival from my father, Henry Nightingale – you might know him.'

'Henry Nightingale?' the landlord shouted back. 'Can't say as I do. A lift, you say?'

Barnaby nodded, but before he could say more the barman's attention was distracted by a scream. Someone had bumped into one of the little waiters, knocking the scalding hot bowl of soup he had been carrying all down the front of his shirt.

'Water somebody!' a man cried as others attempted to strip him to prevent more burns. The barman hurried away.

Most of the other drinkers turned to watch the drama, except one, sitting a little way down the bar. He was a tall, spare man of about fifty, with intelligent eyes and hair the colour of a fox.

'You're a Nightingale, eh?' he said just loud enough for Barnaby to hear over the waiter's shrieks.

'Barnaby Nightingale.' Barnaby stretched out his hand and the man shook it. 'You know my father?'

'By reputation,' the man said. 'After a lift back home, are you?'

'Are you going that way?'

'I wasn't but I can.'

'I don't want to inconvenience you.'

The foxy man raised his hand. 'Not at all. I'm a businessman. I do my business where I can find it. And I'm sure I'll find something worth my while in Beltane as much as anywhere else.'

'Well, thank you,' Barnaby said, adding as lightly as he could, 'and when do you think we might be able to, er, depart?'

The foxy man finished his whisky in one gulp, then pushed out his stool and stood up. 'How about now?'

Barnaby could have hugged him.

He followed the man, whose name was Rattigan, out into the yard. The fellow's horse was a huge, muscular beast with wild eyes and scars criss-crossing its black flanks. Rattigan murmured a few words into its ears then gave it a violent but apparently affectionate slap and swung himself up onto the cart.

'Come on then, Mister Nightingale.' He patted the wooden seat beside him, 'Let's get you home.'

The seat was rock hard and buckled with damp and by the time they reached the outskirts of the town Barnaby's backside was hurting. He shifted around, trying to get comfortable.

'You're soft, boy!' Rattigan grinned. 'Us old soldiers don't feel a thing.'

Barnaby blushed. It was true, he was soft. Soft as horse-shit. He had spent a lifetime doing nothing but what he pleased while the likes of Naomi and Juliet wore themselves out for his comfort. He folded his arms against the cold, and then hated himself even more since this was nothing to the cold and misery they were enduring.

He sensed Rattigan watching him.

'What's wrong?' the man asked.

'Nothing,' Barnaby said.

Rattigan reached into the sack at his feet and drew out a leather bottle, its stitching black with age. 'Whatever it is, this'll cure it.'

Barnaby thanked him and took a large swig, ignoring the sour smell of another man's spit on its rim.

The warmth of the liquor spread in his chest. He would try and perk up a bit for Rattigan's sake. The man would soon tire of such dreary company and might even abandon him on the road.

'So,' he said, 'you have fought in the war?'

'For king and country.'

Barnaby had never thought much about the war. As a child he had loved King Charles for his fine clothes and jewels. He had studied the coins embossed with his image and couldn't imagine why anyone would not want to be ruled by such a fine specimen. Then Oliver Cromwell had come with his ugly uniforms and dour laws banning bear-baiting and dancing, and now the handsome king was in prison. Albeit in more comfort than Grimston gaol.

He decided that he liked Rattigan.

'What will happen to the king, now, do you think?'

'The country will see sense,' the other man said grimly. 'That scoundrel Cromwell's head will be boiled for a Christmas pudding!' He gave a laugh that turned into a wet cough.

Rattigan had plenty of good stories. He had fought at Edgehill and at Naseby, where he had been one of the only Royalist foot soldiers not taken by enemy. The only high point of the battle had been when he managed to capture a Roundhead horse whose rider had been unseated – the very beast that now pulled them. He had carried his new master bravely into every skirmish that followed, sustaining all the cuts that now scarred his flank with barely a whinny of complaint.

'And now he must pull a rickety cart from town to town while I try to scrape enough money to feed us both.'

For a time there was no sound but the steady clip of hooves and the rumble of wheels.

Barnaby broke the silence: 'When we get back I will see that you are generously recompensed for this. My father might even be able to find you some work.'

'No need,' the man said in a clipped voice. Barnaby feared he had somehow offended him. They continued on in silence.

At noon they shared a loaf of bread and hunk of cheese that Rattigan had purchased from the inn at Grimston. Barnaby was starting to feel discomfort at the inconvenience and expense he was putting Rattigan to and barely ate a crumb.

They managed to resume an awkward, stuttering conversation for the rest of the journey, although Rattigan seemed to be holding something back, and Barnaby had no desire to reveal what had brought him to Grimston. It was altogether disappointing that what could have been an interesting journey had become an ordeal for both of them and he was sure Rattigan shared his sense of relief when the spire of St Mary's came into view. The need for conversation receded as the sky bloomed into a magnificent sunset. The golden weathercock that tipped the church spire flashed fire from its open beak, the snow-covered thatches burned crimson, and through the gaps in the trees he could see the red disc of the lake. Only the forest was dull: the sky above it brooding with oncoming night.

Without warning Rattigan started speaking rapidly:

'The trouble is, now that the war's over there ain't nothing for us. No work, no relief from the parish. My own

218

village don't want me. My sweetheart found another. It's enough to turn a decent man into a desperate one. I ain't a bad man but I done bad things and this ain't the worst of them but it won't be nothing for me to boast about neither.'

Barnaby frowned at him. 'I don't understand.'

They were coming into the village now and he could smell the woodsmoke of the hearths, sweet and welcoming.

'It ain't personal. You're a nice lad and I wish you the best of luck. Don't say nothing. Make 'em prove it.'

Rattigan pulled on the reins and the horse came to a stop outside the Boar.

'My house is a little further,' Barnaby said.

Rattigan turned away from him, put two fingers to his lips and gave a shrill whistle. A moment later the inn door was opened by the landlady. Oddly enough, as soon as Mistress Spenlow saw Barnaby she vanished inside again.

'I suppose it's as good a place as any,' Barnaby said, climbing down from the cart. He had begun to feel uncomfortable in the man's company and would rather walk the last few hundred yards. 'If you wait here I shall go and fetch your payment.'

'I will receive that presently,' Rattigan said quietly.

The inn door was kicked open and two large men burst out. Before Barnaby knew what was happening they had him in an armlock. He didn't think to struggle, presuming there had been some mistake. He said as much but they ignored him. He called to Rattigan, asked him what was happening, but the man turned his face away.

Then the inn door opened for a third time and two more men stepped out into the ebbing daylight.

'Barnaby Nightingale,' the first one said, 'you are hereby charged with witchcraft, of making a compact with the devil, of summoning imps to commit murder and grievous injury upon your neighbours, and of . . .'

Hopkins broke off, coughing, and a fine mist of blood dissipated in the air before him.

Barnaby stared. His eyes flicked to the second man.

Abel wasn't smiling. At least not with his mouth.

14
Flea bites

The house was in darkness as they approached, and when Abel opened the door a smell of must and decay wafted out.

'Where are our parents?' Barnaby said.

'They decided to seek you themselves. Fortunately they did not find you, for if they had hidden you from us they too would have been guilty.'

'Who says that *I'm* guilty?'

Now Abel did smile. 'We shall see.'

As Barnaby went to step over the threshold Abel shoved him in the back, making him stumble.

'All right, Abel,' Hopkins said softly. 'While he is co-operating we will treat him with gentleness.'

'He is Satan's creature,' Abel hissed, 'and must be abhorred as such.'

'When it is proven,' Hopkins said and closed the door behind them. For a moment the three of them stood in the gloom while Abel lit the lanterns. To Barnaby's relief there had been few people who had seen their journey here. Those they had passed hurried on, their faces averted. The only one to stand and follow their progress was the deaf boy, Luke. Barnaby had held his gaze defiantly but the boy's expression was unreadable.

'Upstairs,' Abel said.

Barnaby climbed the staircase, making for his own room at the front of the house.

'No. My room.'

It became apparent why as soon as they entered. Always lacking in ornamentation or comforts, the room had now been stripped of all its furniture except for a wooden stool in the centre of the room.

'Sit.'

Barnaby sat.

Abel stepped back and Hopkins came forwards.

'Art thou,' he said, aiming a white finger at Barnaby's chest, 'in league with the armies of Satan?'

And so the questioning began.

Barnaby began by laughing at them. His denials were wearily insolent. He sing-songed his 'no's (*Was the contract with Satan in his own blood?*) and sighed his 'yes's (*Did he believe in the Holy Trinity?*). They seemed to go round in circles, with a word changed here and there and increasingly strange construction. *Did he imagine that God could not see the work of the devil's servants?* Yes. No. *Had he become acquainted with the devil in the past year?* No. *Earlier then?* No. *Ah, so more recently.*

Barnaby asked for water and something to eat. He had not supped properly since the previous night at the inn. Later, he was told.

The questions went on. The sky coloured with the first tendrils of dawn. Hopkins' monotone was soporific. Barnaby's head nodded, managing to answer the odd yes and no in the gaps in the conversation. He answered yes to something before the meaning of the question had penetrated his dozy brain – *Had he sent an imp to kill the Parsleys' child?* – and came to with a start.

'No!'

'No, what?' Hopkins asked innocently.

'The last question you asked, the answer is no.'

'The last question,' Abel said, 'was do you accept the lord Jesus Christ as your saviour?'

'No, it wasn't!' Barnaby shouted.

Hopkins and Abel shared a glance. Barnaby sprang up from the chair and drew his fist, his sights fixed on his brother's vile smirk. There was a flash to his left and something came crashing down on his head.

He awoke to find himself tied to the stool. Someone was supporting his back but they moved away when he stirred and he almost toppled backwards.

The room was bright as day, and when he winced at the glare the whole left side of his head throbbed. But it was not day. The black square of window reflected the two other figures in the room back at him: the pale ghost of Hopkins shadowed by the black crow of Abel.

'Now,' Hopkins said softly. 'Let us talk of fairies.'

Barnaby was cold. They had let the fire go out. He waggled his fingers behind his back to get the blood moving.

'Do you pretend to make a distinction between black and white magic, like others of your kind?'

'My kind?'

'Witches,' Abel hissed.

'I have no idea what witches think.'

Hopkins ignored him. 'Fairies,' he said with a lip curled in distaste, 'are nought but the devil's imps in disguise.'

Something in Barnaby's subconscious woke up and he felt the first pricklings of fear.

'Do you have truck with the fairies?'

'No.'

'When did this cease?'

'I never had truck with them.'

'You certainly did in the earliest days of your life. Is it not the case that you were stolen by these creatures and only returned when the changeling they had replaced you with was left upon the dung heap?'

Barnaby paused before replying. He was starting to get cramp in his left calf muscle and the contractions it made were distracting. He needed to be careful.

'That is the story I was told,' he said.

'Do you have memories of this time?'

'No.'

'And yet these "fairies" continued to watch over you; almost as if they saw you as one of their own, to be protected and nurtured as their own.'

'What gives you that idea?'

His leg was spasming now and he tried to adjust its position, but found that the bindings were too tight.

'Can you loosen these cords?' he asked Hopkins. 'I am in pain.'

Hopkins ignored him.

'You visited them in the forest, did you not? At an hour when most would be afeared. But not you. You went into the forest to commune with these imps and they guided you safely home.'

'I went to the forest to try and impress my friends,' he said. 'And I claimed to have seen the fairies for the same reason.'

'You lied.'

'Yes.'

'Are you lying now?'

'No. Please loosen these cords. I am in pain.'

'And was it also a lie that the imps left a trail of berries for you?'

Barnaby hesitated before replying. It would be a risk to deny this in case someone else had seen them.

'There was a trail, but anyone could have left it.'

'When you communed with these imps, what did they offer you in return for your soul?'

'Nothing.'

'So you did their bidding out of love for their master?'

'No!'

Hopkins was still perfectly calm but Barnaby felt his anger rising. His leg was extremely uncomfortable and now he had pins and needles in his fingers. The room was growing colder by the moment.

It was Abel who spoke next. 'You found a list. Written in blood. The names of the damned.'

'What happened to it?' Hopkins said evenly.

'It blew out of my hands. It may not even have been such a list. I could not read it.'

225

'You destroyed it,' Abel hissed. 'When you read your own name upon it.'

'More likely I should have read yours,' Barnaby snapped. 'Thief, liar—'

Abel gave him a backhanded slap and his bony knuckle split Barnaby's bottom lip.

The questions went on for more, long minutes. Barnaby felt his attention slide dangerously, and tried to focus, but he was tired and thirsty and in pain. He became aware of a scritching sound and saw that Abel was writing down all that was said.

He leaned as far as he could to get into his brother's line of vision.

'I hope you are writing that I am bound too tight.' The scritching paused, but Abel didn't look up. 'That I have been deprived of food, drink and rest, and stripped to my shirt in the bitter cold. Are you writing that, Abel? Don't forget now. Shall I spell "bitter" for you?'

'Do you know the name Lolly?' Hopkins said loudly.

Barnaby blinked.

'Lolly,' Hopkins repeated. 'Is that familiar to you?'

'No. Yes.'

Hopkins smiled. 'Which is it?'

'Lolly is a crow that my maid used to feed.'

'Are you referring to Juliet?'

Barnaby nodded.

'The confessed witch?'

Barnaby caught his breath, then said through gritted teeth, 'Confessions drawn out by torment.'

Hopkins's smile froze. 'Nothing of the sort, boy. Your maid confessed freely. It was she who named you.'

'What . . . what did she say?' Barnaby said hoarsely.

'We asked her if you had presided over the sabbats and she assented to this.'

Barnaby threw himself forward, straining at the bindings across his chest.

'She would have assented to being a March hare to get you to leave her alone!'

'Where did you make the cut with which to draw the blood to sign the contract?'

'Give me a drink,' he said flatly.

'Is it the scar on your belly?'

'Give me a drink.'

'Whose effigy is the corn doll on your windowsill?'

The questions went on. Sometimes he nodded in the chair but woke when he was about to fall and righted himself. The pain was constant now, in every part of him that wasn't numb with cold. He tried to stay focused on Hopkins's words but they ran away from him. For one long stretch that might have gone on for hours he simply said, 'I deny everything,' at another, 'This is all lies,' and another, 'Horse shit and pig swill.' At some point dawn broke and when he next glanced at the window the pale disc of the sun was resting on the roofs. Where was the time going?

Scritch, scritch went Abel's pen. He was sitting in a chair now, with a blanket about his shoulders. Hopkins too had acquired a blanket from somewhere without Barnaby noticing. His own teeth were chattering and there was no spit left in his mouth to wet his lips. The room began slowly to revolve.

'What form of bewitchment did you use to usurp your brother from your parents' affections?'

227

Barnaby smiled and as he did so his lips cracked.

'Handsomeness and charm,' he tried to say, but his voice rasped like tearing paper. He was gratified to hear the scritching of the pen pause.

'Is the devil as handsome, Barnaby?'

'Not at all,' Barnaby said. 'He's ugly as a horse's arse compared to me.'

Hopkins gave a friendly laugh.

'Is he dark or fair?'

'Dark as a mole, like Abel.'

Hopkins laughed again. The scritching paused.

Barnaby was going to continue but his eye was caught by a movement in the corner of the room. Two black demons hovered by the roof beam. Rams' horns curled from their heads and they clacked their teeth together, grinning. Even from where he sat Barnaby could smell their stench of decay.

He stole a look at Hopkins and found he was watching him.

'What is it, Barnaby? What do you see?'

'Nothing. What do *you* see?'

Hopkins turned, and after a moment turned back. 'I am of the Lord's party, boy. I see only the wall and the roof beam.'

Something changed now. The questions became harsher, more rapid, more confusing.

Did he make waxen effigies of those he hated?

Did he stick bent pins into them?

Did he bury the foetuses of animals in hallowed ground?

Did he pray backwards?

Did he lame the horse of Lord Fairfax?

Had he sent fleas to torment Abel in his bed at Cambridge?

'Gladly!' Barnaby cried, jerking up his lolling head. 'Fleas and slugs and rats and leeches – even they would find his blood too foul to suck; the devil's pen would melt at the touch of it!'

Still Hopkins went on. The stars came out and danced for Barnaby in the little square of window. He could move no part of his body beneath his neck. Someone had opened a window and moths were crawling all over the lanterns. One landed on his knee, fat and furry and heavy as a mouse. He could not twitch his leg to shift it. His vision blurred and blackened at the edges, as if singed. He was covered in vomit but couldn't remember being sick.

Hopkins droned on. Barnaby's head lolled back and he stared at the pulsating colours on the ceiling.

And then a blast of wind blew a flurry of snow through the window. A few flakes fell into his open mouth, moistening it. It was enough to wake him briefly from his torpor. He found that a piece of paper had been thrust onto his lap. The spidery writing scuttled across the page every time he tried to focus on it.

'Sign,' Abel said.

Barnaby tried to read it but his head wouldn't stay still.

'Just sign and this will all be over,' Hopkins said.

Barnaby picked up the pen. A spot of ink dripped onto the paper, where it began to morph into outlandish shapes.

'Sign it and you can sleep,' Abel said.

Barnaby's head swayed and he squinted up at Abel, trying to focus on his brother's dark eyes.

'What is it?' he slurred.

229

Abel's eyes flicked to Hopkins and back.

'Just a transcript of everything you have told us,' Hopkins said, behind him.

'Read it to me.'

Abel glanced again at Hopkins then lowered his head and began to read.

'This is the testimony of Barnaby Nightingale . . .'

But as he went on Barnaby frowned. Abel was a fluent reader but he seemed to be stumbling over the words, as if he wasn't actually reading the testimony as it was written at all. As if he was making it all up as he went along.

With his last ounce of strength Barnaby lifted the pen and hurled it across the room. It hit the wall and black ink spattered the whitewash.

Abel made to strike him again but Hopkins stepped between them.

'Enough, Abel.'

He turned to Barnaby. 'Many thanks.' A whisper of a smile passed across his sickly face. 'We have all we need.'

Barnaby awoke to a woman's gentle murmurs. Soothing hands were passing over his body. He was lying on his front and the cramps had gone, but he was still freezing cold. Why hadn't they covered him? The hands paused at his elbow and rested there.

'What's this?' the woman said quietly.

'Nothing but an old graze,' another said.

They resumed their explorations up and down each arm before moving onto his back.

He opened his eyes. A woman's broad hips were before them. The skirts smelled nice. A hand came to rest on the mattress by his cheek. The fingers were plump and pink, the nails clean and neat. He had a sudden urge to hold them. That was when he found he was still bound.

'Try beneath his hair.'

The voice was Abel's.

Now he could feel that he was naked. The cold breeze from the window chilled his buttocks. His balls had shrunk to peanuts. Had they already probed the other side of him? A hand moved between his thighs, and he jerked and cried out.

'Hush, boy,' the woman said. 'We are nearly done.'

'Check the hairline,' Abel said again, and Barnaby moved his head to try and see him but he was out of his sphere of vision.

The motherly fingers moved to his temple and began probing his hair, in just the same way Agnes had checked him for lice when he was a child.

'There is nothing,' the woman said. 'His body is unblemished.'

'The nape of his neck,' Abel said.

The fingers moved over his scalp to the back of his head and it dawned on him what Abel meant.

Plenty of times he had sat in the kitchen with his head bowed while Juliet pressed a handkerchief to the mole that bled so easily.

The fingers stopped.

'Bring the clippers, Grace.'

They cut away the hair at the nape of his neck.

'It is a strange colour,' Grace said.

'Like a large flea-bite.'

'It's ragged at the edges, as if it has been gnawed recently.'

'It's a birthmark,' Barnaby croaked.

'Come and see, Mr Hopkins.'

'No, no, ladies, this is your job. You must decide if you have seen such an unusual blemish before or whether it might perhaps be the cunningly concealed mark of an imp's teat.'

There was a beat of silence.

'I believe it is, Grace.'

'Yes, Marjorie. I have never seen such a mark before. It's shape is . . .'

'Infernal?' Barnaby croaked, but no-one answered him.

'What happens if you touch it with your nail, Mistress Tatley?' This was Abel.

'You know it will bleed, you dog!' Barnaby shouted but the women pressed his face into the mattress. He jumped at the sharp nick of a nail followed by a pinch. They were squeezing it to get the blood to come, and sure enough a moment later he felt a warm trickle down his neck.

'It bleeds for me most willingly,' Marjorie said.

'Enough to sup on?' said Hopkins.

'Certainly, for a small familiar such as a mouse or spider.'

It's a birthmark! Barnaby tried to shout, but his voice was muffled by the mattress.

'Prepare him for the watching,' Hopkins said.

After the third blow he allowed them to dress him without a struggle. They weren't his clothes. These garments were drab and patched: the garments of a peasant farmer. When they tied him to the chair, for some reason they left his legs outstretched. Then they went away, leaving him alone with their henchman, Leech.

He managed to catch a few moments' sleep but woke with a cricked neck and the grumblings of cramp in his upper arms. He rolled his shoulders as much as he could and wriggled his feet to get rid of the pins and needles.

Leech was asleep so Barnaby made a few half-hearted attempts to get out of the bindings, but when the chair legs banged against the floor the thug stirred at once. Even if he did free himself the door would be locked, and if he did get out of the room there was the problem of getting out of the village unseen, then finding shelter before the cold killed him, then trying to make his way to a town where he wasn't known. But there was one deciding factor against escape: he would be abandoning Juliet and Naomi to their deaths. At least if he remained he might find some way to save them.

His brother wanted him dead, that was plain enough, and perhaps during the interrogation he had said things that might go against him, but in a court he would deny them. True, they had found that damned birthmark, but if he was allowed to show it to the magistrate it would surely be dismissed. Whatever this 'watching' was that had to come next, he would be strong and admit nothing. He would have to try and withstand the physical discomfort for one more night. It was night, wasn't it? He glanced at the window but they had pulled a curtain across it now, perhaps to disorient him. Besides, his parents would be working hard for his release, talking to everyone they knew of any stature. The Slabbers must surely be doing all they could, and Griff's family would vouch for his good character. In fact, apart from his brother there was no-one who really disliked him.

Then he remembered: the deaf boy.

A chill crept into his bones. The furrier had no standing in the village so there was no reason why his son should be listened to, but if he repeated his story that Barnaby had killed his mother, there might be some who believed it. Barnaby had been trapped here so long he had no idea what was going on in the village. Perhaps it had been gripped by the witch hysteria he had heard of in other towns, with people accusing their own mothers and grandmothers, or even the village priest. If so it might be a good thing for him and Naomi and Juliet. They could hardly burn all five hundred villagers.

Or perhaps they could . . .

He heard voices on the stairs, laughter. The key turned in the lock and the two women were back, alone this time.

Their dresses were spotted with grease stains and as they smiled he saw bits of food caught in their teeth.

'Upsy-daisy, Mister Leech,' Grace sang and the big man stirred and farted.

'Let's get a fire going,' Marjorie said. 'I ain't sitting here all night in the bleeding cold.' Her words were slightly slurred.

'You sure? Hopkins won't like it.'

'Don't be stupid; the talking bit's done now. And besides, the creatures will be drawn to the warmth.'

'Get a fire going, Leech,' she said, 'then go and wait downstairs. Any trouble and we'll call you.'

When he had kindled the fire and gone down, Marjorie produced a bottle of wine from her skirts.

'Heaven be praised,' Grace chuckled.

They sat by the fire, drinking.

Every glug into the pewter cups, or slurp from the women, was agony to watch. The fire just made it worse.

'Will you at least let me wet my lips?'

Marjorie swung her head round to him. 'What?'

'I'm so thirsty.'

With a sigh she got up and walked over to him unsteadily.

'Thank you, Goodwife,' he said, opening his mouth, but she merely dipped her fingers into the wine and wiped them across his lips. The fire dried them at once and they became more cracked than they were before.

Crouching down beside the chair she stroked his cheek, breathing wine fumes in his face.

'You're a beauty, aren't you? You got a girl?'

He nodded, trying to smile to play for their sympathy.

Marjorie sighed. 'Poor thing.'

'Why?'

'Why, because she'll be taken too, of course.'

She got up but he grasped a scrap of her skirt between his fingers.

'Is there any hope for us?'

'Well,' she smiled sadly, 'you have not confessed much, the mark is, I should say, equivocal, and no familiar has yet appeared, so . . .'

'Shut up, Marge!' Grace snapped.

Marjorie pressed her lips together and scuttled back to the fire.

The house ticked and creaked. Occasionally a log crashed down, jerking him from his doze. The old women murmured and burped. He developed unbearable itches that had him close to shouting that he would confess anything Abel wanted, but eventually, through gritted teeth and strained muscles, subsided.

The sun came up and Grace opened the curtain while Marjorie slumbered.

She went back and lifted the dregs of her wine to her lips, then put the pewter cup down in a shaft of sunlight.

The bang on the window was so loud they all three cried out in fright.

Footsteps thundered up the stairs and Leech burst in.

'What is it?' he shouted.

'I don't know,' Marjorie gasped, her hand pressed to her chest.

The three of them stood in the middle of the room staring at the window.

For some minutes there was nothing. And then a great black shape came flapping up. It balanced for a minute on the frame, and stared through the glass with glittering black eyes. Then it rapped on the pane with its grey beak.

The women's eyes were out on stalks.

'Should I open the window?' Leech whispered.

'No!' they cried in unison. 'It might be Satan himself!'

'It is my maid's pet ...' Barnaby began then hung his head: he had just damned Juliet.

'It is looking at the boy,' Grace whispered. 'Everyone move into the shadows.'

The three adults melted to the edges of the room. The bird remained, and now there was no getting away from the fact that its attention was fixed upon Barnaby.

'Yah!' he cried. 'Begone, you pest!'

Tap, tap, tap went the cruel, hooked beak.

15
Black Kisses

The cart hurtled along the rutted road to Grimston, throwing him from side to side, striking his head against the frame so that he bit his tongue and jarred his back.

When it eventually came to a halt and the driver opened the door he was momentarily blinded by the glare. But the man did not wait until he could see to walk. Hauling him out like a sack of turnips, he dragged Barnaby to the door of the gaol, his bare toes carving runnels in the snow crust.

The gaoler did not recognise him and spent the whole descent to the cells complaining that he was not paid to look after so many and was rushed off his feet with all their unreasonable demands.

'Comfort yourself that they will soon be dead,' said the driver.

Barnaby could not orientate himself in the shivering lantern light. It took him a while to realise that the icy water he was paddling in was the channel of human filth that ran down the central aisle. The lantern stopped moving. Keys clanked, a door opened and he was flung to the ground. The door slammed shut again, the keys turned, and the lantern light retreated.

He was alone in the pitch-dark.

He spread his arms and found the wall of the cell and behind it a wooden structure that might be a pallet. Clambering up onto it he found it occupied by an ice-cold body. He got down and crawled across to a pile of straw on the other side. This too was occupied by something half naked and rank-smelling. He crawled over to the bars of the cell, a barely perceptible gleam in the sea of darkness.

'Naomi?' he called.

There was a faint rustling and then, shockingly close by, she spoke.

'Barnaby? Oh God, not you too?'

'Are you all right? Is Juliet better?'

A moment's silence.

'She came round after we saw you and I tried to get her to eat something, but she was too distraught. She said Hopkins and your brother had twisted her words and confused her and she believed she had said something to damn you.'

'It's all right,' he called. 'Tell her it's all right. Abel would have got me somehow. It wasn't her fault.'

But there was no reply from Naomi.

'Are you there?' he called. 'Is she still with you?'

'Yes,' Naomi said. 'She is here, but . . .'

'But what? Is she well?'

Naomi's voice lowered to a murmur and he pressed his ear to the bars to make out her words.

'There is a sickness here. The Widow Moone had it and

now she is gone. It begins with a cough and then these strange black lumps appear and … and then …' She paused. 'Juliet has them in her neck.'

Her voice was a thread in the huge silence. And then he began to make out a new sound. A sound that came from the same direction as her voice: rasping, laboured breathing.

'Is that her?' he said.

'Yes.'

He squeezed his eyes shut and pressed his forehead against the bars until his skull hurt.

'How long did it take for the widow to die?' he murmured.

'Two days,' Naomi breathed. 'But she was old and weak. Juliet is—'

He staggered to his feet. 'Jules!' he cried. 'Jules! Can you hear me?'

The ragged breathing caught and then there came the weakest, frailest croak of a voice he'd ever heard.

'Barney, I'm sorry.'

'It doesn't matter, Jules! It wasn't your fault. You must take some water, for strength.'

He had to strain to hear her reply.

'My … throat … is too … sore.'

'Please, for me!'

There was some movement, a slow rustling followed by the chink of a jug or cup.

'That's it,' Naomi said. 'Just a few sips and you'll feel much better.'

Juliet began to cough.

Naomi spoke some words of comfort but the coughing

continued and the cup clanked to the floor. Barnaby strained to try and see into their cell but could only make out splinters of the distant lamplight in the stream of excrement. The coughing grew worse, tearing the silence into ragged shreds.

'Can't you do something?' he cried.

And then there was a violent retching, followed by a splash, followed by silence.

He panted against the bars, breathless with relief.

'Naomi? Has she been sick?'

Very quietly Naomi said, 'It doesn't smell like sick.'

Barnaby swallowed hard.

Then another voice threaded through the darkness: an old woman's.

'Tell your friend to keep away from that blood.'

Barnaby stared wildly in the direction of the voice. 'But she might be able to help her!'

''Twill poison her. I kept away from the poor old dear as shared this cell, while the other tended her. They were both dead in a week. Once you have the marks of the devil's kiss upon you there ain't no hope.'

Barnaby took a deep breath. 'Get away from her, Naomi,' he said loudly, 'Right away. To the other end of the cell.'

'No!' Naomi cried. 'I could not be so cruel.'

'GET AWAY, NOW!'

She gave a small sob.

'Are you away from her?'

There was a rustling and then she said, 'Yes.'

'What a fool I was to hide from those black kisses,' the old woman continued. 'By now I should have been enfolded in His warm embrace!'

240

'Hush, Goodwife,' Naomi called softly. 'Do not let them hear you speaking that way.'

'Oh, I care not, child! Either the fire will warm me or the rope will hug my poor empty throat. Whatever happens it will soon be over and I will be with my master.'

'Your Lord,' Naomi said. 'Call him your Lord or they will think you mean Satan.'

'Ahh, sweet girl, it is too late to care what men think of us.'

A dreadful gurgling began.

'There,' the woman said. ''Twill soon be over.'

There was a low rustling from the cell opposite.

'Stay where you are, Naomi!' he snapped.

'I must go to her. I can't let her die alone.'

Barnaby squeezed his fists, pressing the nails into his own palms. 'No,' he said. 'It's too late for Juliet. Please, Naomi,' he lowered his voice, 'please.'

Though his ears strained in the silence there were no more rustlings.

But the gurglings went on, hour after hour through the night. He sat on the wet floor and rocked backwards and forwards, pressing his palms against his ears, though it did little to help. Then, just when he thought it couldn't get any worse, the gurgles became horrible choking grunts, like an animal trying to give birth.

He couldn't help the prayer that rolled around in his head: *Please let it stop, please let it stop . . .*

Eventually the prayer was answered. The grunts were replaced by a strange rattling sound, like a stone grinding across a washboard. Between these awful rattles he could hear Naomi weeping.

Then another voice drifted through the darkness.

'Through his own most tender mercy may the Lord pardon thee whatever sins or faults thou hast committed. May He who frees you from sin save you and raise you up to His side.'

Barnaby lifted his head. 'Amen,' he said.

'Amen,' said Naomi.

There were faint amens, from all along the corridor.

Juliet took another breath and this time the rattling exhalation seemed to go on forever: like pebbles endlessly tumbling across the seabed as the wave ebbs.

And then there was silence.

16
The Beetle

When Barnaby opened his eyes the cell was filled with a damp, grey light.

A figure was hunched in the corner of the cell opposite. On the bed was another shape, contorted and somehow inhuman.

He pulled himself to his feet and Naomi raised her head at the sound, gazing at him with hollow eyes.

'Gaoler!' he shouted. 'Get this corpse out of here.'

A few minutes later the gaoler's slow footsteps came splashing down the aisle.

He reached Naomi's cell and peered in.

'Get the corpse out,' Barnaby said, 'before it putrefies and infects us all.'

The man turned on him with a sneer. 'I don't have to answer to the likes of you.'

'You do if you want to keep getting generously paid for my keep,' Barnaby said.

The gaoler went off grumbling and returned with a wheelbarrow.

Barnaby flinched as Juliet's body hit the ground and the gaoler began dragging it out. He knew he should not look at her but he couldn't stop himself.

Her face was like a clumsy wax impression made by fairies to be left in place of the real thing: grey of flesh with sunken, malformed features. Her chin was covered in blood and black lumps clustered around her throat. Her nose was black, as were the tips of her fingers, screwed into claws at the ends of her stiff arms. Only her hair was the same. He remembered the smell of it, brushing his face as she bent to plump his pillow or fasten his collar. The man heaved her into the barrow like a rotten tree trunk.

The wheel of the barrow squeaked under the weight of her and her protruding feet rattled against the bars of the other cells as he pushed her away.

'Oh, Barnaby,' Naomi whispered when she had gone. 'I'm so sorry.'

He gripped the bars between numb fingers.

'Don't be sorry,' he said thickly. 'Her suffering is over.'

Then he sat heavily on the ground and covered his head with his hands.

Things began to happen. During the course of the day there were various visitors, muttered conversations with the gaoler: people were taken up and didn't return. From outside came the rhythmic thud of a hammer against wood. A little later feet jostled about the window as a crowd formed in the square above. They were hushed at first, but exploded into life at the crack of a rope. The remaining

244

prisoners prayed and moaned. The man on the mattress died and his body was removed as unceremoniously as Juliet's. Barnaby developed a cough and phantom twinges in his arms and neck. He kept feeling for lumps, but his fingers could not be trusted and beneath them his flesh seemed to creep as if insects burrowed through it. The cough became worse and, trying to clear his chest, he hacked a few drops of blood into his hand. *Please let it be quick*, he thought.

While he was devouring the congealed pottage that would be that day's only meal his parents came.

He heard rapid footsteps and raised his head to see Frances running through the stream, heedless of the filth splashing up her dress. Henry came tip-toeing along behind with his handkerchief pressed to his nose.

'I have spoken to my father,' she said, breathlessly, pressing herself against the bars. 'And he believes he can get an audience with Cromwell himself!'

'What's the point?' Barnaby said. 'Cromwell approves of what Hopkins is doing.' He went back to his pottage.

'Yes, but you are just a boy! And from a respectable family!'

'And what of Naomi?' he snapped. 'And the other poor wretches rotting down here?'

His father lifted the handkerchief from his nose. 'We cannot hope to save everyone. Good God, what is that you're eating?'

Barnaby stared at him, then shovelled another handful of the lukewarm slop into his mouth. 'It tastes pretty good to me.'

'Something must be done. I'm going to speak to the gaoler.'

Barnaby called after him: 'Lobster cocktail followed by spitted lark!'

His bitter laugh died as his gaze met his mother's. She looked old and ill. Without Juliet to do the linen her dress was grubby and creased. But there was something else: an air of defeat, less fitted to a merchant's pampered wife than a broken old drudge in an almshouse.

'I'm sorry I failed you,' she whispered.

His breath caught in his throat. All that stuff about Cromwell had been for his father's benefit. She was saying goodbye.

He laid the bowl down on the floor and wiped his hands on his shirt. He could not catch her eye when he spoke. 'You didn't fail me. I wanted for nothing.'

'Except love.'

He swallowed hard. 'I had my father's.'

'You deserved your mother's.'

'Then why . . .' He had to pause and begin again. 'Then why was I not worthy of it?'

Her voice became almost inaudible. 'There was another child, Barnaby.'

'The changeling.'

She closed her eyes. 'If that is what you wish to call him.'

'Not me, Mother, everyone.'

'Whatever he was, I loved him a great deal and when he was taken from me a part of my heart died.'

In the silence Barnaby could hear his father remonstrating with the gaoler, his voice shrill and ugly in the quiet.

Tears crept out from beneath his mother's eyelashes but

Barnaby felt no sympathy. A great pit had opened up somewhere deep inside him.

'Enough of it remained to love Abel,' he said.

Now she opened her eyes and gave a haunted smile.

'He looked so much like my first darling. For a while I could pretend that he had been returned to me.'

'Well, I am glad he has proved so worthy of your adoration.'

The raised voices had stopped and now they could both hear the footsteps approaching.

'It was I who was not worthy of you, Barnaby. Can you forgive me?'

They stared at one another through the bars. And wasn't this the way it had always been? There had always been a wall between them that, as a child, he had tried so hard to break through before eventually giving up. All the love he may once have had for her had long since turned to dust. They were now perfect strangers. Or not quite strangers.

Perhaps now, at the very end, they could be friends.

He stood and went over to the bars and took her hand in his. Then he dipped his head and allowed her to kiss his forehead. And for the first time in his life his mother's love flowed over him, soft and warm and safe, and his legs melted and he crumpled against the cold iron.

For a long time after they had gone he lay curled up on the floor of the cell. At some point he must have fallen asleep. He dreamed he was at home; his mother was reading him a story. Juliet was preparing dinner and delicious smells wafted from the kitchen: something warm and spicy for a winter's afternoon – a casserole of squash and cinnamon, perhaps, or a beef and ale stew. The heat of the fire radiated on his back.

Then something jolted him awake. For a moment he thought he was still at home, dozing in front of the fire, but then he saw that it was only the warm glow of sunset making its brief passage across his window.

The footsteps that had woken him clacked down the tunnel. These were the shoes of a gentleman, and he was being escorted by the gaoler.

'Just a little further, Sir.'

Fear sprang up in his heart. Had they come for Naomi?

The footsteps halted and the visitor's black shape detached itself from the shadows.

There was a beat of silence, then Barnaby said, 'Hello, brother.'

Abel dismissed the gaoler with a wave of his hand and the old man melted back into the shadows.

Barnaby stepped forwards and straightened up to his full height, even though it hurt his chest to do so. 'Come in,' he said, gesturing at the suppurating filth behind him. 'Make yourself comfortable.'

Abel said nothing.

'Have you come to gloat?' Barnaby said. 'Be my guest. I'm pissing in the corner and coughing up blood. You win. Well done.'

When Abel spoke, his voice was soft.

'How are the mighty fallen.'

Barnaby sighed and closed his eyes.

'The sword of the Lord is indeed swift and terrible.'

Abel came close to the bars, his mouth twisted in that familiar sneer.

'You have deceived my parents and the rest of that foolish village for long enough. Tomorrow you will be tried, convicted and sent back from whence you came.'

'The dung heap?' Barnaby said coolly, though inside he was reeling from Abel's words: *tomorrow*? His parents must have told Abel of the plan to speak to Cromwell, forcing him to act quickly.

'Hell!' Abel hissed, his spittle striking Barnaby's forehead.

'Hell is the place for murderers,' Barnaby said. 'You have murdered Juliet.'

'A confessed witch,' Abel spat. 'She admitted being in league with Satan.'

'What exactly did she say?'

'She named you as her partner in evil.'

'Did she really? Or did you say that and then confuse her into agreeing?'

'She had the devil's mark, and the same diabolical raven of yours came to her when we were watching.'

'It was a crow, Abel,' Barnaby said. 'They're quite common. You will be laughed out of the court.'

'Not at all. The evidence against you is strong.'

'A birthmark and a hungry crow?' He forced a laugh.

'And the things you said.'

'I never confessed, I never signed anything.'

'You said things.'

'You deprived me of sleep, starved me and stripped me.'

A sheen of sweat had burst out on Abel's high forehead and he licked his lips.

'Why exactly did you come?' Barnaby said.

'Oh, not to see you,' he smiled. 'No-one cares about your fate any more. I have come to speak with Miss Waters.'

Abruptly he turned away. Walking across the aisle he almost tumbled into the stream of filth and gave a yelp of distaste. On the other side he straightened his back and clasped his hands behind his back – evidently trying to look imposing and authoritative. But Naomi didn't raise her head and when he cleared his throat to speak she interrupted him in a hollow voice.

'I do not wish to hear what you have to say.'

She was huddled in the corner, her bare feet drawn up close to be out of the blood congealing on the floor.

'Miss Waters,' Abel said, 'you were kind to me once, and I did not intend it to go so badly for you.'

'And what did you *intend*, Abel Nightingale?'

Abel shifted from foot to foot and the fingers behind his back knotted.

'When I heard that Mr Hopkins was on his way to try the Widow Moone, I spoke to him of my fears of my brother's origins and he agreed to investigate them.'

'Shame on you.'

'It is not my fault that . . .' He tailed off and began again. 'Mr Hopkins is very thorough in his investigations and he discovered a nest of wickedness I had heretofore never even suspected.'

Even in the gloom Barnaby could see her eyes flash with fury.

'Not you,' Abel added quickly, then he glanced over his shoulder and his eye caught Barnaby's. He turned back.

'Perhaps we can speak somewhere more comfortable.'

'I would not accompany you anywhere.'

'As you wish.' His voice became even quieter. 'I wanted to make a . . . a suggestion to you.'

250

'Juliet was my friend.'

'A suggestion that might save your life.'

If he expected his announcement to be greeted with enthusiasm he was disappointed. Naomi's dry monotone did not waver. '*You* are the devil, not Barnaby.'

Abel took a deep breath and continued as if he had not heard her. 'You could leave this foul pit and be home at your farm by the morning.' He took a step closer to the cell. 'With your dear little brother.'

She did not reply to this but her breathing quickened, as if she was about to cry.

'To my mind,' Abel murmured, 'there has only ever been one of Satan's servants in Beltane Ridge. Somehow, with his wiles and his infernal bewitchments, he managed to ensnare poor innocents like Juliet. If you will agree to testify against him – only what you know to be true – that he is vain and arrogant and crushes those weaker than him. That you believe he set his familiars upon you to injure you in such a way that it made suspicion fall upon you. That he sent the cat to make us think—'

'You brought the cat,' she said.

He stammered a little as he continued, 'If you do these things then the magistrate will pardon and release you. My master, Mr Hopkins, has arranged such bargains many times in the past.'

Naomi stood up and walked through the blood until she stood directly in front of Abel. Though she was shorter, pale as a ghost, and shivering with cold, he started back.

'Shame upon him, too,' she said.

'I'm trying to help you,' Abel hissed.

'You do not wish to save me, only to damn Barnaby.'

Abel straightened and took a step back.

'I will give you until tomorrow to think on this, thereafter your fate will be in the hands of the magistrate.'

He walked a few steps away from the cell, then turned. 'The scaffold has already seen much use.'

His footsteps receded up the corridor, like the clicking of a beetle.

When he had gone, Naomi leaned against the bars and sobbed.

The last flares of daylight illuminated the full horror of their situation. The blood on the floor of her cell was bright scarlet, clotted with crimson. The water in the stinking runnel was brown and flecked with rat shit. Green slime covered the walls. Naomi's skin was grey and waxy, her once glossy hair dull, her dress stained and torn. Barnaby did not need to turn around to see for himself that the man on the bed behind him had developed the purplish buboes of the sickness – he could hear it in the man's cough and gurgling chest.

Eventually Naomi's sobs subsided to sniffles. She wiped her eyes on her dress and began running her fingers through her shorn hair, tearing savagely at the clumps and knots.

'When Abel comes back,' Barnaby said, 'you must agree to testify against me.'

She stopped what she was doing and stared at him as if he had spoken in a foreign language.

'What's the point of both of us dying?' he went on. 'Go home to your brother.'

She paused before replying and somewhere far away the death-watch beetle continued its clicking, up the steps and out into the chill winter air.

'If you think I would consider it for a moment you do not know me at all.'

She got up and went to lie on the bed, facing the wall.

He tried again but she said nothing more that night. Eventually he crawled to the back of the cell and lay down on the dead man's straw. Though he was freezing cold and his chest ached, he fell asleep almost immediately.

When he woke he knew exactly what he had to do.

17
The Pact

Barnaby's bare feet slapped on the wooden floor of the empty courtroom as he walked towards the benches at the far end. The room was lined in wood and so still retained some of the warmth of the dead fire in the imposing hearth. Everything about the place was imposing, from the carved cherubs scowling down from the cornicing, to the bookcases of huge ledgers that must contain the names and deeds of a thousand dead men. He tried to take it all in so that it wouldn't come as a shock the following day.

Abel was sitting on a kind of throne at the top of a flight of steps. The gaoler jerked him to a halt a few paces from the steps, then pulled up a stool and pushed Barnaby into it.

'I shall be waiting outside, Sir,' he said to Abel, bowing.

'Aren't you going to bind him?' Abel said.

'Oh. I haven't brought any rope. He isn't armed.'

'Fool. This man is known to be violent.'

'Shall I get some?'

'And leave me alone with him? No!'

The gaoler hurried away, mumbling apologies.

'Where's Hopkins?' Barnaby said. 'I asked to see him not you.'

Abel gave a small smile. 'He's a very busy man. He has done what he came to do. The wheels of justice are now in motion. From now on I speak for him.'

At the sight of Barnaby's expression his smile spread across his cheeks.

'You can always go back to your cell. Although you seemed very keen for us to talk elsewhere. Unlike poor, brave Naomi, who refused to be interviewed in comfort.'

'I did not want her to hear what I had to say.'

'Oh, so you will betray her now, will you?' Abel sneered. 'Well, it will not save your sorry neck. We have enough on you as it—'

'No you don't. Not to be certain of my execution. Not without a confession.'

'Nonsense,' Abel snorted but his fingers twitched on the arms of the chair.

'You need me to confess, Abel. And I need something from you.'

Abel blinked. The fingers went still. 'What?' he said.

Barnaby took a deep breath. 'I will admit to anything you like if you have Naomi freed.'

Abel did not speak for a few minutes.

The cries from the market traders outside echoed in the empty hall. They had set up their stalls around the scaffold. On the way here Barnaby had watched the customers bustle heedlessly by as the rope swung in the wind above them. Would they cheer for him? Would they call for the hangman to have mercy? Would they give him back his shoes? He hoped so: he didn't want to die like a beggar.

Then Abel spoke again, thoughtfully. 'She has a mark and there was the business with the cat, but she did not confess.'

'What if I say that the Widow Moone, Juliet and I wanted to get her to join our coven and we sent the cat familiar to torment her? That I made the corn doll in her image in order to bring her under my control?'

'You would damn your precious Juliet?' Abel widened his eyes in mock surprise.

'Nothing I say can harm her now. Answer me, would that work?'

Abel thought for a moment, then shrugged. 'I suppose it might. Juliet never named *her*, after all, only you, and the only accusation against her was retracted.'

'That's not good enough. Swear on the Bible that she will be freed or I will not confess.'

They stared at one another. The pupils of Abel's watery eyes were large in the gloom, his index finger stroked the comb of a wooden cockerel carved into the arm of the chair. There was a distant cry that might have come from the cells beneath their feet, or just a gull wheeling in the leaden sky.

'I will stand as character witness for her,' Abel said. 'I will say that I saw you feeding the cat, that I heard you telling a flea to go and bite her arm to cause a mark that would put her under suspicion.'

His eyes slid away from Barnaby's to gaze out of the window.

'Will that be enough?' Barnaby said.

Abel chuckled. 'They may not believe *you*, brother, but my word carries a great deal of weight these days.'

'Shake on it,' Barnaby said, rising from the chair.

Abel started as Barnaby climbed the stairs towards him, seeming to shrink and darken as Barnaby's shadow fell upon him. Barnaby stood over him, holding out his hand.

'Have we a pact?'

The bird cry came again, closer this time: out in the square perhaps. It was a crow. Calling to its friends, telling them that there would soon be a feast of carrion.

A white hand snaked up to Barnaby's and they shook.

'We have,' Abel said softly.

When it was written and signed the gaoler took him back down to the cells. Naomi was asleep. She slept through the afternoon, not even waking when the gaoler thrust some black bread through the bars, just out of reach from the skeletal hand that stretched across from the adjacent cell.

But perhaps it was better after all if he kept silent.

He lay down on the mattress and gazed up at the roof of the cell, pitted and cracked with rot.

She was woken by a shaft of the setting sun and came straight over to the bars.

'Where did you go?' she said, ignoring the bread. 'I was worried.'

He stayed silent.

'Barnaby?' she whispered. 'Are you asleep?'

He snored quietly so that she wouldn't fear he was dead.

Eventually she gave up, tugged the bread out from between the bars and shuffled away again.

Every so often throughout the evening she would come back to the bars and call his name, and he was able to snatch glimpses of her between his eyelashes, but then it grew too dark to see. He heard the creak of the pallet as she lay back down and the rustle of the thin blanket as she pulled it over herself.

'Goodnight, Barnaby,' she murmured.

The night crept by. At first he whispered some prayers but the words hung in the vast empty darkness, and he didn't believe anyone was listening.

At least it wouldn't be the pyre. Hanging was quick. If he could manage not to cry or faint then he would have made as good an exit as anyone. At least his mother would not be too distraught. His father would be inconsolable, of course. The thought of Henry's distress brought tears to Barnaby's own eyes. He tried to keep silent, but his sinuses blocked up and in the end he had to sniff. Immediately there was a sharp rustling from the other cell.

'Barnaby? Are you all right?'

He swallowed to clear the thickness from his voice. 'Yes, fine. Are you?'

'Yes.'

She paused. 'I'm glad we're together.'

He blinked quickly, which made the tears dribble down his temples. 'Me too.'

That was all that needed to be said. He rolled over to face the wall and counted the seconds to morning.

18
The Trial

They came for him early, before Naomi had awoken, passing silently down the darkened tunnel with no lanterns.

He did not recognise the voices that whispered to him from the shadows.

'Come now, boy, it's time.'

He felt amazingly calm as allowed himself to be led out of the cell, pausing in the tunnel while it was locked behind him.

Naomi's cell was a sea of darkness. He touched the bars, at the place where she had pulled the bread through.

His legs only turned to water when they started leading him up the staircase. At the sight of the grey rectangle of dawn awaiting him at the top he shrank back, but one of the men was behind him, urging him on. He concentrated on lifting one foot and then the other, keeping his gaze fixed on the new boots they had given him to walk through the snow. They were too large: the dead man they had belonged to must have been a giant, and he felt like a child walking in his father's shoes.

When they got outside he saw that the constables were good men, simple hard-working townsmen who didn't like what they had been tasked with. They dawdled in the cold dawn light, scratching under their hats, discussing whether or not there was time to smoke a pipe. There wasn't. With a sigh they led him around the side of the building towards the steps of the court.

The market square was empty but for the gallows. The rope hung straight down, utterly still. Barnaby's chest tightened. The men must have heard his choked breaths because one of them hung back to walk beside him.

'It may yet be all right, boy,' he said gently. 'You have Judge Godbold. The old man frees as many as he convicts.'

He nodded and tried to bring his breathing back under control. Naomi would win that particular fifty-fifty chance.

'Your case is due to be heard first so you will know soon enough. Better that way. Better that it be done quick.'

Barnaby swallowed and nodded again.

The steps came into view. A small group of men waited at the top.

'Here we are, son,' the constable said. 'Be brave, now. If you've done nothing wrong you have nothing to fear.'

At this his colleague glanced at him and the man cleared his throat and looked away.

One of the figures on the steps was Abel. He wouldn't catch Barnaby's eye as he climbed. Another of the men said something to him and he answered in a high, brittle voice that sent a clutch of birds flying from a nearby roof.

The little knot of men paid Barnaby no attention as he passed. As if he was already dead.

The doors opened with blast of cold air that set Barnaby's teeth chattering. The chattering carried on all the way down the corridor, gradually spreading to the rest of him, so that by the time they arrived outside the doors of the hall he was shivering violently. The constable went to announce his arrival and as he waited Barnaby forced himself to go through the routine his father had taught him all those years ago to overcome the terror of his nightmares. But no matter how hard he tried – stretching and loosening his muscles, breathing in-two-three-four, out-two-three-four – he could not stop himself trembling and panting like a dog.

He knew then that he would not make a brave end after all and his lip began to quiver as the constable returned to lead him into the hall.

The sight of the deaf boy stopped it at once.

If he had seen his parents first he would certainly have cried, but the sight of Luke sitting in the front row staring directly ahead was disconcerting enough to shake him out of his fear.

Had the boy come to gloat? It didn't seem so. He would not even meet Barnaby's eye and, as Barnaby passed him, his jaw clenched and his fingers tightened around a sheet of paper in his lap. Was this more evidence to damn him?

Henry and Frances were further along the front row, near the lectern behind which he would be standing. His father's gaze burned into him for the entire duration of his passage up the hall. His mother looked down at her lap, but when he passed her she reached out and gripped his hand so tightly he almost stumbled.

'My darling,' she murmured.

She looked up and there was such emotion in her liquid brown eyes that his breath caught in his throat.

'Mother,' he said, his voice cracking, and this was the cue for the room to erupt.

The benches were filled with people he knew: tenants, workers at the Boar, his father's business colleagues, Father Nicholas, Juliet's family, the Hockets, the Slabbers, the Rawboods. There seemed to be an even split between those who wanted him freed and those who wanted him hanged. People he barely recognised spat curses and waved charms, the Hockets glared and muttered, a barman he had joked with during many drunken evenings threw a rotten turnip that struck his shoulder. Of all people it was Richard, for so long Barnaby's mortal foe, who climbed over the benches and threw an ineffectual punch at the barman, starting a mini-brawl.

Griff and Flora were crying. The Waters family sat stiff and white-faced, and Naomi's little brother, barely visible above the back of the bench in front, watched him with wide, fearful eyes. From somewhere Barnaby dredged up a smile and waggled his fingers. The boy's fingers crept over the seat and waved back.

The furthest bench, directly opposite the lectern, was occupied by grim-faced strangers. This must be the jury. He tried to read their characters in their faces but apart from one middle-aged woman who crossed herself at the sight of him, they all looked like sober-minded townspeople.

He climbed the three steps of the lectern, to face the grand chair Abel had sat in the previous day. Seated there now was a man of about sixty: presumably Judge Godbold. He was fat, with heavy bulbous features and the purplish blotchiness of a drinker. His eyes were closed and Barnaby wondered how he could sleep through all the noise but then the man's chest heaved in a sigh and he opened them.

'Silence,' he said.

Though he had not spoken loudly the single word seemed to penetrate every corner of the room and a hush descended.

'Is this the prisoner?'

'Barnaby Nightingale of Beltane Ridge, Sir,' the constable said, 'accused of witchcraft.'

The judge sighed again. 'What age are you, boy?'

'Sixteen,' Barnaby said, relieved at the steadiness of his voice.

'This is young for such a charge,' the judge said. 'Who is here to prosecute?

Abel stood up. 'I, your honour.'

Godbold looked him up and down. 'Very well, begin.'

First there was a report – this from the mayor – of all the misfortune that had befallen the town that past year: crop failures, sick animals and farm accidents, the strange deaths of infants and the elderly, the harsh winter that had killed even more. He spoke of the Widow Moone and how she had admitted her guilt in sending a familiar to kill the Hockets' child.

'And where is the widow?' Judge Godbold said.

'Dead, Sir.'

'But we can assume she was telling the truth,' Abel

263

butted in from where he perched on the edge of the front bench. 'She would have no reason to lie.'

'Unless she had *lost* her reason,' the judge said. 'Go on, Mayor.'

'The widow admitted that there had been a coven, and another suspect gave us the name of the accused.'

'This other suspect? Where is she?'

'Dead, Sir.'

The judge raised his eyes to the ceiling.

'The accused tried to flee but was caught and questioned, and so now,' the mayor continued quickly, as if in a hurry to be done, 'I hand over to Master Abel Nightingale for his report on this interview and the subsequent searching and watching of the accused.'

'Abel *Nightingale*?' the judge said.

'Yes, Sir,' Abel said, standing up to his full height. 'The accused is my brother. But I did not let this interfere with the exercising of my duty. The very soul of Beltane Ridge was at stake.'

He lifted his chin defiantly and there was a quiet hiss from the crowd.

The judge regarded him from beneath hooded lids. 'How old are you, boy?' he said.

'Fifteen,' Abel said. 'But I am here on the authority of Matthew Hopkins himself.'

The judge winced at the name.

'So, where is Hopkins?'

'Gone to help others in their tribulation, Sir. He is most busy in these times of wickedness.'

'Indeed,' the judge said drily. 'Proceed.'

Barnaby's heart gave a little leap. Judge Godbold seemed

264

a reasonable man and he didn't seem to be impressed with what he had heard so far: perhaps if Barnaby insisted upon his innocence . . . but no. It was too much of a risk. According to the constable the judge still hanged half the witches he tried. He might release Barnaby and hang Naomi.

Abel's gaze caught his and Barnaby gave an almost imperceptible nod.

Abel picked up a ream of papers from the floor and stood up.

'I should now like to read my report of the questioning of the accused, which took place on the thirteenth of December sixteen hundred and forty-six, led by the esteemed Matthew Hopkins with myself as deputy.'

The judge exhaled impatiently.

'Mr Hopkins is accustomed to using the services of Grace and Marjorie Fowler, renowned experts in finding wounds where blood has been taken to sign the devil's contract, and locating marks where familiars have supped. The accused displayed both of these.'

A ripple of shock passed through the room.

'Are the women here?'

'No, Sir.'

'Where were the marks?'

'There was a scar on his belly where the blood was drawn, and beneath his hairline is a teat from which his familiars suckled.'

Seemingly unable to restrain himself any longer Henry leaped to his feet: 'That's a birthmark, you fool!'

'Sit down!' Godbold barked at him. 'If you rise or speak again you will leave my courtroom. Now, let me see this mark.'

'The hair has grown back,' Abel said. 'It will be hidden.'

The judge ignored him and beckoned Barnaby over. Barnaby stepped down from the lectern and walked across to the chair. Turning round he lifted his hair at the back of his neck. The chair creaked as the judge leaned forwards.

'You won't be able to see it properly, Sir . . .' Abel said.

'I can see it,' Godbold said, then he gently pushed Barnaby away. 'Show the jury.'

He went over to the bench and lifted his hair. They stood up and crowded in on him, their breaths hot on his neck. Somebody tutted. When they had sat down he walked back to the lectern.

Though he hadn't been able to see the jurors' expressions, his parents were now looking at one another with hope in their eyes.

But Abel was not so easily discouraged. His eyes narrowed.

'These may seem like trivialities to some,' he said, 'though they are tried and tested methods for finding out witches and many have perished on such evidence alone, but in the case of the accused there is something not so easily dismissed.'

He glanced around at the crowd. It seemed as if he was starting to enjoy himself. 'Let us talk about his beginnings.'

The room fell silent. All eyes were fixed on Abel. Barnaby bent his head.

His heart sank even lower as the familiar tale was retold, more sensationally and shockingly than ever. Children who had not heard it before nudged their parents to confirm the truth of it, the townsfolk of Grimston stared, openmouthed. When Abel got to the part where Barnaby was discovered alive and well on the dung heap there were gasps all round. The jury looked at one another, then to the judge.

'That is indeed a strange story,' Godbold said when the tale was done. 'Do we have witnesses here of this event?'

Slowly hands went up around the room.

Abel gestured towards his parents. The judge looked across at them. Henry hesitated, then nodded.

'Is that the way it happened, Mistress?' Godbold said, gently.

Frances raised her face, which was wet with tears, and nodded.

'And you, Father,' he addressed Father Nicholas. 'Did it happen as the boy describes?'

Father Nicholas rubbed his brow and nodded.

'As you know,' Abel went on, 'the Church does not recognise a difference between good and bad magic. All are bewitchments of the devil. These so-called fairies that took my so-called brother were no more than Satan's imps. And during his time in fairyland or as we know it better *hell* . . .' he paused for the murmurings to die down, 'the accused accepted the devil as his master, and when he grew old enough began to do that master's bidding. When a list of Satan's accomplices was found in the woods, the accused made sure it was destroyed so that others would not read his name inscribed upon it in blood.'

The judge frowned but this time Abel did not wait for permission to go on.

'Now, perhaps you would like to hear exactly what maleficium Barnaby Nightingale perpetrated in his lifetime . . . in his own words.'

There was a collective gasp and then the room exploded.

Abel waved a paper over his head, shouting above the din: 'A confession!'

Griff and Richard were on their feet, spittle flying from their mouths as they hurled abuse at Abel. Flora was shrieking. His father bellowed his name. His mother's head was in her hands.

'SILENCE!' Judge Godbold roared, but this time it took several minutes for the demand to take effect. In that time Barnaby saw little Benjamin scramble out of his seat and streak out of the doors. When a hush had once more descended the judge turned to Barnaby.

'This confession was freely given?'

Barnaby nodded.

'You were under no duress? No threats? No torture? Deprivation of sleep or the administration of medicine or alcohol?'

He shook his head.

The judge sighed and turned once more to Frances and Henry. 'Is your son of sound mind?'

'He cannot be!' Henry cried. 'Barnaby, what are you doing?'

The judge held up his hand to silence him, then turned back to Barnaby.

'Read it, then, child. I wish to hear it from your own lips.'

It was fortunate that Abel had gone through it with him several times before sending him back to the cell because the words were a jumble, the letters seeming to weave and somersault beneath his shaking grasp.

'I, Barnaby Nightingale of Beltane Ridge, do solemnly

swear that what I am about to read is the truth and nothing but the truth.'

He glanced up to check that he'd said it right. Abel nodded for him to proceed, but he felt other eyes upon him and saw that the deaf boy was watching him with violent intensity.

Momentarily disconcerted, he struggled to remember what he had to say and in that moment, rising above the sound of Flora and his mother's sobs, he heard a distant wail of anguish from below. Benjamin must have told his sister what Barnaby was doing. The paper shook in his hand and his eyes clouded.

'The coven,' Abel murmured.

Ah, yes, the coven. That was where he should begin.

He spoke of the coven he had led, with the Widow Moone as his second, and diverse other old ladies whose identities he had not bothered to learn. He knew he had written down Juliet's name and felt that he had to speak it if he wanted to sound convincing. When he did so there were sobs from the bench where her family sat and shouts that he was a liar. He continued. He had given each member of his coven her own familiars and demonstrated how to feed the creatures from her own body. He had produced contracts on behalf of the devil and overseen the signing of these, with the promises that good fortune would be delivered to each signatory and dire torments to her enemies. There had indeed been a list of those who had signed, written in the blood of a murdered infant, but he had burned it for fear of discovery. He had promised all the things the devil told him to, in the full knowledge that these were all deceits and that the women were forfeiting their souls to torment.

'For eternity,' Abel added.

'For eternity,' Barnaby clarified.

He had personally taken hair and nail trimmings from a five-year-old child in order to take possession of its will, then forced it to run under the wheels of a cart. He had stolen away a child in the dead of night to suck its blood, then when the child died and was buried he dug it up and distributed its body parts for his coven to cook and eat, using the rest to make ointment that would render them invisible.

This was particularly inventive of Abel, Barnaby felt: perhaps he had read of such a thing in one of his pamphlets, and his brother couldn't resist a smirk at the shouts of consternation produced by his words. The jury muttered behind their hands.

Barnaby ploughed on.

He had opened the chicken coop of Farmer Tilly and sent an imp in the guise of a fox to tear apart his whole brood. He had given the cooper's wife a tumour on her leg the size of a turnip. He had transformed himself into a piebald dog and attacked the tanner.

He paused to take a breath and cast an eye around the crowd.

His parents were in one another's arms. Griff and Richard scowled. Flora hid her face in her mother's shawl. And the furrier's son just stared at him, the paper he held becoming limp in his hands.

Barnaby went back to the sheet. Where was he? Had he mentioned the bit about bewitching his parents against Abel?

It was too long. People grew restless. He began to get his

words wrong: misreading *wicket* for *wicked* and *spit* for *spirit*. Abel had to prompt him more and more. He started to sweat. Down below, Naomi was shouting and banging on the bars of her cell. He decided to finish up. He had probably said enough.

Raising his head, he stated clearly that he had no remorse for what he had done and looked forward to the day when his soul would be united with his master in hell.

Nobody spoke.

He flicked a glance at Judge Godbold, who turned to the jury, his expression unreadable.

'Is there anything you would like the boy to repeat?'

They shook their heads.

'Very well.'

Barnaby gripped the top of the lectern. His mouth had gone bone dry.

'We have heard from the accused's own mouth,' the judge said to the jurors, 'That he committed acts of maleficium against his neighbours, denied God and contracted his soul to Satan. You have seen the markings that some take to be infernal, and you have heard the strange story of his birth in which he first became acquainted with the devil and his imps.

'It is my experience that none of these factors in isolation can be trusted to indicate guilt, but when taken together, as in the case of the accused, you must use your discretion as to whether you think this a case of madness and malice, or of true maleficium. You must now come to a verdict, whether you believe Barnaby Nightingale to be guilty or not guilty.'

After a moment's discussion one of the townsmen stood up, 'We are united in our decision, my Lord.'

'Are you certain?' Judge Godbold said. 'A child's life is at stake.'

'We are certain, my Lord.'

The judge pulled something from his pocket: a piece of black fabric. Barnaby's heart stuttered. This was what Judge Godbold would place over his head when passing the sentence of death.

'Very well, you may sp—'

But before he could finish, there was the screech of a bench against the floor followed by an inarticulate cry.

The voice was strangely thick and guttural but Barnaby understood what the deaf boy had said.

Wait.

'What?' the judge said, turning to face him. 'Is this some new evidence? Why was it not put forward earlier?'

'I am sorry,' said the boy, 'I am deaf. It was dif . . . difficult for me to follow what was happening.'

'Is this important?' the judge asked impatiently.

Luke nodded and held up the piece of paper. 'Yes. Important.'

'I shall be the judge of that.' Godbold waggled his fingers and Luke walked forward and handed it to him, then waited while he read. Barnaby looked down at him from the lectern. He was tall and well-built, with dark hair as glossy as a conker. Barnaby realised now that Luke could easily have hurt him that day in the churchyard if he had wished to.

The judge looked up at the boy and then to Barnaby, then he frowned and reread the paper. A moment later he passed it back to Luke.

272

'Read it. Take your time. Make sure everyone under-stands.'

Luke nodded, turned to face the courtroom and, in that odd, thick voice of his, began to read.

'My name is Luke Armitage and I am sixteen years old. I was brought up by James and Susannah Armitage. But they were not my parents. I only discovered this after my mother's death, two months ago. She left me a letter explaining my true origins. My real parents, she said, were rich and of high standing, and if I chose to do so I could go to them and demand my birthright.

'I did not choose to.

'I have never wanted more than the loving family who brought me up. But the events of the past several weeks have forced me to bring the contents of her letter out in the open.'

He paused.

Barnaby's eyes flicked to his parents and he was sur-prised to see they had both turned white.

'As you can hear from my voice I am deaf. This was a defect from birth.'

A tiny whimper made Barnaby glance back at his par-ents: his mother was pressing her handkerchief to her mouth.

'At the time, however, it was not recognised as that. My parents, along with the priest and my nursemaid, believed I was not a real child at all, but a fairy changeling that had been left in the place of the true child. They agreed upon a well-known method to retrieve the true child – to leave the changeling upon a dung heap. Supposedly unable to watch their own kind torn apart by wild animals or frozen to death, the fairies would swap it back with the true, human child.'

He paused and swallowed.

There were now moans coming from both his parents but Barnaby could not tear his eyes away from Luke's lips as they parted to continue.

'News of the plan passed around the village and came to the attention of the furrier, James Armitage, and his wife. They had recently been blessed with a son of their own: a fine golden-haired boy who had already grown fat and pink with health.'

Silence.

'But much as they loved their son, they could not bear to see an innocent child murdered for the sake of superstition and ignorance.'

Barnaby tried to swallow but his throat was too dry.

'For pity's sake they decided to give up their own, perfect child, to save the life of the deaf child. They followed the family to the forest and watched them leave the child, they sheltered it and comforted it for the whole of the long cold night, and in the morning, when they heard the sounds of the returning parents, left their own golden-haired boy on the dung heap and took the deaf one home with them.

'They brought me up as their own and the golden-haired child, the true child of the furrier and his wife, grew up the lauded son of the esteemed Nightingales.'

He looked up from the paper and cast a cold eye around the paralysed court.

'Barnaby Nightingale was never stolen by fairies, he never visited Fairyland. He was given as a gift to rich fools

274

who should have known better and I pity him for the love he did not receive from a far nobler and better family.'

Something had gone wrong with Barnaby's vision. It was as if he was looking at a picture of the courtroom and the picture had begun to pucker and burn at the edges.

The hand holding the paper dropped to Luke's side and he looked up at the judge.

'These are the facts. It is my opinion that Abel Nightingale, my own brother in blood, developed a violent jealousy against Barnaby and determined to destroy him. I only came forward to prevent this great wrong, as my parents came forward sixteen years ago to prevent a similar one.'

Finally he turned to Barnaby and their eyes locked.

For a few minutes nobody moved or spoke. And then somewhere to Barnaby's left there was movement. The square of black that had dominated his attention for the past long minutes disappeared from sight. The judge cleared his throat.

'Barnaby Nightingale,' he said and Barnaby swayed round to face him. 'For perjuring yourself with a fabricated confession I sentence you to three months in prison. As for the charge of witchcraft,' he turned to the blinking jury-men, 'I instruct you to find the defendant innocent.'

There was split second of absolute silence, then all hell broke loose.

Barnaby fell backwards and was caught by strong arms and passed from person to person until the constables arrived. Hooking his arms over their shoulders they carried him down the central aisle, thrusting aside the shouting people, the grabbing hands, the waving shawls and hats. A fight broke out, a woman screamed. His father's face swam into view, twisted and wet with tears.

But this man was not his father.

His mother was there, her mouth moving, her eyes wide and shocked.

But this woman was not his mother.

And then Luke was there. His brother? No, not his brother. His saviour? His . . .

Tearing himself from the constables' grasp, he threw himself onto Luke's shoulders and clung there, as if this poor, deaf boy was driftwood on a heaving sea. Luke's chest shuddered against his own and the arms that clamped around him didn't seem to know whether they wanted to embrace him or squeeze the life out of him.

Barnaby wanted to say something – *thank you, sorry, forgive me* – but his chest was a churning sea and his mouth was numb.

And then the two boys were wrenched apart and Barnaby was propelled out into the violent whiteness of the December morning.

March 1647

Barnaby shivered and drew the blanket across his shoulders. The room had grown very cold, but he didn't dare put any more dung on. There wasn't much left and he was still too weak from the sickness he had contracted in prison to go looking for more. He'd been lucky not to die. It had run through the place like wildfire and those wretches who didn't have sponsors died within days. As much as he had tried to reject the financial assistance offered by the Nightingales, it ensured he had a cell to himself with blankets and a bed, hot food, a plentiful supply of ale, and his own lantern. As a consequence of which he had been strong enough to survive. For which he did not thank them.

The one good thing about the tiny cottage was that everything was close by. He leaned forwards and ladled out another cup of warm ale to fill his empty stomach. Though Frances Nightingale brought pies and cakes to his door, he usually left them to be eaten by animals and birds.

Sometimes he succumbed. Evidently starvation was a very painful way to die.

She'd had nothing, his mother: barely a stick of furniture, a single pan with a bottom worn thin as paper, a straw mattress in a cubbyhole in the wall. There must once have been another, for Luke, but the spare had probably been used for fuel after her death.

It had taken a lot to get Luke out of here. Legally the place was Barnaby's now that he'd turned sixteen; just as legally the Nightingale fortune would go to Luke. The deaf boy had fought though. Refused to leave, stating rights of 'adverse possession', but when it was established that he would have had to have held the land for thirty years before this law came into effect, Luke finally allowed the bailiffs to evict him, taking just his paints and brushes.

Barnaby had moved straight in, having spent the intervening time following his release from prison at the Boar. He had at least agreed to let the Nightingales pay for that. Luke refused to live with them and, after accepting an annuity from these, his blood parents, left the village to apprentice himself to a painter in London.

He and Barnaby had not said goodbye. They did not speak again after the trial. Barnaby hadn't spoken to anyone much. Only the landlady of the Boar, the Grimston merchant who bought his fine clothes and sold him some more fitting to a furrier's orphan, and the baker who had taken his last pennies for a loaf of bread three days ago. He would have to try and earn some more, but he had no idea how. When spring finally came he might be able to get work as a farmhand, although if he performed as badly as he had the previous year he wouldn't make much: for now he was destitute. He had considered begging, but at the moment he felt too ill to go out. It was March and still the bitter cold showed no signs of abating.

There was a knock at the door.

Richard again.

He closed his eyes and let his head thunk against the rickety chair back.

After the first few rebuffs Griff had given up, but strangely Richard, his former enemy, persisted: waiting outside the locked door, or peering through the windows, cajoling, scolding, threatening, before eventually going home to warm up before coming back the next day. Idiot. He had always known Barnaby for the fraud he was, and now he was acting like all the creeping sycophants of Barnaby's illusory past.

Another knock, louder.

Needless to say, Flora had not visited. She had been in such a hurry to return Frances's ring she sent her maid down to the cells with it. Barnaby wore it for two and a half months to stop it being stolen, before selling it to the first gold merchant he saw upon his release.

The knock again. A voice called his name. The voice was not Richard's.

He stared at the pulsating embers.

'Barnaby?'

Predictably enough Henry had turned to drink. Once or twice he had staggered round to the hut, sobbing and begging forgiveness, but after receiving no response he'd staggered off again. Frances had written him a letter. He had fed it page by page into the fire unread.

'Barnaby?'

Abel was gone. He had slipped away during all the commotion that followed the trial. No-one was quite sure where, according to Richard, but he would certainly have to stay away for a decade or two if he didn't want to be torn apart by a mob led by Farmer Waters. The man had brought Barnaby a butchered and salted lamb the first week he'd been here, and of all the gifts this was the only one Barnaby could bear to accept. Waters said that Naomi had been ill following her own trial, which had ended in acquittal seeing as there was no-one left to give evidence against her. Barnaby had heard nothing of her since then.

Until now.

'Let me in!' she snapped. 'It's freezing.'

He stared at the embers, his fingers loose around the cup of now cold ale.

'I'm just out of bed from fever, Barnaby Nightingale, and if you don't let me in immediately you will be responsible for my death.'

'Don't call me that.' His voice cracked from lack of use.

'Fine. Armitage then. I don't care. Just let me in.'

He didn't move. She rattled the door a few times and cursed him, but eventually she gave in.

It was getting too cold now. He would have to go to bed. Wrapping the blanket around himself he got up and shuffled towards the cubbyhole. As he did so he caught sight of himself in the tiny window by the door. In those three months he had become a different person. He had lost weight, and his hair fell in lank curls on his bony shoulders. His eye sockets were dark and his cheekbones jutted out. The weight loss had made the bridge of his nose more prominent, like a bird of prey. How could he have ever thought himself a Nightingale? At least he didn't look like the Lucifer of Luke's mural any more. More like John the Baptist after years in the desert eating locusts.

An ear-splitting thud made him jump out of his skin.

Something hit the door with such force the thing nearly came off its hinges: a line of splintered wood now scarred it right through the centre.

She had got the axe from the outhouse.

'What the hell are you doing?'

'Coming in.'

CRASH – the axe struck again, and this time the blade broke through.

'Stop! You're destroying my door!'

'Are you going to let me in?'

For a moment he stood his ground, his fists clenched at his sides, but then the axe was wrenched out and she began to count down: *five . . . four . . . three . . .* His shoulders slumped and he trudged to the door.

She looked better than he did. A lot better.

Where before she had been plump and pretty as a cat she was now lean and elegant. Her hair had started to grow and curled in glossy ringlets about her temples, framing her green eyes with their jet-black lashes. The cold had reddened her cheeks and nose, and the hands that clutched a bundle of blankets in her arms.

The snow was still falling, speckling her hair like stars in a clear night sky. All the warmth in the room rushed out and was swallowed by the night.

When he made no move to usher her in she pushed past him and kicked the door shut with her foot.

They regarded each other silently for a moment.

'It's cold in here,' she said.

He gave no reply and went back to sit by the fire.

'You have done a very good job of hiding from the world. It has almost forgotten your existence.'

He heard her walking around the room: it didn't take more than a few seconds.

'It's a sturdy little place,' she said. 'The floor is solid. And the thatch looks good from outside.'

He stared into the greying embers. The cold air was creeping through every hole in his shirt.

'Where shall I put this?' she said, coming to stand between him and the fire.

'I have enough blankets.'

'It's not just blankets,' she said.

He sighed and looked up at her. She regarded him steadily with those glittering eyes.

'What, then?'

'Rushes from the lake and shoots of willow,' she said. 'My parents helped me harvest them from the forest. I was always a better basket-weaver than I was a maid, and Juliet used to tell me what fine rabbit-skin muffs and hoods you made for her. Perhaps you have your father's skill as a furrier.'

The embers stopped hissing, the mice in the thatch stopped rustling.

'Go home,' he said hoarsely.

'Please, Barnaby. It's all over, now. The things that are lost can't be brought back. All we can do is go on, as best we can.'

'I killed my own mother,' he said.

'You saved my life,' she said. 'You saved my family from

a lifetime of fear and shame. You saved Beltane Ridge from turning on its daughters and mothers and grandmothers.'

'That wasn't me, that was Luke Nightingale.'

She said nothing to this but a moment later placed four willow stalks and a paring knife onto his lap.

He stared at them for a moment. The knife was a stubby thing, only three or four inches long, but strong and sharp. He picked it up and pressed it to the pad of his thumb. A ball of blood swelled up around the tip. It was too sharp to hurt.

Naomi breathed quietly beside him.

The willow stalks were deep conker brown, with gentle swellings, like knuckles, along their length. He picked one up and bent it almost in half. It did not break, although when he allowed it to spring straight again there were wrinkles in the papery bark.

The fire guttered. Still it clung on though there was nothing left to feed on. Even at the very last it would fight for its life, like a coney in a snare, like a man on the gallows clutching the rope above his head to try and lift himself from the pit. Like the blanket on the bed he slept in: so patched and darned that there was barely anything of the original left. In the Nightingale house it would have been thrown away with the vegetable peelings, but here it had been preserved and cherished.

How had she felt, lying on that blanket, with another woman's child slumbering beside her, and her own gone forever? Was life so precious that it should be preserved at any cost?

Barnaby closed his eyes and a single tear whispered down through the dirt on his cheek. When he opened them again the flames were bright flares in his blurred vision: a last dance at the very point of death.

Death was so easy to come by, life so hard to cling to.

What would Juliet think of him simply throwing it away?

He picked up the knife again and, with one swift movement, plunged it into the heart of the willow stalk.

Naomi had brought cinnamon biscuits and salt beef and he attacked them ravenously, while she lit rushlights and fed the fire with some of the willow stalks. It sprang up at once, crackling and dancing, stretching its fingers up the chimney.

Her father's ale tasted ten times better than he remembered and next time he met Farmer Waters he would ask again about the yeast and this time pay attention to his explanation. Perhaps the farmer might even lend him a little to get his own batch started.

'You will need more straw for your bed,' she said. 'This stuff is mouldy. It will hurt your chest.'

He grunted, his mouth packed with salt beef.

'You can have some of ours,' she went on. 'But you ought not to sleep here another night, especially in your weakened condition.'

'I'm not weak,' he said, through his mouthful.

'No,' she said, smiling a little. 'Perhaps, after all, you are not. Have you finished?'

'Well, the *food* is finished, if that's what you mean, but I could eat the same again.'

'Oh, and I suppose you would like me to go and fetch it for you, Master Barnaby?'

He smiled. 'If you like.'

'I have a better idea. Come and dine with us, then sleep with Benjamin this night, and tomorrow I will help you bring some fresh straw and maybe something a little sweeter for your fire than cattle dung.'

'I have nothing to pay you with,' he said quietly.

Already the rushlights were burning low and the last of the willow stalks spat and hissed on the fire as they died. It would be a cold night here all alone.

'You have already paid us,' she said, pulling on her cloak. 'But if you set the price of my life so low then you may assist me in making some basket chairs for children, like the one I made for Benjamin. Henry Nightingale believes they may fetch some money in Grimston market.'

He flinched at the name and his face hardened, but she held his gaze with her clear cool eyes.

'Pride is expensive, Barnaby, and remember, you are a pauper now.'

The rushlights guttered and started to go out one by one. As they did so the reflections in the black windows melted away to be replaced by the deep blue of the night sky. Suddenly he wanted to be out in it: walking through silver pastures beneath the cold moon: up the path that led to the lake, the farm, and beyond it, the forest. It held no fear for him now. Juliet had been right, the spirit of the forest never forgot him. She watched over him with love, and perhaps a little shame: a little disappointment. The Son of the Morning had fallen into darkness. Now he must climb back up into the light.

He stood up and gave a little bow. 'Mistress Waters, I am at your service.'

The night air was bitterly cold, like a rush of lake water down his throat. He remembered the day he had fought her off as she tried to rescue him from drowning. He remembered the Widow Moone.

He took her hand as they climbed over the ditch that divided the Nightingale lands from the common land. The ploughing and muck-spreading had already begun and the rich smell of cold earth and manure rose up as they tramped through the mud. Bats flew overhead and from somewhere in the distance came the churring call of a nightjar. The forest was just visible on the brow of the hill.

She stopped abruptly beside him and her hand slipped from his grasp.

'There's a light in the forest,' she whispered.

She was right. A cool glow radiated from the trees, pulsing silently.

'It's only marsh gas,' he said.

'The Widow Moone said the devil had promised her eternal life,' Naomi murmured. 'I hope he kept to it. I hope that light is the devil's fire and they are there now, dancing infernal jigs with him and his imps, drinking wine and making spells to give boils to the mayor and gout to the aldermen. The Widow Moone, and Juliet and all of them.' Her voice cracked.

The light wavered and shifted, as if there were shadows passing in front of it. The nightjar's call was like distant laughter.

'So do I,' he said. Then he took her hand.

They regarded one another silently. Two peasants just beginning their lives. No doubt these lives would be filled with hardship. Hardship and pain and the loss of those they loved. But at least they would *know* love: the expression in her eyes told him so, and love was as hard to come by as life itself.

'Come on,' she said finally.

The witch tree was silent as they passed beneath its branches and on up the slope towards the glimmering lights of the Waters' farm.

Matthew Hopkins, self-styled 'Witchfinder General',
died of tuberculosis in 1647, aged 27.
He had been responsible for the deaths
of over 200 women.

In 1895 Irishwoman Bridget Cleary was murdered
by her husband who believed she was a changeling
left by the fairies in place of his true wife.

Acknowledgements

As usual deep thanks to my brilliant, supportive, encouraging, stiletto-banning, migraine-scorning agent, Eve White, and her assistant and possessor of the coolest name in publishing, Jack Ramm.

To my lovely editor, Jane Griffiths, to Paul Coomey for his wicked cover designs, to Catherine Ward, Laura Hough and the rest of the team at Simon and Schuster. Thanks for working so hard for this book and for being such a pleasure to work with.

Thanks to Shelley Instone, partly for the excellent writing advice, but mostly for the cackling gossip.

To my dad for offering the occasional reluctant and extremely guarded opinion.

To Mum for telling EVERYONE.

Thanks to my friends: Laura Wilder for the ace workshop ideas, Sarah Baker for the book-chat and nut-free cakes, and both of them for listening to me complain.

To the original golden boy, Barney Shanks, (and equally bling siblings, Gabriel and Echo) whose goblin mother didn't do such a bad job of raising after all.

Thanks to Bert and Bill for letting me write in the evenings (in between putting Bakugans back together and admiring homemade zombie-pirate masks).

And finally, thanks to my husband for his scandalously unappreciated cooking. Sorry, Vince: this one's even longer.

WHAT LURKS IN THE DEPTHS?

COSTA BOOK AWARDS
Shortlist
2013

THE HANGED MAN RISES

SARAH NAUGHTON

1

The boy sat on the end of the jetty, skimming oyster shells across the water. It was too choppy to get many bounces but occasionally a shell would strike the dredger, moored further out, with a satisfying clang. He didn't even bother to prise open the next one before he threw it. The thought of slurping out its slick grey innards, still quivering, made him queasy. A person could get heartily sick of oysters, and Sammy often wished his father had been a cattle drover or a cheesemonger. Anything but an oyster farmer.

Now that he was eight he'd been given more responsibilities, including this afternoon's task of checking the size of the oysters seeded the previous week. He was taking as long as possible about it, to put off the moment he had to return to the shed to carry on de-barnacling with his brother. He'd been at it all morning and the icy water had made his hands too numb to feel when the knife slipped. It had taken this long for his fingers to warm up and now that the feeling had returned they were throbbing. He lowered them into the green water and threads of blood drifted out from them to coil around the oyster ropes. Like hair. Sammy shivered. He wished he hadn't thought of that: not now, not while he was out here all alone. The one who was killing all the children liked to take bits of their hair as a souvenir. That's why they called him the Wigman.

To try and drive the thought from his mind Sammy started

whistling, a cheerful music-hall tune, but the sound drifted mournfully out over the dark water and he soon stopped.

The low sun burned crimson, glinting off the tips of the waves, and making the river appear to flow with blood. A few wisps of fog drifted in. If he waited a little longer he could say he'd got lost in it.

He realised he'd been too long when the water turned black. The fog had become so dense he couldn't see further than his own legs dangling over the jetty's edge, but if the sun had gone down it must be nearly five o'clock. His father would be furious. He'd probably have taken the cart and gone home, leaving Sammy to walk all the way back to Lambeth.

He scrambled to his feet and ran a little way along the slimy boards. Then skidded to a halt.

His father was waiting for him further down the jetty: he could just make out his blurred shape.

'I'm sorry,' Sammy called, 'I didn't know it was so late.'

He set off again, quicker. The fog enclosed him in a little bubble that contained only his scared breaths and the clatter of his footsteps along the boards.

'Tomorrow I'll start early and—'

He stopped. The shape had not moved, either to turn away in disgust or to raise a fist. It merely stood watching him, close now, but still veiled in smog. Perhaps it was a policeman.

'Excuse me, sir,' he said as he hurried up alongside the figure, 'but my father is waiting for me.'

The figure moved sharply and Sammy went sprawling.

'Hey!' he cried as he was roughly turned over, but the cry was cut short as rags were thrust into his mouth and a cord tied around his head to keep them in place.

Then the man was gone. Sammy lay there a moment in

bewilderment, then sat up. The rags were packed so tightly he could hardly breathe. They tasted of honey.

Too late he heard the crunch of pebbles below. The man had merely jumped off the pier onto the beach. Hands reached up and yanked him over. Throwing out his arms to save himself he landed heavily on his wrist, and it gave an audible crack. His scream was muffled by the rags.

As pain overwhelmed him, he was dimly aware of being dragged up the beach and laid down. Then something heavy and smelling of sweat was thrown over him and he was left in darkness.

He knew immediately what was happening. The Wigman had got him. Over the thumping of his heart he could hear the man chanting, a little way off.

Biting his lip to suppress the cries of pain and terror, Sammy used his good hand to lift the coat off. Everything was grey. The smog would shield him from sight and muffle the sounds of his escape. He rolled onto his stomach, then pushed himself up onto all fours. The wall swung into view beside him, wet and black with algae. There were some steps fifty or so yards east of the pier. He began to crawl towards them.

The sand beneath his knees was stinking and black, with tar and muck from the tanner's yard and slaughterhouse.

There was a splash some way behind him and the voice intoned, '*Accept this gift.*' Sammy moved quicker, his left wrist flapping uselessly. A moment later another splash, more distant now. '*Accept this gift.*' Closer and clearer were the booms of Big Ben striking a quarter past the hour. Would his father have gone home or was he on his way here now, his fists rolled and ready? Sammy hoped it was the latter, and was momentarily glad that the Wigman had taken him: at least it was an acceptable excuse.

The wall suddenly zigzagged up away from him. He had reached the steps.

Climbing onto the first tread he allowed himself a moment's relief. Very few had escaped the Wigman to tell the tale, and most of those had wriggled out of his arms before he could do any tying up and chanting. But here Sammy was, nearly free, and with a story that would bathe him in adulation for years to come.

Then he heard voices from above, the first deep and gravelly:

'Can't see him. Fog's too deep.'

The second a bad-tempered whine:

'Prob'ly home by the fire, eating bread and dripping.'

It was his father and brother. He tried to call out to them but his muffled squeak from beneath the gag was drowned by the tidewash.

'He might have fallen asleep on the pier. We shouldn't leave him.' His father again.

'He deserves it. He never does his fair share. I have to work twice as hard to make up for him.'

'He ain't as old as you.'

'Ain't far off. You're too soft on him.'

Sammy wasted a few seconds fumbling at the knot round the back of his head, then continued to climb. It was hard, with only one good hand and the steps so slippery.

'Come on, Pa,' his brother said. 'Let's get on. If he is asleep it'll teach him a lesson.'

'I'm not sure. Not with this Wigman feller about.'

Sucking in as much air as he could through soot-coated nostrils Sammy shouted, 'Dad! Fred!'

It came out as 'Ahhhg! Ehhhh!' but would have been audible, had a barge not come by at just that moment and given several long honks on its horn.

'Asleep?' Fred sniggered. 'On a night like this, with the boats sounding their warnings every five minutes? I tell you, he's home with Ma. Let's go.'

Sammy hauled himself up the next few steps. He was more than halfway now, but could hear his father's heavy footsteps retreating.

He shouted for him to wait.

'Aiighhh!'

The footsteps were growing fainter, but it was all right. He could still catch up with them and bring his father back to the beach. The Wigman wouldn't know what had hit him.

A blow sent Sammy reeling sideways and he crashed down onto the sand, too winded even to scream.

He looked up mutely at his assailant. The Wigman was younger than they said, not more than twenty or so. His face was utterly colourless, like a grub dug up from the soil, and glistened like sweaty lard as the man knelt down beside him. His hands were massive, red and scarred, and Sammy watched in horror as he slipped one of them into his pocket and drew out a knife. He brought it towards Sammy's face. Sammy screwed up his eyes and moaned, but with a flick of the wrist all the man took was a hank of hair.

As the Wigman was tucking the lock into his pocket, Sammy brought his knee up sharply and the knife skittered across the sand. Sammy flipped himself over and went after it, grunting as his wrist collapsed and he lurched sideways, but righting himself and clawing onwards.

The knife glimmered on the black sand and Sammy's fingers were almost touching it when he was hauled into the air. With his good arm he clawed at the Wigman's eyes and throat but the arm was clamped down and his face was pressed into a chest that stank of tallow and sweat. Sammy sank his teeth into the soft flesh until a fist descended on his head.

The blow and the lack of air were making him dizzy and he began to see strange things in the darkness: shadowy figures gathered at the edges of his vision, murmuring to one another. Or was that just the shush of the river on the beach?

The murmuring grew louder and the cold air slapped him alert as he landed on the sand. Water lapped around him, filling his ears, seeping into his clothes. The Wigman knelt down next to him, cut the cord around his head and pulled the rags from his mouth.

'Let me go, please,' Sammy gasped. 'My father's rich, he'll pay you whatever you ask, I won't say who you are I swear . . .'

But the man wasn't listening. He reached into his pocket again, took out an object and pushed it into Sammy's open mouth. The slick congealed thing slipped straight to the back of his throat, its end fitting snugly into the opening of the airway. Then the hands launched him out into the dark water.

Escape was still possible. He could swim well. He would simply roll onto his stomach, cough out the thing, whatever it was, and make for the other shore.

Then something heavy fell across his abdomen and he went under.

As the water surged into his nostrils he looked up to see the shadow of the Wigman step back, leaving just the fog, now endless green stretching all the way to the sky.